Praise for

MW01141588

"A creative take on a ghost story and a ~~~~
— Valentina Cano, *You Gotta Read Reviews*

"The sexual tension runs high and the sensual delights are sizzling hot, tender and poignant."
— Shannon, *The Romance Studio*

A Recommended Read! "...a vivid story complete with well developed characters that keep you on your toes throughout."
— Susan, *Dark Divas Reviews*

"...a dark yet gorgeous romantic novel."
— Miranda, *Joyfully Reviewed*

"...a very intriguing read which provided quite a few shockers."
— Chris, *Night Owl Reviews*

Blood Rite
"...grabs you by throat and does not let go until you have read the very last page."
— Regina, *Coffee Time Romance & More*

Leave Me Breathless
"I highly recommend this erotic adventure; these two men are worth the ride."
— Stephanie Q. McGrath, *Paranormal Romance*

LooseId ®

ISBN 13: 978-1-61118-388-7
DARKNESS FALLS
Copyright © March 2012 by Trista Ann Michaels
Originally released in e-book format in April 2011

Cover Art by Valerie Tibbs
Cover Layout and Design by April Martinez

DISCLAIMER: Many of the acts described in our BDSM/fetish titles can be dangerous. Please do not try any new sexual practice, whether it be fire, rope, or whip play, without the guidance of an experienced practitioner. Neither Loose Id nor its authors will be responsible for any loss, harm, injury or death resulting from use of the information contained in any of its titles.

Printed in the U.S.A. by
Lightning Source, Inc.
1246 Heil Quaker Blvd
La Vergne TN 37086
www.lightningsource.com

DARKNESS FALLS

Trista Ann Michaels

Chapter One

"Are all the cameras on the third floor in place?" Alana asked.

"Oh, yeah. And check out this view."

Alana leaned forward, staring at the massive computer screen over Tray's shoulder. He was her best tech and always got her the best angles.

"Looks perfect," she mumbled as she studied the third-floor landing through the eyes of her infrared camera with a cynical gaze.

Alana James, paranormal-romance author and ghost-hunter extraordinaire, was nothing if not skeptical. She'd become fascinated with ghosts while investigating her first paranormal romance. So fascinated, in fact, ghost hunting had become her second job after writing. Upon the success of her books, she'd approached one of the cable networks and now had one of the highest-rated ghost-hunting shows on television.

But Alana wasn't easily convinced. She debunked a lot of stuff just by looking at it logically, which more often than not pissed off their flashy tech guy, Tray. Now there was a man who saw ghosts everywhere he looked.

Tray glanced at her sideways and frowned. His impatience to begin this latest investigation was evident in the anxious drumming of his fingers on the makeshift desk that took up the back of the small box truck that held all their equipment.

"Is our contact here yet?" he asked.

Sighing, Alana straightened and tapped the edge of her walkie-talkie against her upper arm with growing impatience. "Nope."

"Well...damn," he snipped.

Alana's lips twisted with impatience. She knew how he felt. She was just as ready to get this started as the others were. They'd spent weeks investigating this house and just as many weeks playing phone and e-mail tag with their contact for this project, Councilman Aiden Barns.

Truthfully, she wasn't sure if her excitement was over the house or finally seeing Aiden in person. She knew what he looked like. She'd Googled him almost as soon as he'd contacted her about investigating the house. For one, she liked to know who she would be working for, especially long-term, which this project could prove to be. But also his voice had sent a ripple of pleasure through her she hadn't felt in...well, ever.

Tray snapped his fingers in front of her face, getting her attention. "You're thinking about that politician again. I can see it on your face."

Alana snorted. "He's not a politician. He's a councilman."

Tray's lips twisted. "Same thing. When did he say he'd be here? It will be dark soon, and I want as much time in that house as possible."

"It will take us at least a week, possibly two to go through this house, Tray. It's what? Thirty-five, forty thousand square feet? You can wait until he gets here."

She jumped from the back of the truck and glanced again toward the end of the long, tree-lined drive. What was taking him so long? He'd texted her earlier saying he had a last-minute meeting, but he'd promised he'd be no later than six. It was now six thirty.

"I hate waiting on people," she grumbled under her breath. She spun around and smiled at Tray. To hell with waiting. "You know what? He's running late, so go ahead and send Lisa with one of the cameramen up to the second floor."

Tray grinned. "I already did."

"When?" she asked.

"About ten minutes ago."

She leaned forward and hissed. "You're supposed to wait for me, you ass." Then she grinned wickedly. "But off the record, good job."

They both high-fived with a laugh as Alana lifted the walkie and hit the Talk button. "Lisa, where are you?"

"I'm on the second floor, heading toward the tower," her friend's voice came back.

"Anything going on so far?"

"God, yeah. Tell Tray he's gonna love this place."

Alana smiled. Lisa was one of the senior members of her investigating team. Lisa and Tray had been with her since the beginning, before Alana had her ghost-hunting show, even before she had her first paranormal romance published. Lisa and Tray went with her everywhere.

In the distance, she noticed a set of headlights and sighed in relief. *Finally.*

"Be careful up there. Looks like our contact has finally arrived."

"Careful's no fun," Lisa replied, and Alan could just see her sticking out her lower lip in a playful pout.

LISA MADE HER way down the dark hallway with a broad smile, the show's cameraman, Keith, just a few steps behind her. This house was amazing. It was huge, dark, spooky, and—if all the crap she'd seen in the last ten minutes was any indication—haunted to boot.

Unfortunately, it would take a little more than shadows and a few EVPs—or electronic voice phenomenon—to convince her friend and business partner, Alana.

Lisa heard the slamming of a car door and quickly made her way to one of the windows overlooking the front drive. A tall, gorgeous man climbed from the truck, and Lisa grinned, knowing Alana would be creaming her jeans standing that close to the hunk.

"That the guy you were telling me about?" Keith asked as he looked over her shoulder to see out the window.

"Maybe. If he is, Alana is probably having a cow right about now."

"Why's that?"

"Because he's gorgeous."

The cameraman shrugged. "If you say so. You said the other day Alana needed to get laid. Maybe now's her chance."

"She does need to get laid, but not by the guy who hired us. Are you crazy? Even I know not to do that. If we were out of here in a couple of days, I would say go for it, but he wants us to stay through Halloween and host the spook fest. That would be plenty of time for Alana to fall head over heels and get her heart broken. Not a good combination when the man is writing the checks."

Lisa looked over her shoulder toward Keith and narrowed her eyes. "If you repeat that, I'll cut off your penis, and you can forget about reattaching it because there won't be enough pieces left that are big enough."

Keith laughed. "You're brutal, do you know that?"

"How do you think I got as far as I did in life?" she countered, smiling. "Now let's hit that room Tray was telling us about."

"I'm right behind you," he said as she headed back down the hall.

Lisa opened the door to the large bedroom at the far end of the hall by the tower. It was dark inside, darker than she expected, so she pushed the button at the bottom of her flashlight to turn it on. For a fleeting moment, light penetrated the corners before it faded, leaving her in darkness once again.

"Damn," she said, shaking the flashlight. "I had a battery drain. How's yours?"

"Mine are okay. No, wait... Damn. I just lost battery power too."

She glanced at the small camera she had in her hand. "This one is okay, so far."

Just as she was about to turn, the door slammed shut between her and Keith. She gasped and dropped the camera onto the floor. "What the hell?"

The hairs on the back of her neck stood straight up, and cold air encompassed her entire body. She shivered and crossed her arms over her chest. The sensation of being watched made goose bumps rise along her flesh. "Who's there?"

"Lisa?" Keith called from the other side of the door.

Through the darkness her gaze caught a brief glimpse of a horribly deformed face, its skin ghostly white, its eyes a ghoulish shade of red. She'd never seen anything like it and screamed just as sharp claws caught the side of her face, knocking her off her feet.

ALANA SLOWLY WALKED away from the truck holding their equipment, moving to greet the oversize pickup as it sped down the drive and came to a gravel-grinding halt next to her SUV.

She held her breath as a man opened the door and climbed from behind the steering wheel, a warm smile of welcome across his handsome face. Black hair teased the edge of his shirt collar, the thick strands outlining a rugged, tan face. His lips were full and kissable, and his eyes were the most startling shade of blue-gray.

Her gaze dropped to his chest, and she swallowed at the width. The expanse had been hidden under his jacket in the picture, but without it, the fact he worked out was glaringly obvious.

God, he is so out of my league.

Alana had been out with her share of men. She enjoyed being around them, sometimes more so than women. Unfortunately, she wasn't the beauty-queen type, so guys tended to pass her by, seeing her as more of a friend or "one of the guys" than a girlfriend. Guys like Aiden wanted eye candy, not tomboy.

"I see you made it. I'm so sorry I'm late," he added as he extended his hand to her in greeting.

Alana took it, almost gasping out loud at the tingling warmth that traveled up her arm. She quickly jerked her hand free and tried to cover up her surprise by talking. "It's not a problem. All the cameras are in place, and I just sent one of our investigators to the second floor to begin."

"Excellent," he said with a smile as he rubbed his hands together. "Mind if I watch? I would love to know how one of these shows is done."

With a shrug, Alana turned, expecting him to follow. "Sure. Just don't get in the cameramen's way. They tend to get a little bitchy when too many people get underfoot."

He chuckled softly, and the deep sound made her stomach tighten. Why did he have to be so hot?

"I can certainly understand that," he replied.

"I think we all could," Alana said, smiling at him over her shoulder.

Their eyes met, and she'd swear she felt a jolt clear to her toes. Turning back to the front, she led

Aiden to the truck. Tray spun around in his chair to greet them.

"Aiden, this is my tech guy, Tray Sharp. Tray, this is Councilman Aiden Barns."

Aiden extended his hand to Tray, but all Alana could see was the way the moonlight reflected in his black hair. "Just Aiden, please."

Tray grinned and took his hand. "Just Tray."

Aiden chuckled. "Nice to meet you, Tray."

Her tech guy shot her a sideways knowing grin. Her eyes narrowed in warning. She knew Tray, and Tray knew her, which meant he knew she was attracted to Aiden. Hell, who wouldn't be?

"Not so bad for a politician," Tray said, and Alana rolled her eyes.

"You'll have to excuse him. He spends too much time working with computers and not enough time with humans, so he lacks manners."

Aiden's lips twitched in amusement. "There're days I would give my eyeteeth to trade places with him, I think." He looked at her with those heavenly eyes, and her knees weakened. "Have you given any thought to what we talked about?"

She swallowed, trying her best to remember. "The haunted house deal?"

Aiden wanted to do a month-long Halloweenfest in his town, with this haunted monstrosity at the center and her and her team as the hosts. It was an intriguing idea, one that had never been done, but she still hadn't made up her mind. As she continued to stare at him, she couldn't for the life of her come up with a reason why she shouldn't do it.

"I'll decide after we investigate the house," she replied, a little more breathlessly than she'd intended.

His gaze bored into her, and her heart skipped a beat at the heat she couldn't help but see directed at her. He blinked, and it was instantly gone.

"Fair enough," he replied.

"Don't worry," Tray offered from inside the truck. "The team loves the idea. We'll wear her down."

"Tray—"

"Oh, shut up," he interrupted, making Aiden chuckle.

"Our town could really use something like this to boost the local economy. Most everyone is for it."

"And who's not?" she asked in curiosity.

"The usual uptight characters."

She grinned. "Why, Councilman, surely you're not talking disparagingly about your constituents."

Aiden snorted. "Don't get me started."

Alana couldn't help but laugh at the thoroughly disgusted look on his face. From the sound of things, he'd apparently had more than his fair share of run-ins with those uptight characters.

Another member of her team, Jordan Sanders, stuck his head around the back of the truck, practically jumping in place to get inside. "Can we go in now?" he asked.

Alana nodded, and he waved toward his partner and the cameraman assigned to follow him. "We can go."

"Take the third floor," Alana called out as they headed toward the massive wraparound front porch.

"Who's taking the first?" Jordan asked.

"Tray and I will shortly."

"Can I tag along?" Aiden asked.

Alana looked at him in surprise. She wasn't sure she could have him close to her and still concentrate on what she needed to do.

"Well—"

Suddenly a scream came from the house that made the hairs on the back of her neck stand on end. She jerked around, glancing toward the second-floor window where the scream seemed to have come from.

"Was that Lisa?" Alana waved her hand at Tray, who had stood and walked to the end of the truck bed. "See what you can find on the cameras."

"I don't have anything pointed in that direction. Lisa was supposed to take care of that when she went up there."

Tray jumped from the back of the van while Alana lifted the walkie and pressed the Talk button. "Lisa."

Nothing.

"Damn it, Lisa. Answer me!" she cried anxiously into the walkie.

More screams filled the air, and Alana took off toward the house at a full run, fear for her friend overriding everything else. Behind her, she could hear Tray calling for her, but she ignored him and headed into the double-door entry to the house.

All the lights were out, but there was enough moonlight coming through the windows to light her way. She sprinted up the grand staircase and turned right down the long dark hallway heading toward the room where she believed Lisa had gone.

Keith was up ahead; the soft glow from his LED headlight cast a soft blue light against the wall and helped to guide her to them as he kicked relentlessly at the immobile bedroom door. Behind her, she could hear numerous footsteps as other members of her team ran to Lisa's aid.

Lisa's screams echoed through the halls, and Alana tried not to think too much about what might be happening. Maybe something had just spooked her.

Keith shoved at the door with his shoulder, cussing and yelling, "What the hell is the matter with this damn door!" He looked at her in desperation as she came up. "I can't get it. What the hell is going on in there?"

A loud bang shook the entire wall, as though Lisa had been thrown against it. Alana gasped and pounded her fist against the heavy door.

"Lisa!" She could hear screams and reached for the handle, shaking it as though that would open it. "Lisa!"

"Was anyone in there?" she asked Keith as Tray, Aiden, and a few others joined them in the hall.

Keith shook his head. "I didn't see anyone. Lisa went in first, then the door slammed shut between us, locking me out. That's when the screams started."

"Move," Aiden said as he pushed Alana out of the way.

He turned sideways slightly and rammed the door with his shoulder. The door didn't move. "Son of a bitch." He reached up to rub his shoulder and step back to study the door.

"You okay?" Alana asked, concerned.

Aiden nodded. "Oak. Serves me right."

Alana stepped forward to slap her hand against the wood. "Lisa!"

The room went silent, and everyone froze, listening. Alana could swear they could all hear her beating heart as it slammed out a rhythm within her chest.

"Lisa," she called out, pressing her ear against the wood. "Please."

A moan sounded from the other side, and Alana breathed a short sigh of relief. "We have to get this door open," she said as she again tried the knob.

Aiden moved her out of the way and waved for Keith to join him. "Let's see if the two of us can kick this thing open."

On three, they both kicked, and the door swung open with a loud *crack* as the lock gave way under the force. Alana's worried gaze landed on her friend, huddled in the corner. She rushed forward, oblivious to the men cautioning her.

Deep gouges in Lisa's skin oozed blood over her face, chest, and arms. Alana gasped as she tried to wipe some of the blood from her friend's face. "Lisa," she whispered. "Can you hear me?"

Lisa just continued to stare straight ahead, her eyes glassy and fearful, her hands trembling. Aiden squatted next to her and wiped a strand of blood-soaked hair from Lisa's brow.

"My God," he whispered. "Someone call an ambulance." He turned and stared at several stunned faces. "Now!"

Three members of the team pulled cell phones from their pockets to do his bidding while Tray began to walk a circle around the room, studying the walls. The window was shut, not to mention the fact they were at least twenty feet off the ground, so it was doubtful whoever it was had gone that way.

"Do you see anything?" Alana asked.

"Nothing," he said in exasperation.

She turned to Aiden. "How the hell would whoever did this get out of here? Where did they go?"

Aiden sighed. "This house is full of secret passages."

"Oh, come on," Tray exploded. "The two of you don't really believe that whatever did this was human?"

"Not now, Tray!" Alana snapped.

She glanced back at Lisa, who continued to stare off in the distance as though in a trance, her body shaking from head to toe.

"She's in shock," Aiden said softly.

Alana looked around the floor. "Where's her camera?" Lisa always carried a small handheld with her. It had to be there.

"It's here." Tray bent down to retrieve the small camera from the far corner. "I'll take this down to the van and see what's on it."

Lisa grasped Alana's wrist with a hard grip. Alana met her friend's fearful gaze. Tears sprang to her eyes as she studied the deep scratches over Lisa's face and neck.

"Not," Lisa whispered through chattering teeth. "Not human."

Chapter Two

At the hospital, Aiden stood back, trying to stay out of everyone's way as they awaited answers from the doctor examining Lisa. Alana had remained by her side, holding her hand through everything. She still hadn't said anything beyond "*not human*," at least that Aiden knew of.

What the hell had happened up there?

Alana stepped from the exam room, and Aiden pushed away from the wall. Other members of her team came forward as well, anxious for word of their friend.

They all began to ask questions at once, and Alana held up her hand, silencing them. "Physically, she's going to be okay. Although the cuts look bad, none of them were deep enough to cause any real damage. Mentally is another story. She's still in shock, so they're going to keep her here for a couple of days."

"Did she say who or what it was?" Tray asked.

Alana glanced at him, then shook her head. "No. She hasn't said anything, really. Why don't you all go back to the hotel? They gave her a sedative, so she's going to sleep the rest of the night."

"What about you?" Tray stepped forward and placed a hand on her shoulders. "You need sleep too."

"I know, and I will. I promise. Did you find anything on the camera?"

Tray shook his head. "It had gone dead. Some kind of battery drain, I think. Keith said it happened to his also."

Alana nodded sadly.

Aiden stood back and watched the exchange with a strange feeling of...jealousy. He'd felt an almost unreal sense of longing whenever he looked at her, which was odd considering she wasn't really his type. Aiden and his twin brother Noah both preferred blondes. He'd never in his life been attracted to a redhead.

But there was something about Alana, something he'd felt since the first time he'd talked to her on the phone.

Her eyes were the most unusual shade of deep green he'd ever seen, her hair a bright auburn riot of ringlet curls, and her skin fair. She reminded him of a fairy, and he half expected her to sprout wings and fly away. She wasn't as tall as other women he'd dated— somewhere between five-five and five-six, maybe. Her curves were fuller, more rounded, but God in heaven, she looked good.

She stood just a few feet away from him, perfectly proportioned for her height, her lips full and—he'd bet—soft and delectable. He could feel himself getting hard, and he silently cursed a blue streak. She'd just brought her friend to the hospital, and all he could think about was consoling her between the sheets.

Noah would be having a field day right about now. His twin could always tell what he was thinking and more often than not let him know it.

"You don't have to stay, either."

He frowned at her softly spoken words, realizing she'd said something and he should damn well be paying attention and not thinking about screwing her.

"I'll stay as long as you do," he said. "What's the significance of a battery drain?"

Alana waved to the others as they left, then moved to the sofa at the far side of the waiting room. Aiden followed. "There's a theory that ghosts will drain batteries when they're trying to manifest themselves."

He sat down next to her and let his thigh rest against hers. He could feel the tension in her body and reached out to grasp her trembling hand. Her fingers were ice-cold, and he wrapped them up in his, warming them.

"A theory?" he pried. "You sound skeptical."

"I am skeptical." She shrugged. She wouldn't meet his gaze and instead glanced toward the hall. "Why would someone do this?" Her voice was soft and shaky.

"I was listening to your team while you were with Lisa. They all think it was a ghost of some sort. Is that why you didn't tell them what Lisa said?"

"They already believe it was paranormal; why give them even more reason to think so?"

Her worried gaze met his, and for a second he stopped breathing. She was frightened. He could see it in her eyes.

"I want to stay and really check this house out. Maybe the additional time here will give the police time to find who did it."

Aiden was surprised. Here she was, obviously terrified, yet she wanted to leap forward and keep going. She had guts, and that impressed him. Suddenly, he wanted to know what made this girl tick; how she'd gotten started in all this and why.

"So you don't agree with your team," Aiden said, studying her, "that it was paranormal?"

"Of course not. Ghosts don't do this." She waved her hand toward the door. "At least not to that extent. We've all been scratched before, but this... There's no way."

"I would agree, but I have a feeling getting the others to agree will be harder than finding the responsible party."

She sighed. "Me too."

He reached up and touched the back of her head, allowing her strands to curl around his fingers as he gently combed through them. It had been intended to comfort, to console, but Alana jumped up as though she'd been shot, and walked swiftly over to the coffeepot.

He watched her, wondering if she'd felt the same bolt of electrical current he had the second he'd touched her.

"Why don't I take you back to the hotel?" he asked.

She stared at him, startled, before quickly composing herself. "You don't have to do that, really. I'll be fine here."

"Alana, I don't think you should sleep here." He waved his hand around the room at the various seating. "There's nowhere for you to stretch out. You'll need your rest if you're going to hit that house tomorrow night, right? You won't get it here. Too many people in and out. Not to mention the fact the hospital doesn't allow guests to sleep in here."

She glanced around with a frown. "You're probably right," she reluctantly agreed.

"Come on. The doctors put Lisa out for the night. There's nothing more you can do here. I'll drop you off, then, if it's okay, meet you back at the house tomorrow night around sunset. Deal?"

She nodded, and he escorted her out of the waiting room. She'd ridden in the ambulance, leaving her truck at the house. He wasn't sure if her reluctance was due to not wanting to be a burden or not wanting to be alone with him.

He walked her out to his truck and helped her inside. He already knew what hotel to take her to; he'd made the arrangements for them. She and her friend Lisa had the presidential suite on the seventh floor at the Johnson Hotel. It was a little dated but roomy with two bedrooms, a living room, a small kitchenette, and two and a half baths.

He'd been told they would need something with a lot of room so they could use it to set up the equipment for when they examined everything they'd gotten the night before.

The ride to the hotel was silent as he made his way through the quiet streets of historic downtown Dandridge. Occasionally he would sneak peeks at her from the corner of his eye. She looked adorable as she bit down on her lower lip, her brow creasing with worry. He wanted so badly for some reason to relieve those stresses.

What the hell was wrong with him? Someone would think he was a horny teenager with no self-control.

He stopped at the main entrance and climbed out, tossing the keys to the valet. "Keep it close. I won't be long."

"We can just leave it here, if you want. It's so late, there won't be anyone coming in."

Aiden nodded and reached out to help Alana down from her seat. He probably didn't need to, but he liked the feel of her hand in his. Once on her feet, she pulled her hand free, and he felt the loss like a punch. With a curious frown, he studied his hand as he followed her into the lobby.

She continued to remain silent all the way to her room, and Aiden let her. He was sure she needed time to think, to mull around in her mind what had happened. Without a word, she opened the door to her room and held it open for him to follow.

Once inside, she headed straight for the makeshift bar that had been set up in the far corner. Worried, Aiden stood back and watched her down three small glasses of vodka before finally slowing down.

"Feel better?" he asked as he leaned against the wall.

She snorted before taking another sip. "I think drunk is the only way I'll be able to sleep tonight. I keep hearing her screams in my head."

Aiden pushed away from the wall and walked over to her. He took the glass from her hand and set it on the bar. "That's not how you should deal with this, Alana."

"Who are you? My mother?" she countered, reaching for the glass.

He snatched it from her reach and was rewarded with an adorable scowl. "God, you're cute as hell," he murmured.

Her eyes widened in surprise. "Excuse me?" she croaked.

Aiden was at a loss for words. Had he really just said that out loud? "I said you're cute as hell," he repeated.

"Oh." Her shoulders lifted into a dismissive shrug. "And you're sexy as hell."

A blush moved over her cheeks briefly. He had a feeling the alcohol she'd just downed had a little something to do with that comment. He'd spent a lot of time talking to her on the phone, and he doubted she was the straightforward type. At least not without the help of a little liquid bravado.

He grinned, wanting so desperately to grab her and kiss her senseless, but the last thing he wanted to do was take advantage of a woman when she'd been drinking. Even a little. He didn't do that. If he was going to have sex with a woman, he wanted her in full control of her actions. No regrets later.

Keeping his eyes on hers, he lifted the glass and downed the rest of her vodka. He had a feeling he'd need it to dull the growing ache in his balls. Damned if it didn't make it worse.

"I think you need to go to bed," he said as he set the glass down. "And I think I need to get out of here before I end up in that bed with you."

He turned to leave but didn't miss her softly mumbled reply: "Chicken."

Aiden left the room before chuckling all the way down the hall to the elevator.

ALANA STOOD STARING across the room in stunned silence. Had she seriously just called him chicken? She leaned her hips against the bar and sighed tiredly as she gazed upward toward the ceiling. Her best friend slept quietly in the hospital, her face a maze of cuts and scratches, her screams still echoing in her head.

And where was Alana? she asked herself. She was in her hotel room, daring her gorgeous business acquaintance to kiss her.

She'd lost her mind. That's all there was to it.

Guilt ate at her insides; fear tightened her stomach. Tray slept down the hall, and she knew all she had to do was call, and he'd be here in a flat second. But the one person she really wanted by her side, holding her, keeping her safe and her nightmares at bay, was Aiden.

Why? She barely knew him. Yes, they'd flirted— sort of. That didn't mean he should stay and warm her sheets, make her feel more alive than she had in years.

She glanced down at the bottle of vodka, wavering between wanting to drink herself into a stupor and calling Tray. Or better yet, calling Aiden back.

She squinted her eyes closed. "Stop it, stop it, stop it. God," she whispered. "But I really don't want to be alone tonight."

* * *

Noah lifted his head from the book he was reading just as Aiden came through the front door looking a little worse for wear. He'd been informed of what had happened hours ago. As sheriff, it was his job to remain in the loop.

"Good to see you're still alive, brother."

Aiden shot him a look that clearly said he wasn't in the mood. "Like you didn't know."

Noah smiled. Yes, it was true; Noah knew Aiden wasn't the one who had been hurt. Not because he'd been told, but because if he had been, he would've felt it. That had been the case since they were teens. They had no idea what started it or why. It had just happened one weekend when they were apart and had been a part of their lives ever since. If one of them was physically hurt, the other felt it. If one of them had a hard-on, the other did too. Which reminded him...

"Which one had you horny?" he asked, snickering as Aiden glared at him over the bar separating the kitchen and den area.

"Aren't you the least bit curious about what happened tonight?"

"I already know what happened tonight as well as the girl's current condition. That's one of the perks of being sheriff."

Aiden rolled his eyes in irritation. "You don't have a clue, Noah. I've never seen or *heard* anything like it. Whatever it was that was in there had that woman terrified, but from the looks of things, no one was in that room with her."

"That you know of," Noah added. "That house is full of traps, hidden passageways, and God knows what else, Aiden, and you know it. More than likely he came in through the passageways. Please don't tell me you're starting to fall for all that ghost-hunter nonsense."

"I'm not falling for anything." Aiden grabbed a beer from the fridge and moved to the den to sit in the recliner facing the television. "And to answer your other question, it was Alana."

Noah tipped his head to the side in acknowledgment. "Which one is she?" he asked.

Aiden's hand holding the beer stopped halfway to his mouth as he stared at his brother in exasperation. "Have you not paid any attention to me at all over the last month? Alana is the redhead. The lead investigator and author."

Noah's lips twitched. There was nothing he loved more than pushing his brother's buttons. "God, you sound like a wife, do you know that? I don't need to ever get married; I have you."

"Fuck you," Aiden drawled, making Noah chuckle.

"Well, from the pounding in my balls, and the deep frown on your face, I guess I can surmise you didn't get anywhere with the girl."

Aiden grumbled incoherently before lifting the bottle of beer and taking a sip.

"I'm sorry, I didn't catch that," Noah said as he studied his brother.

"I said I'm not an ass, Noah. Her friend is in the hospital, for crying out loud. Besides, the second she got back to her room, she started downing vodka. I think the attack really freaked her out."

"I would imagine so."

"Did you send anyone to check things out?" Aiden asked.

"Yeah, but so far they haven't found anything."

"Have they looked for another entrance into the room?"

Noah nodded and closed his book. With a sigh, he set it on the table next to him. "I plan on going out there tomorrow sometime when it's light, see if I can find anything. We spent some time in that house as kids. I remember where some of the entrances are, but I'm not sure where the ones on the second floor are at. Maybe if I walk around a bit, some of it might come back to me."

Aiden frowned. "I know there are passageways on the first floor that lead to the third level, and one in the attic on the fourth that will take you back down to the first, but I don't remember any on the second."

Noah gave his brother a firm stare. "I know they're there. I remember Gram telling us the history surrounding some of them. The entrances are there; it's just a matter of remembering where they are. Whoever did this to that girl was flesh and blood, not a ghost. There's no such thing."

"Gram always thought there was. And so did you at one time."

Noah nodded sadly as he ignored Aiden's last comment and thought back to his Gram. She'd practically raised him and his brother. Well, not practically—she had.

Both her and the owner of that house, Karen Sharp. She'd been Gram's best friend since they were kids. When Ms. Sharp had died, she'd left the house to the town, with him and Aiden as trustees.

A couple of developers had tried to buy the place back from the town and turn it into a massive shopping complex, but most of the township wanted to keep the small-town feel and had voted the idea down, especially after hearing the plans for Halloween.

Aiden was the one who'd come up with the Halloweenfest idea. He wanted to play up the house's rich and supposedly haunted history, and it would be a way to bring in a little tourism and boost the local economy. Once Halloween was over, they would have the house refurbished and opened as a haunted bed-and-breakfast. Noah had been all for it. *It's a shame it had to start on such a sour note.*

"Why don't you ever want to talk about it anymore?" Aiden asked gently.

"Talk about what?"

"What you saw that night you stayed with Karen and I went with Gram."

Noah remained quiet, trying not to think about it.

"I know you saw something, Noah. I don't know what you saw, but I know it upset you. When are you going to finally talk about it?"

"There's nothing to talk about because I don't remember what I saw. Not completely."

Aiden sighed but didn't push, and Noah was grateful. He knew his brother believed him. Aiden could feel if he were lying. Noah could also feel Aiden's frustration. Aiden could still fully remember the fear of that night, and because Aiden could, Noah did as well, but he couldn't for the life of him remember what had caused it.

"Alana wants to keep investigating the house," Aiden said so softly Noah wasn't quite sure he'd heard him correctly.

He glanced over at his brother. The worry lines deepened across his brow as he stared into his beer bottle. Noah could understand his concern, especially after what happened.

Noah's lips twisted. "I'm not so sure that's a good idea."

"I'm going to be there as well. I asked her today if I could be a part of it. I don't know that my presence alone would stop it from happening again, but maybe between the cameramen and myself, we can keep our eyes open for anything suspicious. Besides, I'm curious now as to what did this."

"Don't you mean *who* did this?" Noah asked with amusement.

Aiden scowled. "Who. What. Whatever."

Noah fought a grin. Granted, there wasn't anything funny about this situation, but sometimes, despite what was going on, he couldn't help but aggravate Aiden.

He definitely needed to get a glimpse of this Alana to see what all the fuss was about, because there was apparently something about her that had Aiden in knots. His brother tried to hide it, but Noah could feel it just like he felt it every other time. They'd been that way since they were teenagers, and he doubted it would ever change. Even distance didn't lessen the connection.

Noah remained silent for a few seconds, then spoke. "I'll agree to letting the plan continue unless things begin to get out of hand."

"Fair enough. Hopefully last night was a one-time event."

"From your mouth to God's ears," Noah replied drily.

Chapter Three

Alana walked quickly into the hospital, stifling a yawn as she passed the welcome desk. She had hardly slept at all last night. Her mind kept jumping from Lisa's injuries to Aiden and how he'd looked at her while they were at the hotel.

Just thinking about it now made her skin tingle. She could feel the rush of heat over her neck and cheeks, and she took a moment to compose herself before moving on to the elevator.

The doors opened onto the fourth floor, and she stepped out, glancing down the hall toward her friend's room. Lisa's doctor stood at the nurses' station, and Alana rushed forward, anxious for news.

She lightly touched his arm to get his attention. "Dr. Logan?"

He looked up and smiled at her. "Good morning. It's Ms. James, correct?"

"Yes. How's Lisa?"

Dr. Logan closed the file he'd been looking at and set it aside. "Awake and asking for you. I'm glad I saw you first, though." He paused for a moment, and Alana tensed. "Lisa doesn't remember anything from last night."

"What? Nothing at all?"

Dr. Logan shook his head. "The last thing she remembers is boarding the plane in Atlanta. At first, she thought that maybe she'd been in a plane crash."

Alana's mouth dropped open in shock. "Are you serious?"

"I'm afraid so." He held his hand up, stopping her from asking her next question. "This sort of thing isn't uncommon in traumatic events. In time it may come back, or it may not. Don't push her. Let her remember on her own time."

"Do you think she should go back to the house?"

"That's up to her."

Alana nodded. "Thank you, Dr. Logan. When can she go home?"

"I would like to keep her one more day, just as a precaution."

Alana nodded again and walked around the doctor toward Lisa's room. She knocked twice before gently pushing the heavy door open. "Hello? Are you decent?" Alana teased.

"Of course I'm decent. Where the hell have you been?" Lisa asked in her usual brash manner.

Alana smiled, relieved to see her back to normal. She stepped farther into the dark room, letting the door close behind her. "They wouldn't let me stay," she said, then glanced around at the dark interior. "Lord, woman. What do you think you are? A vampire?"

She walked over and opened the blinds, allowing the morning sunshine to stream into the room. Lisa raised her hands to block her face. "No! The light! It burns!"

Alana laughed. "Oh, shut up."

Lisa joined in, and Alana moved to sit on the side of the bed. The scratches on her face and arms looked much better this morning, although a couple of deeper ones still looked red and swollen.

Alana reached out and finger-combed her friend's dark brown curls. "You look so much better this morning."

Lisa's smile faded. "What happened?" she asked softly.

"You really don't remember?"

Lisa shook her head sadly, and Alana's heart ached for her friend. How much should she tell her? Should she tell her anything at all? "You were investigating the house, and someone attacked you," Alana said, deciding to tell her friend at least some of what happened.

"Do you know who?"

"No. No one was in the room except for you. Whatever or whoever it was shut the door, locking Keith out. Your digital camera didn't catch anything either. Apparently there was a battery drain. Even drained that monstrosity the professional guys carry around."

Lisa's eyes widened. "Really? I wish I could remember something."

"No you don't," Alana replied. "Trust me."

Tilting her head to the side, her friend frowned. Alana knew what was going through Lisa's mind. It was obviously something bad if Alana didn't want her to remember. Lisa opened her mouth to say something, but the door burst open and three members of their crew came rushing in.

"Oh my God," Lisa said, clapping her hands and giggling as Tray placed a huge plate of eggs, bacon, and biscuits on Lisa's lap. "Thank you so much. This hospital food sucks."

"Yeah, I thought you might be needing something a little more...edible."

Alana laughed and tilted her head slightly, allowing Tray to kiss her cheek. "What's this?" he asked as he gently fingered Alana's straight hair.

Lisa gasped and reached out to touch her hair as well. "I didn't even notice it. You straightened it. You usually don't do that because it takes so long."

Alana shrugged, dismissing it. "I had time. I couldn't sleep last night."

Tray snickered. "Was it that you couldn't sleep last night or didn't want to sleep because Mr. Councilman had you occupied doing other things? I saw him escorting you down the hall to your room."

Lisa choked on her breakfast. "What? Did I miss something? Who's Mr. Councilman? Is he talking about Aiden Barns?"

"Yes," Alana replied to Lisa first, then turned to scowl at Tray. "And no, he didn't stay. He left right after he dropped me off."

"Oh, a quickie," Tray teased.

Alana grabbed a napkin off Lisa's plate and threw it toward Tray. "Nothing happened, smart-ass."

"Give it time," Tray said with more confidence than Alana felt. "I saw the way he looked at you at the hospital. That man is definitely in lust. And trust me, I know what that looks like."

Alana giggled despite herself. Tray definitely knew what men's lust looked like. He was gay, after all.

"Even if he did, that doesn't mean I'm interested."

"Oh, you're interested."

Alana glanced toward Lisa who watched her with a hint of amusement and just a little concern. No help from that direction.

"You might as well give it up. You can't argue with Tray," Lisa said, her lips twitching as she tried to fight an all-out smile.

Alana scrunched her nose at Lisa. She couldn't get over the difference between Lisa last night and Lisa now. Maybe it was a good thing she didn't remember what had happened. She glanced at Tray, who pointed the tip of his index finger toward his forehead. Apparently, he'd been told as well, and Alana nodded in silent understanding. For now, they would follow Lisa's lead. If she wanted to talk about it, they would. If not, they wouldn't.

* * *

Noah strolled through the massive house, studying the paneling along the second-floor hallway. Where was that damn entrance? He knew it had to be here somewhere. He remembered his Gram talking about using it to sneak into someone's room at the far end of the hall when she was a child.

He hadn't been in this house since he was a teenager, since before he'd left for college. The place gave him the creeps. It had always had this underlying sense of evil about it. It had ever since he and Aiden had spent those few days apart. He frowned. Why were there so many blanks concerning that weekend?

He'd asked Karen numerous times, but she'd brushed things off, telling him not to worry about it. He'd had a bad nightmare, nothing more. Deep down Noah had known it was so much more than that, but could never put it all together and had eventually given up, deciding to trust Karen and her insistence that it had been nothing.

Karen had been like a second mother to him and Aiden. He remembered so little about his own mother. She'd disappeared when he and Aiden were very young, leaving them with an indifferent and mostly absent father. Gram and Karen had been their saviors, keeping him and his brother out of trouble.

With a sigh, he wiped his palm along the smooth paneling, feeling for the hidden mechanism along the raised design in the wainscoting. All the mechanisms were the same throughout the house; it was just a matter of finding where they were hidden.

A cold shudder worked its way down his spine, and he shivered, trying to ignore the icy fingers of dread. He shook his head, fighting the sensations. Frowning, he realized it wasn't the first time he'd felt those sensations, and he knew instinctively it had to do with the house—something that had happened in the house or close to it.

He shook his head, trying to figure it out. Something just out of his reach; something he couldn't quite put his finger on.

This was insane. Ghosts didn't exist. Psychics didn't exist. Premonitions didn't exist. The connection between him and his brother shouldn't exist either, but that one he couldn't deny. He could ignore it, downplay it, or fight it, but he couldn't deny it.

Pushing the sensations aside, he rubbed his palm along the wood. Dust flew into the air, swirling around him, highlighted by the morning sun as it shone through the dusty glass of the bedroom to his left. A breeze blew through the open window at the end of the hall, blowing the dust into his nose. He sneezed, and the sound reverberated through the empty hall.

"Damn." He wiped at his watering eyes.

The hairs on the back of his neck stood on end as the feeling of being watched washed over him. He slowly opened his eyes and glanced toward the end of the hall, unsure what he might see but expecting something. He could feel it.

A young woman, her age indiscernible, stood at the far end staring at him. She had long blonde hair and a slim build. Something about her seemed familiar, as though he'd seen her before, but he couldn't think of where. She was dressed in an old, faded dress and had a look in her eyes that made Noah's muscles tighten.

He'd seen that look in women before—women who'd been abused, tormented.

He frowned. "You shouldn't be in here," he said. "It's dangerous."

The woman just continued to stare, and Noah got a weird sensation in the pit of his stomach. "Who are you? What are you doing here?" he asked.

She glanced around Noah's shoulder toward the other end of the hall in fear, and Noah turned to see what had upset her. There was nothing there, so he turned back to the girl, only to find the end of the hall empty. He scowled and took off running toward that end.

"Hey!" he yelled, looking into the bedrooms for the woman who had disappeared. "I'm not going to hurt you, but you need to get out of this house."

Silence.

He stood at the end of the hall, scowling. Where had she gone?

* * *

Aiden glanced up from the computer screen just as his brother opened the door to his office and stepped in. Noah never wore a uniform and instead dressed in street clothes, jeans and shirts usually. No one minded. Noah was one of the best sheriffs they'd ever had, so how he dressed was of little concern.

Noah had a strange look on his face, one that made Aiden uneasy. The tension and fatigue in Noah washed over Aiden. Something had most definitely startled his brother, and Aiden was curious as to what it was.

"Did you find anything?" Aiden asked.

Noah frowned and dropped into the leather chair across from Aiden's desk. "Yes and no."

"Okay. What does that mean, exactly?"

Noah leaned his elbow onto the armrest and lifted his hand to rub his fingers across his lips. "Well. I didn't find the main entrance on the second floor, at least not yet, but I did find the one on the third floor and the one from the main level to the attic."

Aiden raised an eyebrow. "Yeah? Anything out of place?"

"No. It's just as dusty and filled with cobwebs as I remember, although there are some...footprints, disturbances in the dust covering the floor, like someone's been walking around."

"Well, that is how we believe the guy got into the room without being seen," Aiden pointed out.

Noah narrowed his eyes, glancing at him in irritation.

Aiden's lips twitched slightly. "Isn't there an entrance to the second level within the lower passageway?"

"Maybe. I can't remember." Noah stared thoughtfully out the window.

"What's up, Noah?"

"A very bad feeling." He turned his gaze back to Aiden. "I saw a girl there today. Looked to be somewhere in her twenties, maybe."

Aiden sat back in his chair, stunned. "A girl?"

"Yeah, but she... Something behind me scared her. I turned to see what it was, but by the time I turned back, she was gone."

Aiden raised an eyebrow but remained silent.

Noah scowled. "Don't look at me like that."

"Like what?"

"Like I've lost my mind."

Laughing, Aiden made his chair swivel back and forth. "I don't think you've lost your mind. She has to know where the passages are, that's all, and while you were turned, she ran into one."

Noah looked thoughtful again. "Yeah, I guess you're right."

"So do I need to give you that speech about falling for all this ghost-hunter crap?"

Noah slowly stood. "Oh, you're just loving this, aren't you?" Aiden chuckled softly as his brother pointed a finger at him and continued to bark off orders. "Just keep an eye out, would ya? And keep looking for that entrance. It has to be there somewhere. I thought I could remember where the one in the hall was, but I couldn't find it. The ones in the bedroom have to be opened from inside the passage. You can exit the passage, then reenter through the bedroom, but you can't access it from the bedroom without unlocking it from the inside first. And before you ask, I checked, and the one in the bedroom was locked from the inside."

Aiden frowned. "I always thought that was strange, the way that was set up."

"I can't believe you don't remember any of this. Karen said they were set up that way because her father kept sex slaves locked in the bedrooms for government parties and special occasions concerning the governor. That way the men could secretly get into the room, but the girls couldn't get out."

Aiden shuddered and shook his head. "Karen had a strange family history, didn't she?"

"No kidding," Noah replied drily. "This whole thing with Lisa has to be someone's idea of a sick joke. Whoever it was knew they were coming and set this up. I'd bet my badge on it. That woman I saw today could possibly be part of it. Just keep an eye on things while you're out there tonight. Don't let the women go off alone or even with just one cameraman. Make sure everyone stays together in groups."

"Aren't you coming?"

Noah shook his head and turned to leave. "I have to cover a shift at the station. Derek is on his honeymoon, remember?"

Aiden scratched at his cheek and the stubble he'd forgotten to shave that morning. "Yeah. I forgot."

"And shave before you go out there. You look like something the cat dragged in."

Aiden made a face at his brother's back as he left his office. Yeah, he knew he looked scruffy, but he'd overslept.

"Sue me," he grumbled.

* * *

Alana stood at the van, trying her best not to drool as Aiden walked across the yard toward them. He'd changed into jeans, his freshly shaved face all handsome and tan, his shoulders wide and mouthwatering beneath the cotton of his T-shirt. The blue denim of his jeans hugged lean hips, and the cool early-fall wind ruffled his hair and stirred dead leaves around his feet as he walked. She licked her lips before she could stop herself.

Tray slapped her back, jolting her back to reality. "Ow," she growled, grasping her shoulder with her free hand.

"Don't look so obvious," Tray whispered. "Lisa would tell you to make him work for it. Shame she's still in the hospital. She would miss seeing you all moon-eyed."

Alana rolled her eyes. "Lisa would lecture me on the perils of having sex with the boss, and I'm not obvious or moon-eyed, thank you."

"Please," Tray teased. "You're *blazingly* obvious."

She bit down on her lower lip, embarrassed. Was she really that obvious? "Really?"

"Don't worry, doll. You're no more obvious than he is."

Alana snorted. "I swear I don't know whether to smack you or thank you."

"Why, thank me, of course," Tray replied sweetly.

She couldn't help but grin. Tray was a good friend and would never steer her wrong, even if he was steering her into Aiden's bed. But of course, she wasn't arguing. Tray watched Aiden as well over her shoulder.

"Did you get a look at his hands?" he whispered wickedly in her ear. "He's a good eight inches at least, or I'm a—"

Alana smacked his chest with the back of her hand as Aiden got within earshot. "Stop that," she hissed. "You're early," she added in a louder voice to Aiden.

Aiden's lips widened into an adorable, roguish grin. "I'm dying to get in that house again. I think you're beginning to rub off on me."

Alana giggled as a warm, tingling current of heat traveled along her flesh and settled in the lower region of her stomach. His gaze locked with hers, holding her frozen like a stone just inches from the heat radiating off his body.

She couldn't seem to move or breathe this close to him. She waited, watching breathlessly as his gaze dropped to her lips. The pounding of her heart echoed in her ears so loudly, she wondered if he could hear it as well.

What was wrong with her? She'd never in her life had this kind of reaction to a guy, especially one she barely knew. Well, she wasn't sure she would say *barely*. She had been talking to him through e-mail and on the phone lately, so she knew he had a fun and playful personality.

Her knees went just a little weak as she imagined what he might look like without that shirt. She licked her lips and didn't miss the way his eyes darkened as they followed her tongue's motion along her bottom lip.

Tray's palm landed between her shoulder blades and pushed. The shove caught her off guard, and she fell straight into Aiden's chest with a grunt of surprise. He wrapped his arms around her, holding her close to keep her from falling farther and making more of a fool of herself than she already had.

"Tray," she chastised. The heat of a blush moved over her cheeks as she raised her face to look at Aiden. "I'm so sorry," she murmured.

Aiden's lips twitched as he stared down at her with eyes full of lust. The fact that lust was directed at her made her gasp in shock and anticipation.

"I'm not," he whispered so softly she wasn't sure she'd heard him correctly.

Ohmygod! What the hell do I say? Think…think.

"Alana?" Her producer's voice calling from a few feet away on the front porch of the house broke the spell. "Where do you want to start? First floor or third?"

With a sigh, Alana put some much-needed distance between herself and Aiden before turning to face her producer, Jim. "We're starting on the third tonight. Let's steer clear of the second floor for now."

Jim nodded and turned to head back into the house.

"Organized chaos," she grumbled, giving Aiden a half smile.

"You handle it well."

Her lips twisted with fatigue and frustration. "It's all show. Lisa usually handles a lot of this stuff. Where we'll start, how long to spend on each floor. I tell people what equipment to use and who goes with who." Aiden's intense gaze almost made her forget what she had been talking about. She took a quick breath and continued. "Some investigators work better with others."

Aiden nodded in understanding. "Is there anything I can do?"

Alana had to bite her lip to keep from speaking aloud what went through her mind with that question.

Hell, yeah, there was stuff he could do. Lots of stuff. Lots of hot, sexy, dominant-guy stuff. God, she had to be losing it.

Think of Lisa. Think of your friend in the hospital, attacked by someone in this house. Think of work and the ghosts Tray was convinced occupied those walls. Think of anything other than Aiden.

"Alana?"

He raised an eyebrow in amusement, and she cleared her throat, embarrassed she'd been caught daydreaming. "Um, sure. I would love to have your help. You can go with Tray and me. This place is so big, we can send more than one team in at a time."

She reached into the truck and pulled out a small digital camera, which she handed to Aiden. As he took it, his fingers brushed over hers. Whenever he touched her, every inch of her skin warmed instantly, and she no longer noticed the cool temperature of the night breeze.

Pulling her hand away, she glanced up at the starless night sky in an effort to calm her racing heart and screaming libido. She couldn't ever remember wanting a guy this badly. Getting a handle on her hormones had to be a priority; otherwise she could easily see herself shoving him into a closet somewhere, ripping his clothes off, and climbing him like a tree.

Chapter Four

Aiden walked behind Alana, unable to keep his thoughts on what they were doing. All he could think about was grabbing handfuls of Alana's ass, which he could see perfectly from his position about four feet behind her. Wow, she looked good in those jeans.

He moved his gaze up along her back, watching the camera lights play off her hair. She'd straightened it, but as the night air became damper, her curls began to slowly creep back in.

"Where do you think we should start?"

Aiden blinked as he realized Tray was talking to him. He moved his gaze from Alana, forcing himself to stay focused. "When I was a kid, I remember Gram talking about the library being pretty active. It's down the hall and to the left at the back of the house."

Tray nodded and headed through the entrance and around the back of the main staircase. Alana followed second, then Aiden. Two cameramen followed behind him.

"Let's turn the camera lights off, guys," Alana said without turning around.

Instantly the camera lights went out, leaving the hall in total darkness. Tray and Alana turned on flashlights to make their way to the library.

"Do you normally do this in the dark?" Aiden asked. He kept his gaze on his small digital camera, which displayed an infrared image on the small screen, allowing him to see way ahead of him.

"Usually," Alana replied, still keeping her stare straight ahead. "We've done it both ways, but so far everything we've ever caught was caught in the dark."

"Interesting," Aiden murmured as his mind strayed to other things he could do in the dark with the delectable Alana. God, when had he turned into such a horny-ass teenager? "My brother, Noah, said he saw a woman in the house earlier today when he was looking for the passage entrance on the second floor. But she disappeared on him."

Both Tray and Alana came to an abrupt halt, causing him to almost run into Alana. He jerked to a stop and looked up to see two people staring at him as though he'd suddenly grown two heads.

"What?" he asked.

"Why didn't you tell me this earlier?" Tray demanded. "Where did he see her?"

"Come on, guys," Aiden replied with amusement. "He's positive the girl was real. She looked real, solid, just like us—"

"They can look just like us," Tray argued.

"Tray," Alana said as she frowned at something in Tray's hand. "The EMF gauge is spiking."

Aiden looked as well and noticed the row of lights blinking frantically, indicating a high electromagnetic field was close by. Tray lifted it to read the numbers flashing on the screen just below the lights.

"Whoa," Tray breathed, his voice full of barely contained excitement.

Tray and Alana began to look around the hall. "What's causing it?" Alana asked softly. "I don't see anything that would make it spike like that."

"Power lines in the walls maybe?" Tray asked as he pointed the device toward the wall. As he did, the numbers went down, and the lights dimmed. He pointed it back down the hall, and the numbers went back up.

"Is there a mechanical room or something close by?" Tray asked.

The hairs on the back of Aiden's neck stood on end, and he reached up to rub them. "This house is too old for a mechanical room."

"It's big enough to need one," Alana replied. "The wiring in this house has to be several decades old. Old wiring would spike like that."

"But it goes down when you point it at the wall," Tray reasoned.

Alana waved her hand, indicating they should continue. "Well, let's see if we can figure out where it's coming from."

"The temperature's dropping," one of the cameramen said from behind him.

Aiden frowned as a cold breeze blew past them from behind, as though someone had sped past very quickly.

"Did you feel that?" Tray asked as he placed his hand out, palm down, trying to follow the temperature fluctuations.

Alana swung her flashlight toward the far end of the hall. The dim light illuminated a woman, and Aiden's heart almost stopped.

"What the hell?" he whispered.

"Are you guys getting this?" Tray whispered.

"She's not coming in on the camera," one of the cameramen replied.

Aiden quickly lifted the small infrared one and pointed it at the end of the hall. A light, outlined image appeared, but nothing more. His gaze moved back to the woman, who stood silent, watching them with trepidation. Was this the woman his brother had seen? He gazed back at the camera and the floating, smoky image on the screen.

"She's on this one but as smoke, not a clear image," Aiden said in awe. He'd never seen anything like this.

"Holy shit," Tray said with a giggle.

"Did you bring any audio?" Alana asked as she glanced sideways at Tray.

Tray held up a small digital recorder in response.

"Who are you?" Alana asked as she turned back to the woman. "What are you doing here?"

The woman looked around as though frightened, but she didn't speak. "Did something happen to you?" Alana asked, then added, "Do you need our help?"

The girl's haunted gaze met Alana's, and Aiden's chest tightened. God, she looked so damn familiar, but there was also a darkness in her eyes.

"Something terrible has happened to her," Aiden murmured, and Alana quickly glanced at him over her shoulder before turning back to the woman.

A loud bang sounded from somewhere on the far side of the house, making everyone jump. Even the young woman appeared startled before disappearing right before their eyes.

"No! Wait!" Alana pleaded.

Tray held up the now dark EMF gage and sighed. "She's gone." He swung his flashlight around and pointed the light at Alana's face. She frowned and tilted her head to the side, moving the light to her cheek instead of her forehead. "So, Miss Skeptical," Tray began. "You got a logical explanation for that one?"

Alana's lips twisted. "Give me a second."

"Oh, come on," Tray argued.

"I'm not saying that it wasn't paranormal," she said in frustration. "But—"

"Oh, give me a break with the *buts*."

"Is this normal?" Aiden asked the cameraman standing behind him.

He chuckled. "The ghosts, or those two arguing?"

"Both, I guess."

"We don't normally see ghosts quite like that, but those two arguing... That's normal."

* * *

Alana paced behind the truck while Tray played with the settings on the computer. He wore headphones as he fast-forwarded and rewound his way through the audio. If there was anything there, Tray would find it. The two cameramen and Aiden waited as well, all three of them anxious and talking in excited whispers in the corner.

"Found it," Tray announced, and everyone rushed forward at once to listen. Tray used the mouse to begin the recording from the audio device. Alana could hear her own voice ask, "*Who are you?*"

"*He's here,*" a soft voice replied, and Alana got chills up her spine.

"*What are you doing here?*" Alana asked.

"*Must help. Dangerous.*" The voice was low and garbled, making it hard to understand. Alana had to rewind it twice to make it out.

"*Did something happen to you?*" Alana asked, then added, "*Do you need our help?*"

The loud bang came through the speakers, and Alana sighed, knowing that's when the girl had disappeared.

"Damn," Tray exclaimed excitedly. "That's some of the best damn EVP we've ever gotten."

"What do you suppose she meant by 'must help, dangerous'?" Aiden asked.

"I don't know," Alana said with a shrug, frowning. "But I think I'm more curious as to what she meant by 'he's here.'"

"She could be referring to who or what attacked Lisa," Tray offered.

Her lips twisted. "Possibly, but I'm still not ruling out residual or even something man-made."

"Look, Velma," Tray sneered.

"Velma? Who does that make you? Shaggy?"

"Oh, ha-ha."

"Are you sure the two of you aren't married or something?" Aiden teased as he watched them. "I mean, I'm certainly no expert, but that definitely looked ghostly to me."

"Thank you," Tray sang as he waved his hand. "That's all *I'm* saying."

Alana rolled her eyes and chuckled. "All right, Aiden. What's your impression of the ghost?"

Aiden shrugged. "My gut tells me something bad happened to her."

"Okay, we could go with that. Trapped ghost, wounded, tortured girl. Most of the time that's a residual haunt." Alana said. "Residual haunts are almost impossible to get rid of but easy to prove with evidence."

"So what do we do?" Aiden asked.

"We start with the girl," Alana replied. "Usually by investigating the history behind the house."

Alana studied Aiden, and he gave her a leery half smile. "Why are you looking at me like that?" he asked.

"You grew up in this house."

"Sort of," he replied. "But I don't remember ever seeing that girl. Dead or alive."

"She could be way older than you. Didn't you say this house was over a hundred years old?" Tray asked.

Aiden nodded once. "So why didn't we see her as kids?"

Alana twisted her lips and shrugged her shoulders, pretty much dismissing the question. "That's not unusual. Sometimes things happen in the present that stirs this stuff up."

"Like the attack on Lisa?" Aiden asked.

She pointed at him. "Exactly."

"Interesting," Aiden murmured.

Aiden's cell phone rang, startling him. He pulled it from his pocket and glanced at the screen even though he didn't really need to. He knew it was Noah on the other end.

"Sorry, guys, I need to take this. Don't go in the house without me. Yeah," he said as he jumped from the truck, flipping his phone open.

"Things going okay over there?" Noah asked.

Aiden glanced around the yard and the various people milling about and loading things into cars. "Well, depends on what you mean by *okay*."

"Aiden," Noah drawled tiredly.

"No more attacks, but we definitely saw something interesting."

"Like what?" Aiden could hear the trepidation in his brother's voice.

"That woman you saw."

Noah was silent for a second, then: "She's still there?"

"I think she's always here."

"Aiden..." Noah began.

"Brother, trust me on this. This woman is no normal woman." Aiden's lips twitched. "Do you remember, years ago, Gram telling us about the ghost of a woman who helped them find Laura's husband's will?"

"Yeah, I remember, but that woman wasn't a woman, but a teenager. Gram always thought she was one of the slaves who'd died in the house."

"That's right," Aiden said with a sigh. "This woman can't be her, then. Her clothes were too modern. We could see her, Noah, just a few feet in front of us, but she didn't show up on any of the regular cameras. Only the infrared."

"Have you been drinking?" Noah asked, and Aiden rolled his eyes.

"You know damn good and well I haven't been drinking. If I had, you'd be drunk too. I'm dead serious about this."

"I know you are. That's what concerns me."

"You need to get out here. See all this for yourself. There's also something else."

Noah sighed. "What?"

"She's trying to warn us about something or someone, but we can't figure it out."

"And you think I would be any better at it?"

Aiden grinned. "You *are* the cop. Besides, I think you should meet Alana."

Noah snorted. "You know, I can't seem to stop thinking about her, and I haven't even met her yet."

"You can't because I can't."

"I don't know that I like where this is going. We've fallen for the same woman only once, and that didn't go over very well, Aiden."

He glanced toward the sky and held his breath. The one time they fell for the same girl was a disaster. She couldn't handle both of them, so from then on out, if they became serious about a girl—which was almost never—they tried to keep some distance. Unfortunately, keeping some distance felt wrong.

Jeez, he and Noah were so fucking screwed up because of this connection they had. Sometimes being a twin sucked.

His gaze landed on Alana as she carried a small camera to Tray's car. She handed it to Tray, then, as though she felt him staring at her, turned to meet his gaze before heading back to the two cameramen waiting at the truck.

"Aiden?" Noah asked. "You're looking at her now, aren't you? I can tell because my balls are throbbing."

"Yeah," Aiden replied softly, not really hearing what his brother said. "We are who we are, Noah. We can't change that, so we might as well learn to live with it."

"It's not just us that have to live with it, brother. It's the woman."

Chapter Five

"There you are. What the hell are you doing back here alone?" Aiden snapped, making Alana jump.

She turned to stare at him over her shoulder as she fiddled with the settings on the camera resting on the edge of the veranda. Part of her thrilled that he would be that upset with her, but another part of her bristled at his high-handed tone.

"I'm not alone." She nodded toward one of her cameramen who had come with her to help set up the camera facing the windows.

He stood in the shadows, so it didn't surprise her that Aiden hadn't seen him. Aiden appeared apologetic as he nodded toward the tall man on the far side of the stone veranda.

"Didn't see you there," Aiden said with a wave.

The cameraman smiled. "Yeah. I kinda guessed that. I'm Bill."

"Aiden," he replied, tilting his head in acknowledgment. His stare turned back to Alana, and her heart skipped. "Why are you facing it toward the windows?"

"We sometimes catch things when we're looking in from the outside." She adjusted the tilt and stared toward the second level. "Bill, would you call the truck and tell them to check the angle?"

Bill spoke softly into the walkie before nodding in her direction. "It's good."

Alana breathed a sigh of relief that the small project was done and she could head back to the front of the house. She didn't like it back here. Despite its obvious previous beauty, for some reason the darkened windows on the upper level gave her the creeps. She felt as though she were being watched and constantly glanced upward to check, convinced she would see a face staring back at her. So far, nothing.

"Would you mind giving us a sec," Aiden said to Bill as he made his way toward them. "I'll make sure she gets back safe."

Bill glanced toward Alana, and she gave a small nod, letting him know it would be okay. He walked around the house, leaving her alone with Aiden. She wasn't sure if she was happy about that or not. Her nerves were so frazzled lately, she was sure all it would take for her to fall into his arms would be for him to open them, tempting her with a strong embrace to help her get through the nights.

"Tray confiscated my camera," he grumbled.

Alana couldn't help but laugh at the disgruntled tone in Aiden's voice. "That doesn't surprise me. I'm surprised you're not in the house."

"I could say the same thing about you," he said as he came to a stop much closer than she felt comfortable with.

Was he deliberately invading her space, or was she just overly sensitive? The moon had begun to rise, illuminating the backyard and highlighting his black hair with silver streaks. She turned her attention back to the camera and began adjusting the settings for shooting in minimal light.

"I just needed some air and to adjust the settings on this camera. It can sometimes be a little complicated getting it exactly where I want it."

"Do you need any help with that? I'm pretty good with cameras."

"No. I'm good."

She felt more than heard him as he moved in behind her. The heat from his body seeped into her back, and she fought a sudden and overpowering urge to lean into him. She could use a strong man to lean on at the moment.

She should feel elation at one of the best ghostly finds of her career, but instead she felt guilty that her friend wasn't here with them, that she couldn't stop thinking about the man who'd hired them, and that the man who'd attacked Lisa was still out there. Possibly still in this house.

She shivered at the thought that he could be up there right now, watching them.

"Are you cold?" Aiden asked.

She shook her head.

He moved a few strands of hair off her shoulder, and she held her breath, wondering what he would do next. Wondered if it would be so wrong to let him comfort her, make her forget, if only for a little while. Suddenly ghosts and anything they might have to say didn't seem so important or so exciting. What felt exciting was the touch of his hand, his breath on her neck, and the promise of a wild night of passion that shone in his eyes.

Her fingers shook as she tried to move through the options on the screen. She wanted to adjust the shutter speed, but for some reason, she couldn't remember where it was located.

Hell, what was she thinking? She knew why she couldn't remember. It was because one of the sexiest men she'd ever seen had his mouth inches from her ear. As he spoke, his breath brushed the side of her neck, making her insides quake with need.

"Do you really need to do that right now?" he whispered.

"What? Um...well..."

"This whole ghost thing... It's incredible," he murmured, his breath softly caressing the side of her neck.

She nodded in agreement.

"Part of me wants to be in that truck with Tray. Then I noticed you weren't there. Why weren't you there, Alana? Don't you believe what we saw was a ghost?"

She shook her head, licking her lips as she tried to clear her mind and control the tingling in her body.

"If you don't believe, why do you do it?"

"I didn't say I didn't believe. I just... I just needed some air."

He grasped her hands, pulling them away from the camera. She didn't fight him. She couldn't. He grabbed her elbow and turned her to face him, pinning her between his hard chest and the ledge. She slowly raised her gaze, knowing that if she looked him in the eyes, he would see she wanted him.

The same lust she felt tightening her breasts shone in his eyes as he gazed down at her, and her heart skipped a beat in excitement. He raised his hand, gently cupping her cheek. His thumb brushed across her bottom lip as he leaned down. Alana held her breath, her lips parting in silent invitation for him to plunder her mouth, do whatever he wanted.

She shouldn't be doing this. She knew she shouldn't be doing this, but...

He stopped so close all she had to do was lean in. She could flick her tongue out, touch his lips and savor his taste. His scent was warm, spicy, and all hot male, invading her senses and settling in her womb. She inhaled and licked her lips, swiping the tip of her tongue lightly across his mouth. He drew in a quick, sharp breath and grasped her head with both hands

"Alana."

She blinked, confused by the sound of Tray's voice.

"Alana!" he repeated. She jumped and stared down at the walkie clipped to her side.

No! No! Not now!

"Alana. I swear to God, if you don't answer me this instant, I'm calling in the National Guard."

She closed her eyes and, with a ragged sigh, grabbed the walkie with shaking fingers. Aiden dropped his hands from her face, leaving her feeling cold and alone.

She angrily hit the Talk button and brought the walkie to her mouth. "Do you have to be so overly dramatic?" she snapped.

"Where the hell are you?"

She glanced up at Aiden, who watched her with a mixture of hunger and curiosity. Had she seriously almost let him kiss her? What the hell was wrong with her?

"Alana?"

"I'm getting the camera ready," she quickly replied.

"Not alone, I hope."

"No. I'm not alone." Her voice faded slightly as Aiden's gaze held hers captive.

"You okay? You sound funny."

She blinked, turning away from Aiden's sultry stare. "I'm fine. Did you need something other than my location?"

"We're wrapping things up. It's almost three in the morning. We've got a lot of stuff to go through as it is."

"All right. I'll be right there."

She set the walkie down but couldn't bring herself to look Aiden in the eyes. "I really don't..." She took a deep breath for courage. "I really don't think we should be doing this. It's inappropriate, and besides, I need to be there for Lisa."

"Lisa's in the hospital," Aiden replied.

Alana lifted her head to glare at him. "Exactly."

Aiden sighed. "I didn't mean..." He dragged his hand down his face.

"It's just the wrong time, Aiden. That's all."

She hoped he understood, even though she didn't. She had a house to investigate—an amazingly haunted house—a friend in the hospital, and a sick freak still on the loose. The last thing she needed to do was become entangled in a romance, despite how tempting it might be or how much she might need that comfort right now—that strong embrace that would make her feel safe.

The last thing she felt at the moment was safe. She felt scared, unsure, guilty. Guilty that she would even want to start something with him when her friend needed her.

* * *

He stood at the window, gazing down on the couple from the third floor. He'd been watching them for a while, waiting with impatience for them to leave. This was his place, his sanctuary, and he didn't appreciate it being invaded. He thought he'd gotten rid of them the other night, but apparently they hadn't gotten the hint.

Looked like he would need to step things up a notch. He didn't need or want them here, and he would do whatever it took to get rid of them.

He had projects to finish.

* * *

Aiden stood outside Alana's hotel room door, indecision waging a war with his insides. Noah would tell him to just knock, stop hem-hawing around, as his

Gram used to say. He wasn't like this with women. Usually he had more confidence.

Honestly, confidence wasn't his problem. His problem was the indecision that plagued Alana. He could tell she wanted him just as much as he wanted her, but he also understood her hesitation.

But time wasn't something they had a lot of. Lisa would be getting out of the hospital tomorrow, and this would be the last night he would be able to get her alone.

He ran his hand through his short hair. God, that sounded so bad, even to his ears. *Fuck her before her friend gets out of the hospital and she's consumed with taking care of her.* Even he could admit how crass that was.

Before he could make up his mind, the door opened, and he found himself staring at her startled expression.

"Aiden?" she gasped. "What are you doing here?"

"I just wanted to make sure you were okay," he said. "You looked a little worse for wear when you left the house."

Her lips formed a silent "oh." "I'm fine," she whispered. "Just tired."

"Yeah, me too. It's one thing to stay up till four; it's another to do it and still work a day job."

Alana's lips lifted into a half smile. "I bet. I was just headed to ah...to Tray's room."

He lifted an eyebrow. "Tray's room?"

His gaze dropped to the sweats and T-shirt she wore. He couldn't stop himself from lingering at her nipples that poked through the material of her cotton top. She crossed her arms over her chest, apparently wise to the direction of his stare. Was there more to her and Tray's relationship than friends? A twinge of jealousy played at the back of his mind, and he frowned.

"Yeah, I kinda got..."

Aiden's gaze lifted to her tired, frightened eyes. "Spooked?"

She shrugged. "I probably should've just had him stay here, but I thought I would be okay. I can't believe what happened is affecting me more than it is Lisa."

"She doesn't remember. You do."

"I suppose. I sometimes feel as though it's partly my fault."

"It's not your fault, Alana. You sent someone with her. You didn't force her up there alone."

"Maybe I should have sent two with her. Someone in front and someone behind."

Aiden wanted nothing more at the moment than to pull her into his arms and comfort her, hold her till she no longer felt afraid and vulnerable. He wanted her to know it wasn't her fault, that no one blamed her, but he doubted she would believe him.

"Listen," he began. "Can I come in for a second?"

She frowned in concern. "Is something wrong?"

"No." He was quick to reassure. "I would just like to talk about tonight. The ghost, I mean."

She nodded, but he didn't miss the slight hesitation. "Come on in." She turned back into the room, holding the door open for him to follow.

"I'm not sure I could sleep tonight even if I wanted to. I've never seen anything quite like that in my life. I think Noah has, but he won't talk about it."

"Why?" she asked.

"I'm not sure. I wasn't there when it happened; I was away with Gram. I just remember waking up in the middle of the night, terrified, sweating, and I knew deep down that it wasn't me that was afraid but Noah."

"How old were you?"

"Around fourteen or so, I think. He was staying at the house with Karen while Gram and I were out of town. I know after that he didn't like spending time in that house and hasn't slept there since."

"I've heard of twins having that kind of connection. Never met any that did, though. Or at least any that admitted to it. Never heard of brothers who weren't twins having it."

Aiden's lips twitched slightly. If she only knew the whole of it. Would she be skeptical? Would she accept it or accuse them of playing her?

"Tray is on cloud nine, but I seem to be climbing the walls," Aiden said. "I noticed tonight that you don't seem to be quite as excited as everyone else. Why is that?"

She leaned her back against the wall and shrugged. "Something just doesn't feel right about it."

"Like what? Have you never caught anything like this?"

"No," she whispered. "Although that doesn't mean that what we're seeing isn't truly paranormal. I really don't know how to explain it. I've always been a skeptic. Even when we find stuff, I'm constantly looking for the logical explanation."

Aiden grinned. "Like Velma in Scooby-Doo."

Alana laughed, and the sound grabbed Aiden by the chest and wouldn't let go, settling inside, warming him, sucking him in.

"Yeah, I guess like Velma." Her smile faded as worry tightened the soft lines of her face. "This stuff never used to bother me. I never got scared, spooked, or nervous. Now it seems like I stay in a constant state of tension. I can't sleep." She sighed and shook her head.

Aiden moved to stand in front of her, cupping her cheek. She closed her eyes and leaned into his hand, seeking his comfort, his touch. He gently caressed her soft skin, trying his best to soothe her while fighting his own desire.

He understood her fear, her tension. Hell, after tonight, he wasn't sure he could sleep either.

"My guess is you've never had a friend attacked under your nose before, either," he whispered.

"No," she breathed.

He leaned in closer and brushed the tip of his nose across hers. He could feel the heat of her body, could smell the flowery scent of her hair and the sweet scent of the lotion she'd applied earlier. Her eyes opened, and she gazed up at him, desire darkening the deep green color.

"Seems we're both in the same boat, unable to sleep, tense," he whispered.

She swallowed. "Yeah."

God, he wanted to kiss her. Truthfully, he wanted to do a whole lot more than kiss her. He wanted to carry her into her bedroom and sink into her hot body, make love to her until they both fell asleep exhausted, unable to think about anything else. Especially ghosts.

"I swear I didn't come here to seduce you," he said, his breath coming out in short pants as he fought his growing desire.

Their lips were so close. He could feel her breath against his mouth, smell the minty scent from her toothpaste. They were so close, he'd swear he could almost taste her.

He dipped his head, swiping his lips across hers, and he could feel as well as hear her sudden intake of air. He pulled back, shocked at the sharp spark of heat that flared between them when his lips touched hers. Is that why she'd gasped?

He stared into her pretty green eyes and couldn't seem to remember how to breathe. Such sweet lips, so soft and...irresistible.

He slanted his mouth across hers, swallowing her gasp of surprise as he slid his tongue past her parted lips. Her surprise didn't last long. Her tongue mated with his, twirling and teasing, driving him insane. Her hands fisted in his shirt, holding him tight as he pressed her against the wall and deepened the kiss.

Her body molded to his perfectly, her curves fitting against him like they were meant to be there— like they were meant to be *his*. His fingers shook as they slid down her neck and over her collarbone. They lingered at her breasts, softly kneading. Her nipples beaded beneath his palms, and he pinched them into harder nubs. She gasped, arching her back and thrusting her breast into his touch, silently seeking more.

Her body trembled, and he wrapped his arms around her waist, pulling her lower body against him. He settled his cock into the vee of her thighs, pressing gently to release some of the throbbing pressure building within his balls.

God, he hurt. He hurt so badly. Every inch of his cock pounded and ached to be inside her. He couldn't remember ever wanting someone this badly, and only after one kiss. One hot, wild, glorious kiss that sent his senses careening out of control.

Her taste, the feel of her tongue against his, the way her curves molded along his frame, every inch of their bodies touching was like an aphrodisiac, fueling his already raging lust.

"Aiden," she whimpered into his kiss.

He knew what she wanted. He could feel her need as well as he could his own.

* * *

Noah climbed into his shower, gritting his teeth at the tension in his cock. Four in the fucking morning! He'd kill his damn brother when he got home.

Most of the time, he could block this out, ignore the lust running rampant through his veins whenever his brother had sex. But for some reason, tonight had been harder. He couldn't ignore it, couldn't stop it. It had never been this strong.

He didn't understand what was going on and hoped a cold shower would help lessen the pounding in his balls.

He reached out and turned on the water, wincing as the cold hit his skin. Aiden was having sex with her. He could feel it, sense it, smell it. Hell, he was positive he could even taste her. The scent of roses lingered in his nose, and he closed his eyes, inhaling slowly as he imagined the scent clinging to her skin and hair.

What the hell was going on with him and Aiden lately? What was it about Alana that strengthened their connection?

"Shit," he hissed as the cold of the water got to be too much.

With a twist of his wrists, he turned it to warm, sighing as the steaming water trickled down his tense muscles. His balls were pulled up so damn tight, he could hardly breathe. He reached between his legs, squeezing them gently, then harder as his mind raced with images of entwined naked bodies.

"This is going to be a long night," he sighed.

* * *

Aiden reached for the hem of her T-shirt, anxious to feel her soft skin against his. Nothing separating them, nothing to get between them.

He cupped her breasts, and she sighed, her soft moans of pleasure urging him on. As he kissed her lips, he pinched at her nipples, enjoying the way they hardened and grew.

Her soft mewling sounds vibrated against his lips as he slipped his tongue into her mouth, gliding it around the silken softness. He loved that sound, the way it came from deep in her throat. She held nothing back when aroused, despite the slight hint of vulnerability he'd seen in her eyes.

He definitely liked that about her. He liked a lot of things about her, and the more time he spent with her in person, the more things he found to like.

Was he falling for her?

He broke the kiss and pulled away to stare into her eyes—eyes such a beautiful shade of green, he felt as though he could lose himself in them forever.

He cupped her face, holding her still. He brushed his thumbs over her cheeks, enjoying the smooth feel of her skin. Beautiful green eyes stared back at him, slightly dazed, darkened in passion and surrounded by thick, luscious lashes. He'd never noticed how thick her eyelashes were, how deeply green and expressive her eyes could be.

Through their previous emails and phone conversations, he'd been attracted to her personality, her slightly sarcastic, always unpredictable wit, and her ability to make him smile. But that inner beauty enhanced her outer beauty, making her breathtaking in his eyes.

Was that why he found himself attracted to a woman so different from the ones he normally dated? Was that why he couldn't seem to stop thinking about her?

"What?" she whispered, her brow creasing in concern.

He shook his head, his mouth tilting up just a little. "Nothing."

Bringing her mouth to his, he kissed her again, silencing the questions he could see in her gaze. Her tongue thrust between his lips, and for a brief few seconds, he allowed her control, allowed her to lead. Her hunger, her need drove his own, making him lose what little restraint he had left.

Grasping the base of her head, he held tight as he deepened the kiss, pressing her back toward the wall as he did, pinning her there.

She landed against it with a thump, and he dropped his hand, grabbing her ass and lifting her thighs around his waist. The heat of her pussy penetrated through his jeans, and he groaned, grinding against her hungrily, showing her exactly what he planned to do to her.

Alana met every thrust, every motion of his hips, and the feel of their bodies moving together almost drove him to come in his pants.

"You make me crazy," he growled.

She panted, opening her eyes and staring up at him with a dazed expression.

"How is it you make me want you so fast?" he asked, panting too as he tugged her shirt over her head.

He tossed it to the floor, watching her face as he reached out and pinched her hard nipples. Her eyes closed, and her lips parted in a soft, breathy sigh. It was almost enough to push him over the edge.

With shaking fingers she reached for the wrinkled hem of his shirt. She had to push his arms upward, forcing him to release his hold on her nipples as she tugged the shirt over his head. Her hands feathered down along his chest, brushing across his nipples, and every muscle in his body quivered.

Her touch was soft, gentle, sensual as her fingertips explored his chest. They dropped lower, skimming over the muscles of his abs to the zipper of his jeans. He swallowed, wanting desperately to feel those soft hands gripping his throbbing cock.

Just as her fingers popped the zipper open, he growled and pushed her thighs back down, setting her feet on the floor.

"Bedroom," he ground out. "Which one?"

"The one at the back," she whispered, her voice shaking with need.

"Go," he ordered as he kicked his shoes off.

He followed her, his gaze glued to the sexy sway of her ass as she walked. Once she reached the bed, she turned to face him. Aiden even surprised himself when he raised his hands and shoved her back to land in the middle of the mattress on her back.

She squealed, but not from fear. A tiny, soft, tinkling laugh filled the room as he gripped the waistband of her sweats and tugged them off her hips. He was going mad; he could feel it. The hunger and lust for her coursing through his veins was unlike anything he'd felt before. The intensity made his hands tremble as he grabbed her panties and pulled them off as well.

She lay before him, her lips red and puffy from his kiss, her eyes droopy from passion, her face flushed. She spread her thighs, and his gaze dropped to her glistening pussy. He licked his lips, anxious to taste the juices that coated her clean-shaven labia.

He put one knee on the bed and reached for the pillows piled at the headboard.

"Lift your hips," he ordered and slid two pillows under her ass as she raised it.

Her eyebrow rose in curiosity as he put both feet on the floor and began to remove his pants.

Chapter Six

Alana stared with a mixture of fascination and anticipation. She knew he was large, but she hadn't realized just how big and muscular he was until he'd taken his shirt off. She'd felt every inch of that glorious chest with her fingertips, and as she did, she could feel herself getting even wetter.

The soft blue light from the nightlight in the bathroom bounced off his bronze skin, highlighting the bulges of his washboard abs and hard pecs. God, he looked good—good enough to eat. Her tongue darted out to swipe along her bottom lip, and the spark of lust in his eyes made her insides quiver with anticipation that threatened to eat her alive.

He pushed his jeans down over lean hips and thick thighs. When did he have time to work out? From what she understood, he sat behind a desk most of the day.

Her gaze locked onto his thick cock, and she swallowed, unsure she'd be able to take all of him. The walls of her pussy clenched as she imagined him filling her with his thick rod. Precum glistened on the purple tip of his engorged cock, catching the light as well as her interest. He wrapped his fingers around himself and pumped upward, forcing more of the liquid out the tiny hole at the tip. He swiped his thumb across it and then leaned onto the bed, putting that cream-coated thumb at her lips.

She opened them and swiped her tongue over the pad of his thumb, licking away the juice. His salty taste filled her mouth as she sucked his thumb between her lips, removing every last drop.

His eyes narrowed as he watched her, and she felt powerful, beautiful, and sexy. He pulled his thumb free and feathered his hand down her chest and stomach as he climbed onto the bed, settling his face between her thighs.

Alana held her breath as she realized what he had in mind. She raised her head, watching as he used the pads of his thumbs to separate her labia. He blew softly against her clit, and she dropped her head back into the mattress with a sigh, her hips lifting toward his face for more.

"Like that?" he whispered, his breath teasing her clit as he spoke.

She could hardly breathe, much less answer. He pressed two fingers deep into her pussy, and she cried out, lifting her hips higher, trying to take more of his fingers inside her. Juices dripped from her pussy to run between the cheeks of her ass and dampen the pillow beneath her.

Her body wanted more, needed more. The walls of her pussy throbbed and ached to feel his thick girth stretching her, filling her till she wanted to scream. And he could definitely make her scream. She wanted to scream now—scream at him to fuck her, to end this misery.

His teeth nipped at her labia, nibbling playfully as his fingers dipped in and out. He slid them between the cheeks of her ass, teasing and circling the tight opening to her anus. She tensed, realizing with just a hint of shock that she wanted him to enter her there. She wanted to feel his fingers sliding into that tight opening, filling her deep.

He moved his fingers back to her pussy, thrusting them inside before pulling back out again, making her moan at the emptiness and the easing of his fingers. His tongue gently circled her clit, tormenting her with light flicks that made her hips jerk and grind.

She fisted her hands, gathering the soft material of the bedspread within her fingers as she fought the growing tide of lust. Every inch of her skin crawled with the need to feel him inside her, filling her, fucking her.

He slowly pressed two fingers as deep as they would go into her anal passage, and she tensed as a dark need rushed through her veins.

"Aiden," she squealed as the first stirring of her climax tightened her womb.

He added a third finger, stretching the tight passage, and she winced as the bite of pain transformed to a pleasure she'd never known existed. No one had ever touched her there, not like that, and she found she liked it. She liked it a lot.

Growling softly, he licked along her slit, lapping at the juices she could feel pouring out from her opening.

"Yes," she hissed over and over. "Yes. Yes."

He thrust his fingers in and out of her ass, teasing her channel from the other side as his mouth ate at her pussy and clit. She panted and squealed, her hips lifting and grinding, wanting more but at the same time not wanting it to end.

She was so close—so very close. Aiden seemed to know just what to do to keep her on that edge, to keep her dangling so close to the precipice she struggled to keep from, begging him to put her out of her misery.

"Don't stop," she panted as her fingers clenched and unclenched within the bedspread.

He shoved his fingers deeper, pumping them into her harder as he flattened his tongue against her clit and sucked. She gasped loudly, forcing her hips into his face as her orgasm slammed through her with an intensity that made her feel light-headed and ready to black out. Her limbs trembled as the throbs tightened the walls of her pussy and anus. She could feel them squeezing at his fingers, milking them as they came one after another.

Aiden removed his fingers and climbed over her just as the last of the throbs began to ease. He pressed the head of his cock at her dripping entrance, and in one, hard, long thrust, entered her pussy balls-deep.

Alana screamed and lifted her legs around his waist, holding tight to his arms as he rotated his hips, hitting her sensitive clit and sending sharp tingles of pleasure straight to her womb.

"Fuck, you feel good," he growled.

She looked up at him, stared into eyes so dark with passion, they were almost navy blue. He pulled out slowly, sighing before ever so gently pushing back in with a groan, her juices easing the way for his overly thick rod. She moaned as he pressed deep, stretching her tight passage around his cock.

She could feel so much. His heat, his heartbeat as blood rushed through the thick vein that ran the underside of his shaft and teased her walls, making her wild.

"Oh God," she gasped as he pulled almost out, then pressed back in slowly, inch by gloriously thick inch.

He growled deep in his throat like an animal, and the sound made her womb tighten. She liked that sound. It made her tremble from head to toe in pleasure so great, she wanted to scream.

She dropped her hands to his hips, digging her nails into the tight mounds of his ass as he continued his slow pumping.

"Faster," she begged, wrapping her legs around his lower back.

"Not yet," he whispered, his voice vibrating with a deep, sexy timbre.

He lowered his head, burying his face in the side of her neck, his lips teasing the sensitive spot behind her ear.

"I like the way you feel," he murmured as he pressed deep, grinding against her clit.

She moaned and scratched at his lower back, trying to force him even farther inside her, trying to make him a part of her.

"I like how your pussy squeezes my cock," he sighed as he pulled out, then pressed back in hard. "I like how you squeal when I shove every inch of it inside you."

Had she squealed? She wasn't sure. At the moment, she didn't care.

"Aiden," she groaned.

God, she was close. She was so close, she could taste it. Every part of her body shook with the rising intensity, the burning need to feel that glorious pleasure again and again.

Her stomach tightened, clenched, quivered as he increased his speed, thrusting faster, grinding against her clit on the down thrust and making her cry out with every glorious flick of his hips. His balls slapped against her ass, teasing her; his chest rubbed against her nipples as he moved, making them harden and throb.

One of his hands moved to cup her ass, then moved lower to the back of her thigh. He pushed, lifting it over his arm and forcing her to take even more of him.

Alana panted as the walls of her pussy throbbed and pulsed around his invading cock. Her womb clenched, then released a pleasure so wild and intense, she actually screamed.

Aiden pumped into her hard, over and over, hitting her cervix until one orgasm rolled into another. Her head lolled from side to side as she rode out one shockingly intense wave after another until he tensed above her, shouting as he lost himself in his own release.

His grip on her thigh eased, and her legs fell to the bed, limp and useless. Aiden dropped his forehead, resting it against hers as their breathing slowly returned to normal. He took a deep breath, then let it out with a soft chuckle.

"You're a little wildcat," he murmured, a sexy grin tugging at his lips. "I like wildcats."

"I could tell," she replied, returning the playful quirk of his lips.

He chuckled again, and the sound vibrated against her nipples, making her shiver. She shifted her hips, and he gasped, pressing into her.

"Fuck," he growled, rising up on his elbows.

The shocked, almost fearful look on his face made her nervous, and she tensed. "What?"

"We forgot condoms. I can't believe I forgot a fucking condom. Alana, I'm so sorry."

Her eyes widened as what he said sank in. She was on the pill, so pregnancy wasn't a worry, but...

"I get tested often, and I'm on the pill," she whispered. "I know I'm safe. Please tell me you're okay."

Aiden dropped his forehead to hers in relief. "I'm fine. We're fine. So's Noah."

"Oh, shit. That was stupid." Alana sighed. She frowned at his mention of Noah but decided to push it from her mind for the moment.

Aiden snorted. "That's how crazy you make me."

He raised his head and stared down at her in a mixture of awe and uncertainty. He cupped her cheek, softly rubbing his thumb along her bottom lip. The way he looked at her made her feel so safe, pretty, but at the same time scared as hell.

She came here to investigate a house, not get involved with a guy.

"When do you pick up Lisa?" he whispered.

She blinked, her chest tightening with guilt as she realized she'd temporarily forgotten about her friend.

"This morning," she replied. "By ten."

He nodded and gently kissed the tip of her nose before brushing his lips along her jaw. His teeth scraped at the skin on the side of her neck, making it hard to concentrate, to think of anything other than what he made her feel. At the moment, there were no ghosts, no crazy weirdos, no deadlines or crew members. There was just her and Aiden.

He pulled the pillows from under her hips and moved them to the side. She lowered her hips to the bed, and Aiden's sank with her. He kept his cock inside her, his half-hard length sliding against her walls as they followed each other's movements to find a more comfortable position. She sighed, shifting her hips against his and making him moan as the heat of his skin warmed hers.

His lips brushed over her temple, and she closed her eyes, stroking her hands slowly up and over the hard muscles of his back. His muscles twitched beneath her exploring fingers.

"That's nice," he sighed in her ear, his breath tickling her neck. "Can you meet me at my office for a late lunch?" he asked.

"Are you going in?" she asked.

"I have to, whether I sleep or not. And right now, the last thing I want to do is sleep."

He brushed his lips over hers, and instantly she realized just how easily she could lose her heart to this man. She needed to remember to keep it strictly physical. Get all she could for as long as she could, then go home with her heart intact.

Or at least that was the plan anyway. Alana knew plans didn't always go as they were meant to.

Chapter Seven

"Good morning," Alana sang as she stepped into Lisa's hospital room.

Her friend's hair was fixed this morning, her makeup once again perfect. The cuts had begun to fade, but Alana still worried what might happen if and when Lisa regained the memory of her attack.

Lisa turned to her and smiled. "There you are." Her smile faded as Alana came farther into the room.

She knew what was coming, what Lisa saw when she looked at her: the lack of sleep, the hickey on her neck. Alana felt the heat of a blush move over her cheeks as Lisa's eyes narrowed.

"Oh my God. You slept with him."

"Lisa—"

"Don't 'Lisa' me. We're working with him, Alana. Not just investigating the house, but he wants us to stay in town and host Halloweenfest. Have you lost your mind?"

"I know what I'm doing," Alana snapped as she dropped her purse on the bed. "It's just a physical thing, nothing personal. We can stay and do Halloween, then we move on."

"Uh-huh. Then Tray and I pick up the pieces once we do."

"Lisa—"

"I know you, Alana. You can do one-night stands. I've seen you do them. You do them well. But this isn't a one-night stand. He's not going to disappear the next day."

"Don't start lecturing me," Alana snapped and narrowed her eyes in anger.

Although, truthfully, she wasn't sure who she was really angry with: Lisa for pointing out the truth, or herself for getting into a situation she knew would break her heart.

"I don't want to lecture you," Lisa said softly, worry clouding her eyes. "You're my best friend. I just don't want to see you get hurt."

"How do you know I'll get hurt?"

Lisa sighed and shrugged. "I don't, I guess. I probably shouldn't say anything. You're the one who's been talking to this guy for weeks. The two of you have been flirting and tiptoeing around each other for a while. Who am I to jump to conclusions and assume he'll hurt you?"

Alana scowled and handed Lisa her jacket. "Maybe I'm the one who will break his heart."

Lisa snorted. "You couldn't break someone's heart if you tried. You're too sweet."

"Oh, I don't know," Tray said as he walked into the room and held the door open for the nurse to bring in Lisa's wheelchair. "Alana can be quite the devious bitch when she wants to be."

Lisa snickered.

Alana frowned. "Well, Tray. Thanks...I think."

Tray chuckled and leaned over to kiss her cheek. Standing straight, he softly touched the side of her neck, his mouth quirking into an amused grin. "You should have worn a turtleneck today, sugar."

Alana's lips twisted as she glanced at the nurse, who tried her best to hide her grin. With a *harrumph*, she shoved his hand away. "Help Lisa, you queen."

Tray laughed and turned to offer Lisa his hand as she made herself comfortable in the wheelchair. "I don't know why I even need this," she grumbled.

"It's the rules, dear," the nurse replied as she turned the chair and pushed it out into the hallway.

"So when did he get there?" Tray asked.

"Who?" Alana responded, deliberately being coy.

"Alana," he chastised. "It's me, remember?"

Alana sighed, relenting. "Not long after we got back to the hotel."

"Did you get any sleep last night at all?" Tray asked as they followed the nurse down the hall.

"I got about two hours after he left to get cleaned up for work."

Tray's brow rose. "He went to work?"

She shrugged. "He's a glutton for punishment like us, I guess." She glanced at him from the corner of her eye. "Have I lost my mind, do you think?"

Tray scoffed. "No way. Honey, I'm all for it. I think Aiden is one hot hunk, and if you hadn't fucked his brains out, I would have."

Alana snorted.

He shot her a sideways glance, his lips sticking out in a pout that made Alana want to grin. "What's that snort for? Don't think I could?"

"I have no doubt you could if it were the right guy, but Aiden's straight."

Tray grinned, then drawled, "Well, I guess you would know."

Alana slapped the back of her hand across his hard abs. Tray grasped it and brought her fingers to his lips, laughing. "I love you, Alana."

"I know," she said with a smile.

"Hey, what about me?" Lisa asked, glancing back at them over her shoulder.

"We love you too," Alana and Tray sang together, making even the nurse giggle.

"Has anyone got a car?" the nurse asked.

"I have mine right outside the door," Tray replied. He glanced at Alana. "I thought Lisa might want to run some errands with me, get out for a while."

"I'd love that," Lisa said with a wide smile.

Alana couldn't help but smile back. It was amazing how good and happy she looked, despite what had happened. The loss of memory didn't seem to be bothering her. The doctor thought that might also be part of her blocking mechanism. In her mind, nothing terrible had happened, and maybe that wasn't such a bad thing.

"Do you want to tag along?" Tray asked. "Or do you have other plans?"

"I'm supposed to meet Aiden for lunch, but I can tag along for a while. Where are you going?"

"Best Buy," Tray replied. "We need more cable." Tray waved his hand with an excited flourish. "Lots more cable, and a couple more audio recorders."

The automatic doors opened, letting in the cool fall air, and Alana pulled her leather jacket tighter across her chest. Despite the warm morning sun, a cold front had moved through, dropping the temperatures dramatically.

Tray hit the button on his key fob and unlocked the doors to his car. "Can you believe our luck with this house?" he said, smiling. "I want to get as much proof as I can. Especially of that woman."

"What woman?" Lisa asked as she slid into the passenger seat of the car.

"Tray hasn't told you about that?" Alana asked.

"I kept the house talk to a minimum," Tray replied softly to Alana. "You know..."

Lisa scowled up at them. "Okay, let's get something straight real quick, guys. You do not have to baby me, keep me in the dark, or otherwise coddle me. Are we clear?"

Alana snickered at her friend's usual brash manner. "As glass, my queen."

"Got it," Tray replied with a curt nod and kissed the tip of her nose.

"Good. Now let's go." With that final command, Lisa slammed the car door closed, leaving Alana and Tray outside the car, giggling.

* * *

Noah stood in his brother's office, staring at the various pictures on the wall of family members, friends, and local celebrities. Aiden had always been popular, even as a kid. Noah had been quieter, more discreet.

They'd learned at a young age the only way people could tell them apart was by their personalities, so they'd defined themselves early on. Aiden had been the sports jock, the talkative one. He'd run for class president and had been editor of his college paper for three years.

Noah had been the bookworm, the intellectual, and was usually quieter than his brother. He kept a smaller circle of friends, and Noah liked it that way. He wasn't the partier like his brother. He didn't enjoy politics. He hated them, as a matter of fact.

He just wanted to do his job, keep his town clean and safe, and enjoy an occasional weekend barbecue on the houseboat they owned together. And maybe one day find a woman who could put up with his and his brother's unusual quirks.

"Hi," a soft, sexy female voice called from behind him, and he slowly turned, knowing instinctively who it was.

Alana.

His gaze roamed over her curly auburn hair, her laughing green eyes, and full, sensual lips that were perfectly made for kissing. She wore jeans that clung to her hips. Her orange-and-cream sweater hugged her chest and outlined the curve of her breasts and waist to mouthwatering perfection. A brown leather jacket was slung over her crossed arms as she leaned against the doorjamb. His perusing gaze caught sight of a small hickey just below her ear, and he grinned, knowing exactly who'd put it there.

Noah didn't say anything, just watched mesmerized as she pushed away from the door and walked over. She reached up and wrapped her arm around his neck, sliding her fingers through his short hair.

She thought he was Aiden; he could see it in her passion-filled eyes. Eyes so pretty and emerald green he could drown in them. God, her picture didn't do her justice...at all.

Standing on tiptoe, she tugged his head down to hers and slanted her lips, covering his in a sweet kiss he couldn't have pulled away from if his life depended on it.

He should be shot for this. She'd be pissed if she knew who he was and that he'd let her do this without saying a word. But after last night, after all the physical pain and pleasure he'd gone through as he'd felt every sensation his brother had, he couldn't not have one taste.

He put his hands at the small of her back and under the hem of her sweater. Splaying his fingers against her warm skim, he pulled her closer just as he thrust his tongue past her parted lips. She tasted of coffee—warm, white chocolate coffee—and he deepened the kiss, letting his tongue devour the taste and the feel of her tongue as it twirled around his.

His whole body sparked to life as her mouth molded perfectly to his own. No wonder his brother was smitten. There was something about her that set every inch of his flesh on fire.

Noah barely heard the sound of Aiden clearing his throat just before Alana jerked back out of his arms. Her cheeks turned the most adorable shade of red as she tried to compose herself and turn to face the intruder. Noah braced himself for the inevitable anger.

Her gaze landed on Aiden and widened in shock.

"Alana, I'd like for you to meet my brother, Noah," Aiden said as he leaned casually against the doorjamb.

"Oh my God," she whispered as she turned to stare at Noah.

Then those beautiful green eyes narrowed in anger. Anger he deserved.

"Why the hell didn't you say something?" she demanded.

Noah shrugged, trying to think of anything to say that might make even the smallest amount of sense.

"It wouldn't be the first time," Aiden said, his lips quirking with just a hint of amusement.

Noah scowled at his brother, who didn't appear to be helping at all.

"What do you mean it wouldn't be the first time?" Alana snapped, apparently just as pissed at Aiden's obvious enjoyment of the whole situation.

"He's not painting this in the best light," Noah murmured as he glared at his brother.

"Painting what in the best light?" Alana asked as her gaze moved from one brother to another. "Is this what you brought me here for? Some sick sex game with your brother?"

"No," Aiden exclaimed as he pushed away from the doorjamb.

"Then what?"

"I didn't even know Noah was here. I thought we were meeting him at the restaurant." Aiden shrugged. "I wanted you to meet him."

"You need to be honest with her, Aiden," Noah said, staring pointedly at his brother.

Aiden's eyes narrowed. "Not now."

"Honest about what?" she demanded. "And don't you dare say not now! It better be now!"

"It's kind of hard to explain," Aiden began as he reached behind him to shut the door and give them a little more privacy.

"Try me."

"Obviously Aiden and I are twins," Noah began, trying to find the right words.

He should've never let her kiss him. This would have gone so much easier if he hadn't.

"Obviously," she drawled, crossing her arms over her chest. "What? Are you going to try to tell me that not only do you share a mental connection but you share girlfriends?"

Aiden and Noah both looked at her a little shocked that she'd hit it on the head so damn fast.

"Not always," Noah tried to reason. "But this time the connection is pretty...well, it's pretty strong. Stronger than it's been before."

Aiden frowned at him. "What?"

Noah opened his mouth to explain, but Alana's snort of disgust stopped him cold. He took a deep breath and tried again. For some reason it was important to him that she understand—then she could hopefully accept it.

"I know that Aiden had sex with you last night. I could feel it."

"Feel it?" Alana sneered. "Did you feel it when he came? Is that what you're trying to tell me? That you came every time he did?"

"Yes," Noah snapped, his own anger rising to the surface.

"Noah," Aiden cautioned.

"You know what? Forget it." Alana held her palm up, her stance rigid, her face tense in anger. "I'm going to finish investigating the house, then we're leaving. I'm done."

"Alana," Aiden began as she stormed past him.

At the door, she turned to glare at him. "You know, I might've been okay with sharing if you'd just been honest about it instead of having your brother take your place without my knowing."

She left, slamming the door behind her. Noah wanted to run after her, stop her, make her understand.

"Goddamn it, Noah!" Aiden shouted. "What the hell were you thinking, kissing her back like that?"

"I wasn't thinking," he said quietly, and his brother stared at him as though he'd grown three heads.

"And what the hell do you mean you came every time I did? Are you serious?"

Noah sighed tiredly. "Yes. I'm dead serious. It's never been that strong, Aiden. Never. That has to mean something."

Aiden shook his head and walked behind his desk, dropping into his chair as though defeated.

"I had no control over it. I couldn't stop it, couldn't ignore it," Noah added.

His brother rubbed his hand over his eyes. "I felt it too, when you were kissing her. I thought it was because I was watching you and became aroused. Apparently, I was feeling your arousal, not mine."

Noah sighed and closed his eyes. "Imagine how it would feel if I were fucking her."

Aiden snorted. "You need to find her and talk to her."

"Me?" Noah asked, his eyes snapping open.

"Yeah, you. It was you that started all this shit by not opening your damn mouth and telling her who you were and for not finding me sooner and letting me know what was going on."

"She's not going to talk to me, Aiden. Not now."

Aiden shrugged. "Then I guess you better pour on that thick Southern charm. I know you can. I've seen you do it."

"For what purpose?" Noah asked in exasperation. "What are we talking about here, Aiden? A threesome? You know damn good and well that's not going to work."

"What I know," Aiden snarled, "is that I don't want to lose her, Noah. So I suggest you figure it out."

Noah placed his palms flat down on Aiden's desk. Leaning in, he growled at his brother in a low angry tone that sent most men running. "What if I seduce her? Are you okay with that? Are you okay with sharing her?"

"We've done it before."

"For a short period of time. Most of the women we've been with were okay with it for a weekend but couldn't handle it beyond that. A threesome could scare her off."

Aiden's eyes narrowed as he looked up at him. "What are you getting at, brother? Just spit it out."

"I'm not going to go through the rest of my life masturbating in the damn shower every time you fuck your girlfriend. If I go talk to her and try to fix this, it's with the intent there will be a threesome. Plain and simple. Is she worth it to you?"

Aiden was silent for several seconds as a laundry list of emotions flashed across his eyes until he finally spoke. "Yeah, Noah. She's worth it, and after five minutes with her, I think you'll think she's worth it too."

Chapter Eight

Alana sat in her truck, parked outside the hotel just staring out the window at the clear blue sky. She wished her emotions were as clear.

She couldn't believe two grown men would come up with something so outlandish. Part of her became excited at the idea of twins wanting to share her. Wasn't that every girl's fantasy? Two men showering her with attention and affection?

With a sigh, she squeezed her temples, closing her eyes against the massive headache she could feel coming on.

"Just accept the fact you've been played, Alana," she mumbled to herself. "That's all there is to it."

They were twins who enjoyed sharing and thought she would be their next conquest.

"God, why do I keep falling for jerks like this?" She sighed, dropping her head onto the steering wheel.

A knock sounded at her window, and she jumped with a squeal, lifting her head to see who had hit her window so hard, it rattled.

Tray stared at her with a frown, rolling his hand to indicate she should lower the window.

"What the hell are you doing?" he asked, his brow creasing in concern. "I thought you had a lunch date."

Lisa stood behind him, the same concerned expression on her face.

"Change of plans," she replied, not really wanting to get into it.

"What happened?" Lisa asked in her usual demanding tone.

Alana shook her head and opened the truck door. As she climbed out, she grabbed the bag of supplies from Tray's hand. "Is this the cable the guys needed?" she asked, peeking into it.

"Yeah." Tray nodded. "We were just putting it in the truck so we wouldn't forget it."

"Alana," Lisa said.

"I don't want to talk about this right now," she said a bit more snappish than she meant to. "I'm sorry." She sighed and rubbed at her forehead again. "I just need a little while to myself. I think I'm going to take off for a while, drive around maybe."

"Alone?" Tray asked.

"Didn't I just say that? I'll be fine. I promise. I just need to do this. Okay?"

She climbed into the truck, ignoring their shocked and concerned expressions and threw the bag into the passenger seat. "I'll be back in time to eat dinner with you guys, then we'll talk."

Without waiting for a response, she started the truck, threw it into drive, and headed out of the parking lot.

* * *

Noah had spent over an hour driving around, looking for Alana's truck. When he'd finally spotted it at the house, he'd wanted to put her over his knee. Her friend had been attacked here, and the culprit was still loose. She should know better than to come here alone.

He stepped out of his truck and headed up the front steps of the house, all the while unable to keep his mind off their kiss earlier. He would go to hell for all this one day. He just knew it.

Today wasn't the first time he and his brother had played each other. They'd done it as kids all the time. As they became adults, they grew out of it, but on occasion, they would trade places, just to see if they still could.

He had no more intentions of misleading Alana. He'd tell her the truth. Because of his brother's attraction to her, he couldn't stop thinking about her.

Noah stood in the grand entrance of the abandoned house and snorted toward the glass dome above him in the ceiling.

"I'm not sure I would believe that load of crock, either," he said to himself.

His stare moved to the curving staircase, and he sighed. Now where the hell would she be? And more importantly, what the hell was she doing here alone?

"Alana?" he called.

* * *

He stood in the shadows, watching the light play off her auburn curls. She was pretty, although not as pretty as the other one. He could still imagine all the things he could do to her body. All the sexual things.

He closed his eyes briefly, inhaling the sweet smell of roses that floated through the air as she moved. He imagined that smell filling his senses as he buried his cock in her ass, riding her hard before sinking the blade of his knife into her spine, severing the nerves.

Just a head on a stick was what she'd be by the time he was done with her. Unable to move, to get away, to fight. The last thing she'd feel would be his cock buried in her throat.

He opened his eyes, a soft smile pulling at his lips. He could feel his cock getting hard already in anticipation. It had been too long since his last girl. Too long since he'd fed the beast that existed within him. Is that why he found himself attracted to a redhead and not a brunette? It had definitely been too long.

He preferred the other girl. He could still hear her screams, could still smell the scent of her blood as his claws had ripped at her flesh. He'd had a small taste of her, and he wanted more. His fingers clenched at his sides as he tried to control the rage, the hunger that seemed to burn him from the inside out.

Control... He needed to maintain control.

* * *

Alana fiddled with the camera wiring and tried not to listen to the moans and creaks of the house. It was like the damn thing was alive, and she'd begun to regret her decision to come here alone. Tray would have her head if he knew. And truthfully, he should.

The hairs on the back of her neck stood on end as the creepy sensation of being watched traveled up her spine. She froze, holding her breath and listening. Her heart jumped in her chest as a barely audible noise sounded from behind her. Was someone in the room with her? The temperature felt as though it had dropped a few degrees, and she shivered. She should turn and look; she really should, but she was almost too afraid. She had a terrible feeling in the pit of her stomach that if she did, she wouldn't like what she saw.

Swallowing, she reached for the small digital camcorder lying on the table. Not much of a weapon, but it would do in a pinch if used correctly.

"Alana?"

The sound of her name brought both relief and a tinge of unease. Was it Noah or Aiden?

"Great," she snarled. "I'm up here," she called out, albeit reluctantly as she turned to study the empty room behind her with a frown.

She really didn't want to talk to either of them right now, but at the same time she didn't want to be alone, either. Not after that creepy feeling.

"Up where?" he called, and Alana sighed.

"Second door on the right."

She turned just as Noah stepped into the doorway. He looked identical to Aiden. The only way she knew it was him was by his clothes. Aiden had been dressed in slacks and a tie. Noah was in jeans and a form-fitting T-shirt that outlined his wide shoulders to perfection. The blue material made his eyes appear darker, more blue than gray.

"What the hell are you doing here alone?" he demanded, his voice rough and commanding.

She bristled at his tone, despite how his deep voice made her stomach flutter.

"Don't start with me. I'm a grown woman; I can go where I want to. Why are you here? Back for more?" she snapped, unable to curb her anger, especially with her body humming to life at the sight of him staring at her like a hunter looking at his prey.

"Don't be snippy," he said.

She raised an eyebrow, her ire rising. "Excuse me? I think I have a right to be snippy."

He spread his hands as he came farther into the room. "I pretended to be my brother so you would kiss me. I admit it, but I'm not the first twin to do it, Alana."

"Did you think it was fun?" she asked, hand on her hip.

She placed the camera down on the small table next to the closet while she waited for his answer. She'd been amazed when she arrived at just how much furniture was still in the house.

"I thought your kiss was fun," he said, his lips quirking just a little. "I do regret making you angry, though. I'm sorry for that."

"Fair enough, I suppose."

"Am I forgiven?"

She scowled. "I don't know that I would go quite that far."

He smiled, and her stomach jumped in a patty-cake rhythm that caught her by surprise.

"Did your brother send you out here?" she asked, trying to cover up her sudden urge to kiss him again.

All she'd been able to think about while at this house was the two of them seducing her as a pair. Was she nuts? Had that even been their intent, or had Noah just been playing a game?

"Yes and no," he replied, taking a couple of steps into the room.

The closer he got, the more her flesh tingled. Was it because he looked so much like Aiden? He kissed like Aiden...sort of. His kiss had been more demanding where Aiden's was more sensual, slower.

She studied him from the corner of her eye. Now that she really looked at him, she could see he carried himself differently from Aiden. His brother was a people person. He was approachable. Noah was less approachable, more stern and arrogant. He had a darker look in his eyes.

One side of her lips quirked in a half smile. Was it that simple? Aiden was light, the good twin, the gentle twin, and Noah was dark, the dangerous, naughty, and rough twin? She could see that.

His blue-gray gaze met hers, and her breath caught in her chest. Oh, yeah. She could definitely see that. Looking at Noah made her think of hot, sweaty nights between black satin sheets. She licked her lips and looked back down at the camera, trying to take her mind off sex with the twins.

"Alana?"

His deep voice carried across the room and smoothed over her skin like a caress. Too late. So much for not thinking about sex.

"Yes?" she croaked, then cleared her throat to try again. "So if Aiden sending you to apologize is one reason why you're here, what's the other?"

He stepped close behind her, so close she could feel the heat off his body against her back.

"I couldn't stop thinking about that kiss," he replied, his voice so soft and sensual he might as well have just stroked his hand down her back.

"I'm sleeping with your brother," she whispered, although it sounded more like she wanted to convince herself more so than him, even to her own ears.

He snorted softly. "Trust me, I know."

"Are you really going to stick with that story? That you came when he did? I get the whole *twins feel each other's pain*, but pleasure?"

He shrugged. "It is what it is."

"Do you do this often?" she snipped over her shoulder.

"Do what?" he asked, all innocent.

"Seduce your brother's girlfriends?"

"Is that what I'm doing?" Alana could hear the amusement in his voice and bristled.

"I don't know. Is it?"

"If I were, you would know it."

Alana huffed. Of all the arrogant, conceited—

Rolling her eyes, she did what she knew she shouldn't, but she couldn't seem to stop herself. She turned to face him. Craning her neck, she looked into pretty eyes that left her feeling weak-kneed and speechless.

"Honestly? You want the truth?" he asked.

Alana nodded, but couldn't speak past the rising lump of lust.

"Aiden and I have shared women. You wouldn't be the first, but I have a feeling you could be the last."

"What if I'm not into sharing?" she asked, her heart racing wildly in her chest at the idea.

He moved just a little closer, crowding her against the table, and she reached back, grasping the edge with shaking hands. Her fingers tightened around the wood as he invaded her space, bringing his body so close to hers, she could swear she felt his heart beating against her breasts. She had to hold on to something; otherwise she'd jump his ass right there, Aiden's brother or not.

"Think about it," he whispered.

She swallowed. Oh, she had been thinking about it. A lot. Which would probably explain why her breasts were so full and firm, they ached, and her panties were soaking wet.

He crooked his finger and placed it under her chin, forcing it up. With the pad of his thumb, he pulled her lower lip down, making her lips part. She couldn't move—wasn't even sure she wanted to move. His lust-filled gaze had her so mesmerized, she wasn't sure she could even breathe.

She held her breath as he bent down, then stopped just a hairbreadth away from her lips. His eyes stared into hers, watching, holding her immobile with the desire shining in their depths.

In a move so fast it startled her, he planted his mouth on hers. It was demanding, wild just like back at Aiden's office. She drew in a sharp breath of utter delight. It felt as though she'd waited forever for that touch, and when it finally happened, she almost swooned.

There was no gentle swiping of his tongue, no brush of his lips over hers, but a full-on, senses-overloading, tongue-delving kiss that made her knees buckle. His arm wrapped around the small of her back, shoving her up against him so tight, her breasts flattened against his hard-as-steel chest.

She lifted her hands and grabbed fingers full of his shirt to hold on to. His kiss was wild and intense, and God help her, she had the most insane urge to spread her legs and wrap them around his waist, grind her pussy against the hard ridge of his cock that currently pressed into her stomach, and ride him till she came.

It was over way too soon, and she moaned as his mouth left hers, her body leaning back into him, unconsciously seeking more. He pulled back and smiled, his eyes twinkling with a devilish light that made her insides flutter and the heat of a blush move over her cheeks.

"Think about it," he repeated before turning and walking from the room, leaving her alone and trembling.

She blindly reached for the table behind her to keep from falling. Her legs trembled so badly, she could hardly hold herself upright. "Holy crap," she sighed, trying her best to get her breathing back under control.

The sound of a car door slamming made her jump, and she stumbled to the window overlooking the front yard. Now what? Two of her camera crew had arrived, and farther down the driveway she could see Jordan's van approaching. No sign of Tray, though.

She quickly made her way out of the house to meet up with her team. As she came down the front step, she saw Noah shaking hands with Jordan and one of the two cameramen. She slowed, waiting for him to walk away before approaching Jordan.

"There you are," he said and pointed his thumb toward Noah's retreating back. "I was about to chew you out for coming out here alone until I saw Noah. Did you know Aiden had a twin?"

"Yeah," she said with a sigh as she crossed her arms over her chest to ward off the chilly wind. "I found out earlier."

"Guess you can't be any safer than with the sheriff," he said with a grin.

Alana's mouth dropped open slightly in surprise. "What?"

"You knew he was the sheriff, didn't you?" Jordan reached into the van and grabbed his jacket. As he slipped his arms inside, he studied her with a worried expression.

"Yeah," she said with a dismissive wave of her hand.

"You okay? You seem a little distracted."

His eyes narrowed as he glanced toward Noah's Dodge Ram pulling out of the drive and onto the road. He turned back to her, and Alana could feel the heat of a blush moving over her cheeks. She wasn't sure why she felt so guilty. She hadn't done anything wrong.

"Where's Tray and Lisa?" she asked, trying to quickly change the subject.

"They're waiting on you."

"Oh, man." She rubbed at the back of her neck with a sigh. "I forgot."

"The camera crew and I decided to come over early while we still have light and see if we can find the passageways."

Alana snorted. "Good luck with that."

Jordan pointed a finger at her nose, and she reached out, grasping it within her hand. "You better get to the hotel before Tray sends out the guard."

"Tray always threatens to send out the guard," she replied as she pulled at his finger playfully.

Jordan chuckled and patted the back of her hand before pulling his finger free of her grasp.

"He worries about you. We all do, especially after what happened to Lisa. Never, ever come out here alone, Alana. I know you're my boss, but in this matter, I'm pulling rank."

Alana smiled slightly at Jordan's protective nature. Her smile faded, and she gave him a firm stare of her own, this time pointing her finger at his nose. "I'll let you get away with that this time."

Jordan just grinned, knowing full well she was only teasing. To her, they weren't her employees; they were her partners, her family. The only family she had.

"Now get," he ordered and with a smile, headed toward the house.

Chuckling, Alana jumped into her truck and headed down the driveway.

* * *

He stood in the shadows of the attic window, growling softly to himself. These people were becoming a damn pain in his ass.

Chapter Nine

Alana stopped just outside the door to her hotel room. They'd flipped the security bar over, letting the door rest against it and leaving it open a crack. She could hear Lisa and Tray talking softly, debating theories on the recording they had of their young ghost.

Through the crack, she could see her friends sitting at the small dining table, their eyes glued to the screen. Alana assumed they were looking at the footage Aiden's camera had caught of the ghostly image. The smoky ghost was some of the best footage they'd ever caught, and if she hadn't been there in person, she wasn't sure she would believe it was real.

She continued to watch them for a few seconds. She wanted to go in. She wanted to talk about what had happened earlier today. She wanted to talk about her confusion and

her strange desire to want to take the twins up on their unusual offer.

What would that make her? A slut? Easy? Adventurous? Or would it make her anything at all?

She rolled her eyes toward the ceiling, disgusted with herself. Why was she even considering this? Sure, the idea sounded intriguing, but it wasn't her.

With a sigh, she put the palm of her hand against the door and pushed it open.

"Honey, I'm home," she called out, trying to cover her inner turmoil with humor. "What's for dinner?"

"What's for dinner, my ass," Tray growled as he leaned back in his chair and stared at her in annoyance. "What the hell were you doing at that house all alone?"

Alana huffed and tossed her purse into the chair. "I see Jordan called you."

"Yeah, he called."

"I wasn't alone," Alana argued as she dropped onto the sofa. "Didn't he tell you Noah was there?"

"Who the hell is Noah?" Lisa asked as she turned in her chair to sit sideways and rest her arm over the back.

"Noah is Aiden's twin, and he's also the sheriff."

"Twin?" Tray repeated with interest.

"Forget it. He's not gay."

"How do you know?" Tray's lips twitched. "Some men can hide that sort of thing."

"Down, boy," Lisa teased before turning her attention back to Alana, although Alana would have preferred it remain on Tray at the moment. She really wasn't sure she was ready to talk about it.

"Trust me, he's not gay," Alana grumbled.

"What's going on?" Lisa asked. "Something happened earlier that you're not telling us. Like it or not, I'm putting my foot down here. Whatever it was is making you do things you know you shouldn't, such as go to that house alone, especially after what happened to me. Now spill, girlfriend."

"Did you remember something?" Alana asked as she stared at her friend, half hoping she had so they wouldn't have to talk about her dilemma.

"No, and stop trying to change the subject."

Alana dropped her head into her hands and took a deep breath, letting it out slowly. There was no point putting this off, not really. Both Tray and Lisa knew her too well.

"I went by Aiden's office to meet him for lunch."

She stopped, and Tray's eyes narrowed. "Please tell me that jerk isn't married."

Alana shook her head. "No. I wish it were that simple."

"It's worse than being married?" Lisa asked, her eyes wide with worry.

"Well, maybe. I don't know," she replied, sighing. "I...I accidentally kissed Noah, thinking he was Aiden. The two of them look identical; it's amazing."

Tray snorted. "What? That's it?"

"Noah kissed me back, and Aiden walked in on us."

"Awkward," Tray sang. "He shouldn't have been mad, Alana. At least not at you."

"He wasn't mad." Alana began to tug at her fingers, popping her knuckles. "They came up with this ridiculous story that... Well, it was just stupid. But Noah later just admitted that they share."

"Share?" Lisa gapped, her eyes widening in surprise. "As in share you?"

"Yeah."

She bit her lower lip and looked at the two of them. If the suggestion didn't have her stomach tied in knots, the shocked looks on their faces would've made her laugh out loud.

"Well," Lisa said before licking her lips and frowning. "I have to say, I didn't see that coming."

"Me either," Alana whispered. "It wouldn't be so bad if they hadn't tried to trick me by trading places with each other. Noah told me they feel each other's pain and pleasure. He claims he came every time Aiden did when Aiden and I were together."

"Well, that's a new one," Lisa said.

"As well as that, they feel each other's emotions, and when I'm there, it's stronger."

Tray shrugged one shoulder and tilted his head to the side thoughtfully. "Sharing's not so bad...if they know what they're doing."

Lisa scowled at Tray. "You're not seriously suggesting she do this, are you? And how do you know anything about sharing?"

"I've shared," he argued, sounding just a little offended.

"Only because you were after the guy, not the girl," Alana pointed out.

"Hey, whatever works. I'm not above a little slap and tickle with the opposite sex if it gets me the ultimate goal I'm after—which it did, by the way. But we're not talking about me. We're talking about you."

"I'd rather we didn't talk about me," Alana grumbled as she stood and walked over to the coffeepot.

She lifted it and swirled the contents. "How fresh is this?" she asked.

"I just made it," Lisa replied.

Alana poured herself a cup, trying to ignore the two pairs of eyes she could feel boring into her back. "I was played," she said with a shrug as she placed the pot back onto the warmer. "I think it's what they were after all along. They claim they have some sort of psychic physical connection and... It doesn't matter anyway. I got a good night of sex out of it. Let's just hurry and finish with this house and move on."

"Alana, you are so full of shit," Tray said with amusement, and Alana turned to glare at him, but before she could get a word in edgewise, he spoke again. "You cannot stand there and tell us you haven't thought about it."

"Of course I've thought about it. They're gorgeous. Who wouldn't?"

"Like I said, if a threesome is done right, it can be very pleasurable for the woman. You know," he added with a shrug and a wicked gleam in his eyes, "just in case you didn't hear me the first time."

Alana stared at Tray for a brief second, trying not to giggle at his wiggling eyebrows before speaking. "If I didn't know any better, I'd swear you were trying to talk me into it."

"I'm not trying to talk you into it. I know you, Alana. If you decide you want to do it, you will. If you don't, you'll wonder about this for the rest of your—"

Alana frowned. "I will not."

"Really?" Tray drawled, studying her closely.

With a sigh, Alana dropped onto the sofa and twisted her lips. "You haven't said much, Lisa. What's your opinion? I know you have one."

"I just don't want you to get hurt. Guys are dogs. You know it, and I know it. I agree that they probably had this in mind all along, but now that it's been offered—"

"I don't know that it has been offered, at least not in threesome form. All Noah said was that they shared and for me to think about it."

"Sharing usually involves a threesome, hon," Tray said.

"I don't know," she said, letting out a tired breath. "Let's stop thinking about this for now."

"I'm all for that," Tray teased. "All this talk of threesomes and hot guys has me all aflutter."

He shuddered, smiling like a loon. Alana and Lisa both laughed. Tray was definitely good at lightening the mood. He never failed to make her smile when she needed it. He could also listen, sometimes better than Lisa, who often wanted to give advice. And sometimes Alana didn't want to be told what to do but just to talk about it.

"Have you eaten?" Lisa asked.

"No, and I'm starving."

Tray leaned over and grabbed his cell phone off the table that was closest to them. "Let's order some pizzas, and then we'll head on over to the house. I'm dying to get back onto the second floor tonight."

A dark shadow passed over Lisa's eyes. Alana watched her closely as the shadow faded, but a slight hint of confusion lingered on her face.

"Lisa? You okay?" Alana asked.

Lisa blinked and looked at Alana as though coming from a trance. "What?"

"Are you okay?"

"Yeah," she replied after a brief pause. "It's just when he mentioned the second floor..." She waved her hand in dismissal. "It was nothing."

"Lisa—"

"I'm fine. I promise. I'm not about to let you guys keep me out of this investigation. I'm dying to see the inside of this house."

Alana let it go, but concern for her friend lingered. Despite Lisa's resolve, Alana wasn't about to let anything happen to her again. Lisa liked to act tough, but Alana knew just how vulnerable Lisa really was. What happened to her had terrified her enough that she'd blocked it out.

Alana would prefer it stayed blocked for her friend's sake.

* * *

Aiden pulled his tie from his shirt collar and tossed it onto the bed just as his brother walked into the room. Noah leaned against the doorjamb, a frown wrinkling his brow. He crossed his arms over his chest just as Aiden stepped into the walk-in closet to grab a pair of jeans and a jacket.

"Well?" Aiden pulled the jeans from the hanger and tossed them onto the bed from inside the closet. "How'd it go?"

"Not sure yet."

Aiden frowned toward the door then continued sifting through his shirts, looking for something warm. The nighttime temps were dropping tonight, and he wanted to make sure he was warm while investigating the house.

"Care to elaborate?" Aiden asked.

"I kissed her. She kissed me back."

Aiden paused pulling the shirt off the hanger. "That's it?"

"You should know if that's it or not."

"Actually I do, but that's not what I meant."

He stepped from the closet and stared at his brother, who remained inside the door frame, his stare locked on something across the room.

"What's wrong with you?" Aiden asked as he shrugged out of his shirt. "Did she slap you or something?"

Noah used his middle finger to scratch at his nose, making Aiden snicker. "Cute, Noah."

"I found her at the house alone."

Aiden froze. "What? What the hell was she thinking?"

Noah pushed away from the door frame and moved to sit on the foot of the bed. "I'm sure she was freaked out and wanted a minute or two to think, although I'm a little surprised she went there without someone with her."

"And whose fault was that?" Aiden asked as he removed his slacks then stepped into his jeans.

"It was mine," Noah sneered.

"Just making sure we were on the same page. You didn't leave her there alone, did you?"

Noah glared at him through narrowed eyes. "No. Other members of her team arrived."

Aiden's lips twitched slightly as he watched his brother. Noah wasn't one to be underconfident or hesitant, but something had him weirded out. "What's up, Noah?"

Noah glanced at Aiden, then grinned. "I really like her."

Aiden chuckled. "Me too."

"This isn't going to be easy. You know that, right?"

"I know," Aiden replied, sighing. "We'll have to work together on this. Seduce her, really bombard her, both individually and as a team."

Noah shook his head. "You've got this all worked out, huh?"

Aiden slipped his arms into the soft leather jacket. "You got any better ideas, genius?"

"Not at the moment. We should probably just play it by ear, see how things go. I don't want to force her into it."

Aiden scowled. "I never said anything about forcing her. But I don't want to let her get away, either. When you kissed her at the house today, I felt it. I understand now what you meant about not being able to turn it off. We've never felt the connection that strong with anyone else. That has to mean something, and I want to explore this and find out what that is."

"Just make sure tonight at the house you keep your eyes open. We still haven't gotten anywhere with the attack on Lisa. Whoever the damn son of a bitch was didn't even leave fingerprints."

Aiden grabbed his wallet from his slacks and slipped it into the back pocket of his jeans. "You're coming tonight, aren't you?"

"I'll be there later. I have some things I need to take care of at the station."

Aiden nodded and headed out of the bedroom. "All right. See you there."

* * *

"Did you get that camera fixed earlier, Alana?" Tray asked.

Alana nodded as she reached behind the seat for the two new audio recorders they'd bought. After what had happened last time, they wanted to make sure everyone had a recorder. As she shut the truck door, her gaze landed on Lisa.

She stood off to the side, staring at the house, her eyes glazed over, her face pale. Alana walked over and placed her hand on her arm. Lisa jumped and turned to stare at her with wide, frightened eyes.

"I don't think I can go in there," she whispered.

"Do you remember something?"

Lisa shook her head and looked back to the house. "I just get a... I'm afraid looking at that house. Terrified, but I can't remember why."

Alana patted the back of her shoulder in an effort to soothe her friend. "It's okay. You don't have to go in there. Truthfully, I would feel better if you didn't."

"This house has the potential to be the biggest, most successful investigation we've ever done. I can't believe I have to sit it out."

Smiling, Alana wrapped her arm around her friend's shoulder and gave her a slight hug. "There's still lots of stuff you can do. You're fabulous at editing."

Lisa snorted. "Editing. I'm reduced to editing."

"Trust me," Alana sighed as she glanced up at the second-floor windows. "I don't think you want to relive what happened up there. I don't even like reliving it."

Alana closed her eyes for a brief second, blocking out the sound of her friend's cries that were still so fresh in her mind. She still hadn't told Lisa or anyone in her team what she'd said that night about her attacker not being human. He had to be. Ghosts didn't do this. They couldn't, not to that extreme.

"In some ways I wish I could remember. Maybe then they could catch the son of a bitch. Do you think he's still here?"

"I don't know, but we're not taking any chances. No one goes anywhere alone, and that most definitely includes you."

"I wasn't alone then."

"I know, and we're working on that. Maybe two squeeze into a room at a time or something, I'm not sure. But we'll figure it out. The sheriff sent some officers to help keep things under control, so I think we're good."

"Speaking of officers..."

"Oh, please, don't start," Alana said with a sigh as she tried to ignore Lisa's concerned expression.

"Don't start what? I was just going to say one of them is here."

"What?"

Alana quickly turned to where Lisa indicated and spotted one of the twins over by the van talking with Tray. It infuriated her to no end that she wasn't sure which one he was.

"Can you tell them apart?" Lisa asked.

"If earlier today is any indication, apparently not."

Lisa snickered, and Alana tried her best to ignore her. Whichever one he was, he looked good in the black leather jacket. His hands were in his pockets as he laughed at something Tray said. If she were to guess, she would say Aiden. He appeared more relaxed, his smile genuine and inviting.

The good twin.

Alana snorted softly.

"What was that for?" Lisa asked.

"I was just thinking. The two of them remind me of good and bad, naughty and nice."

"Could be an interesting combination. The best of both worlds, so to speak."

"Mmm," Alana replied. "Maybe."

"I'm your friend. Whatever you decide, I'll back you up. Just be careful. I don't see a threesome as being a long-term thing and—"

"I know. But I'm not looking for long-term, and I doubt they are either. Maybe I should just have a little fun. I've always wondered what it would be like to do two guys at once." Alana shrugged. "Maybe now's my chance. A little fun is all a threesome would be good for. That sort of relationship couldn't really last for long, right?"

"Personally, I think you're insane for even considering it, but..."

Alana giggled. "Like I would have the nerve to go through with it anyway." Aiden spotted her, and after a wave to Tray, he started toward them. "Oh God. Here he comes." She wrapped her arm around Lisa's elbow and held tight. "Don't move. I'm not sure I trust myself alone with him."

Lisa chuckled and patted Alana's hand. "I'm not going anywhere."

"There you are," he said as he came to a stop in front of them.

The moonlight played over his dark hair, dancing across the strands in streaks of silvery light. His full lips lifted into a tiny smile as he watched her, waiting for her to say something. All Alana could think about was the feel of his lips on hers and the fact that she still wasn't sure which one he was.

"Aiden," he said, grinning.

"It's impossible to tell the two of you apart," she said.

"Not once you get to know us. Our personalities are pretty distinct."

Alana nodded. "Yeah. It's a shame I didn't notice that difference earlier."

"Noah told me he apologized," Aiden said.

"Did he also tell you he kissed me?"

She wasn't sure why she'd said that. She'd just blurted it out, but now that she had, she was curious as to what Aiden would say.

"He didn't have to. I already knew, but yes, he told me."

Well. At least they were honest with each other.

"Should I leave the two of you alone?" Lisa asked.

"Yes," Aiden replied.

"No," Alana snapped.

"Okay," Lisa drawled. "I've been friends with her longer, so she wins."

Aiden nodded, chuckling. "Fair enough." His intense stare pinned Alana to the spot as he began to speak once more. "But you and I need to talk...soon, Alana."

His stare and tone left no mistake he was serious, and she had a feeling he'd find her alone one way or another.

Chapter Ten

Noah climbed out of his truck and stared at all the commotion going on around him. It apparently took a lot of people to make a reality show. He counted at least three cameramen. By the van, he saw his brother studying the small camera in his hands. Next to him was Lisa.

He frowned. Why was she here?

He made his way over to Aiden and Lisa. "What are you doing here?" he asked, a bit more abruptly than he'd intended.

Lisa stiffened. "Excuse me?"

"Noah, relax. Alana is making her stay in the truck with the equipment, and I got one of the officers to agree to stay with her."

"So you're Noah," she said, letting her gaze wander down his chest and legs.

Noah raised an eyebrow at her brazen appraisal. "Did I pass inspection?" he asked, grinning.

"I haven't decided yet."

"I've already been read the riot act. Might as well brace yourself," Aiden replied with amusement.

"Nah. I figure you can pass it along," Lisa said.

She smiled, but Noah didn't miss the warning in her eyes. She was protective of her friend. Noah didn't mind. It was good Alana had friends that cared so much for her. It said a lot about her.

"Alana went into the house with Tray," Lisa offered.

Noah glared at his brother. After what had happened to Lisa, he didn't like the idea of either woman being in that house, regardless of who was with them.

Aiden sighed. "What? She sneaked off while my back was turned. Besides, she has Tray and two cameramen with her. I'm sure she's fine." Aiden stepped closer and lowered his voice. "She's still skittish. Don't push it."

Noah's lips twisted. Patience wasn't one of his strong suits. He wanted to talk to her. Hell, if he were honest with himself he would admit to wanting to see her, touch her. Her taste had lingered all day, driving him crazy for more. He looked toward the house, wondering what floor they were on. He didn't see any flashlights in the windows, so it was possible they were toward the back.

"How many cameramen are here?" Noah asked. "I saw three out here when I pulled up."

"Normally, three is all we have, but because of the sheer size of the house, Alana called and requested more. They arrived this afternoon," Lisa said.

"How many investigators?" Noah asked.

"Normally four. Myself, Tray, Jordan, and Alana, but because of what happened to me, we're down to three."

"You have me," Aiden said.

Lisa smiled, but the smile didn't reach her eyes. Noah could tell she was frightened but doing her best to hide it.

"You're not really an investigator."

"You have to be trained for this?" Noah asked with amusement.

Lisa frowned, obviously offended that he found her profession to be anything other than serious. "Actually, yes."

"My apologies," he said. "But I honestly wouldn't have thought that. I assumed anyone could take a camera and a voice recorder and investigate."

Lisa shrugged. "Just because you have those things, that doesn't make you an investigator."

Aiden and Noah shared an amused look before Noah's attention returned to the house. He really wanted to go inside and find Alana. He hated standing around out here. But once he did find her, what would he say?

I want you now; drop your pants. Yep, he could see that going over real well. Even Aiden would smack him upside the head for that one.

A movement in the bottom-floor window to the right of the front door caught his attention. His eyes narrowed, his vision focused on the woman standing on the other side of the glass. It was the same girl he'd seen before.

"What is it?" Aiden asked.

"Do you see her?"

"See who?" Lisa asked as she looked as well.

"The window to the right of the door, fourth one down," Noah replied.

"I don't see anything," Aiden said, frowning toward the window.

Noah blinked, then looked again. She still stood there watching him, her eyes pleading and fearful, her hair matted, her face pale.

"You have to see her," Noah said.

Lisa snapped her fingers three times in rapid succession, getting one of the cameramen's attention. "Film the window—fourth one on the right, bottom floor."

"What are we looking for?"

"I don't know yet," she replied.

Noah shook his head. "Screw this, I'm going in."

"Noah!" Aiden called as he headed toward the front door, a cameraman close on his heels.

Noah glanced over his shoulder. "If you're going to follow me, stay out of my way."

"I know the drill," he replied, grinning.

Shaking his head, Noah stepped into the entry hall. Aiden joined him just as the cameraman spoke into his walkie. "Sheriff sees something on the first floor. We're headed toward the main living room and parlor."

"What have you got?" Tray asked, his voice barely above a whisper on the other side of the walkie.

"Not sure yet," the cameraman replied.

Noah stopped and glared at him over his shoulder.

The cameraman shrugged. "It's procedure. We have to let them know when another team enters the house."

"I'm not a team," Noah growled.

"Maybe not, but you are in Alana's territory, and you follow her rules."

"This is ridiculous," Noah grumbled as he turned and began to make his way toward the parlor at the far end.

Had he really seen that woman, or was he losing his mind? At the moment, he'd go for the latter. In his opinion, insanity was the better option. He didn't believe in ghosts. He'd convinced himself of that as a teenager. Even after he'd seen...

He froze, and the cameraman almost walked into him before coming to an abrupt stop. Noah tried to think. Even after he'd seen...what? He couldn't remember. Why couldn't he remember?

With a mental shake of his head, he dismissed it for the time being and pushed the door open slowly. He let his eyes adjust to the soft moonlight filtering in through the windows before he took a quick glance around the room.

A thick layer of dust covered everything from the furniture, to the windowsills, to the hardwood floors, but there was no sign of the girl or even prints in the dust to indicate she'd been here.

"Do you still see her?" Aiden asked.

"I'm not sure I ever saw her to begin with," he replied, his voice barely above a whisper.

* * *

Alana ran down the main stairs as fast as possible, curious as to what was happening on the first floor. So far since she and Tray had been upstairs, they'd heard three disembodied voices, heard two doors slam, and felt four cold spots.

Tray was already chomping at the bit to look at the footage and was ready to set up camp here for the next month. It seemed like every time they stepped into this house, something odd happened. It was an investigator's gold mine.

"Alana, wait up, damn it! Don't run down those stairs so fast. You're going to break your neck," Tray called from just behind her.

She still couldn't believe she'd been the first one down. She fully expected Tray to mow her down in order to get there first.

"Who's in the house?" she asked into the walkie. "It's not Lisa, is it?"

"No. It's the sheriff and his brother."

"What?" she exclaimed before coming to a dead stop, causing Tray to barrel into her. She grasped hold of the railing tight to keep from falling. "Tray!"

"Well, don't stop so damn fast. What the hell is the matter with you?"

"Nothing!" she snapped. "You go."

"Me go?" he cried, half-surprised and half full of amusement. His smile widened as though it dawned on him what she was hesitant about, which made Alana scowl.

"Oh get over it!" Tray said with a giggle. "There're too many people around; they're not going to rip your clothes off here."

"Very funny," she sneered as Tray moved past her and headed down the stairs.

She reluctantly followed, both excited and worried that Aiden and Noah were here together. The two of them together was all she needed. The image of being sandwiched between them had played havoc with her libido all day long.

With a quick shake of her head, she tried to forget about sex and focus on the situation at hand. Excitement hung in the air as they quickly made their way to the cameraman at the far end of the hall by following the soft blue light on the top of the camera.

He stood in the hall, filming into the doorway, bouncing back and forth on his heels in excitement. He was one of the new ones who had been sent in and so far had proved to be adventurous and brazen, important traits to have in this line of work.

She and Tray slipped past him and into the room. Aiden stood to one side, his arms crossed over his chest as he watched his brother. Noah paced the room, studying the floor. He wore the same jeans he'd had on earlier with a brown corduroy shirt open over a beige T-shirt that hugged his wide chest. She swallowed, remembering the feel of that chest against her breasts. He apparently worked out just as much as his brother did.

"What's going on?" Tray asked.

"Noah thought he saw a woman watching us out the window. He's the only one who saw her, though. The rest of us didn't."

"Is it the same woman you saw before?" Tray asked.

Noah's head lifted quickly, and he pinned his brother with a glare.

"Yeah, I told them. Get over it," Aiden replied. "Just answer the question."

"Maybe," Noah said, sighing before turning his attention back to the dust on the floor. "I leave footprints. When we came in here, there weren't any."

"Ghosts don't leave footprints," Tray said.

Noah glared at him through his lashes. Alana had to bite back a grin as she watched him. He was good-looking; they both were, but there was a dark, sexy side to Noah that made her heart pound wildly. She looked at Aiden, and he met her gaze over Tray's bent head.

In his dark blue eyes, she could see a reflection of that same dark quality. Had she been wrong about the good and bad thing? Maybe they were both bad.

Her skin tingled just thinking about it.

"Alana!" Tray snapped.

"What?" she snapped back, jumping at the sound of his voice so close to her ear.

Aiden's lips twitched as though he knew she'd been thinking about them, and the heat of a blush moved over her cheeks. She turned away, hoping the dark would conceal her embarrassment.

"Maybe we should get everyone out of here but two people. All the commotion may have scared her off," Tray suggested. "Do you want to stay?"

"No. I think I'll leave it to you. Noah should stay as well since he's the one who initially saw her."

"I agree," Tray said with a nod as he turned to look at Noah. "You ready for this?"

Noah glanced at Alana, and the hungry look in his eyes made her stomach flutter. It only lasted a second before he turned back toward Tray. "Ready for what?" he asked.

"Well, that's twice you've seen her. Maybe she'll talk to you."

Noah put his hands on his hips. "Hasn't she already talked to you?"

"Sort of. But if everyone was looking at the window, and you're the only one who saw her, maybe it's you she's trying to contact."

"Why would she contact me?" he asked skeptically.

"Well, that's what we're trying to find out." Tray grinned. "Come on, Sheriff. You're not afraid of a little ghost, are you?"

"I'm not convinced she is a ghost," Noah replied.

"Then stay here and prove me wrong."

Alana grinned at Tray's enthusiasm. Noah shook his head then shrugged. "Fine," he grumbled.

Alana couldn't help but chuckle at Noah's obvious reluctance. That man was definitely a skeptic, but to her it seemed as though it was something a little more than just disbelief. Aiden put his hand at the small of her back, leading her quietly from the room and down the hall. His touch sent a wave of warmth up her spine that she struggled to ignore.

"How about if the three of us go out for coffee after we're done here? So we can talk?" Aiden asked.

Alana glanced back at him, unsure exactly what she wanted to do. "I'm not sure that's such a great idea."

"I promise we'll keep our hands to ourselves."

Alana snorted. "It's not *your* hands I'm worried about."

Aiden grabbed her elbow, turning her to face him. "Really?"

She stood before him speechless, her heart racing, her breathing becoming more erratic by the second, and her body humming to life with a hunger she'd only imagined before. Ever since she'd found out they were twins and that both of them wanted her, she couldn't seem to keep her body under control.

"Aiden," she whispered as he pulled her closer.

"Have you been thinking about my brother's suggestion?" he asked.

"I've thought about it," she whispered, then licked her lips. "I've never done that sort of thing before."

"Experience is not a requirement, Alana," he murmured as his lips dropped closer to hers.

Behind him, she heard the cameraman clear his throat, and she quickly tried to step away. "We're not alone."

They followed the cameraman back out into the main entrance, quiet for the most part. Clearing her throat, Alana decided to break the silence.

"What's up with Noah?" she asked.

Aiden glanced down at her, the moonlight highlighting the planes of his face as they stepped out the front doors and onto the porch. "What do you mean?"

"He's not just skeptical. It's almost like he doesn't want to believe."

Aiden shrugged. "I don't know. I feel it... His reluctance, his wariness."

"You feel it?" she asked.

Aiden nodded once. "Yes. It's like we were trying to explain earlier. It's how we are. We have no secrets from each other—we can't. Well...except one," he added, frowning.

"The night the two of you were separated? He never remembered what it was that frightened him so much?"

Aiden shrugged. "No. Noah never talked about it either, but ever since that night, we've been able to feel things. It's..." Raising his hand, he rubbed it across his mouth. "It's weird and hard to explain."

"Do you think it could've been ghost related?"

"It would certainly explain his attitude now, I guess. But I couldn't say for sure."

Chapter Eleven

Noah stood back and watched Tray hold the recorder out, asking questions softly. Shaking his head, Noah glanced toward the window and froze. In the panes of the glass, the reflection didn't match the room. He frowned, glancing around the room slowly while still watching the glass.

What the hell?

The furniture was different. It was older, and there was more of it. He squeezed his eyes shut, then reopened them. The image was gone, replaced with a reflection of what was actually there.

The pounding of his heart echoed in his ears as memories from a weekend years ago played through his mind. A weekend he'd spent in this house, without his brother, without his Gram. A weekend he couldn't remember.

"Aiden called?" he asked. "About me?"

"Yes, dear," Karen replied, smiling. "He sensed you were upset."

"How?"

"It's you," Karen whispered as she brushed his bangs from his brow. "Tonight you learned how to use your ability. Tonight you found your strength. You're

the connection, the power, the center, the receiver, and the sender. You're the reason the two of you are the way you are. And when you find your third, the power will increase, the connection strengthen."

"*I don't understand,*" *he whispered.*

Karen handed him a small glass of milk, encouraging him to drink it. "*You will.*"

"*I'm scared, Karen,*" *he whispered.* "*What if he comes back?*"

Karen adjusted the sheets around him, her eyes full of sadness. "*He may,*" *she said.* "*But you'll be protected if he does, just like you were tonight. She won't let anything happen to you. And I promise, when you wake up, you won't remember anything of tonight.*"

Noah remembered falling asleep. What had Karen been talking about? Who was it he was afraid would come back, and who was it that had protected him?

"We've been in here for a few minutes. Why don't we call it done for now? I'll check the recorders and see if we caught anything."

Noah blinked in confusion at Tray. "What?"

Tray snickered. "You haven't been paying the least bit of attention, have you?"

Noah shook his head. "I'm sorry, Tray. No. I was..."

Tray stared at him, waiting for him to finish his sentence. "You okay, Noah?"

"I've been better. I just can't seem to shake the feeling that I know that woman. I've seen her or something."

"Seen her? You mean somewhere besides here?"

"I don't know," he replied, sighing.

"Let's go find Alana and start uploading some of this footage. Once it's on the computers, we can start reviewing it. If you have seen her, it will come to you."

Noah followed him out, deep in thought about the past, the present, and what awaited them in the future.

* * *

Alana stood in the shadows, watching the two brothers talking softly. Did they know she was there, watching them, desiring them? Did they know her body burned to feel their touch? Did they know how confused she felt at the moment, fighting the need to touch them?

She rubbed at the back of her neck and glanced toward the night sky. This was insane. Truly. She so didn't need this complication in her life right now.

"*Alana.*"

She glanced around, convinced she'd heard her name whispered close to her ear, and frowned. No one was close by. A shiver ran down her spine as she began to search the surrounding yard. Noah and Aiden had walked closer to the van. Aiden was talking while Noah glanced around as though looking for someone.

His gaze met hers, and Alana got the distinct impression he wasn't surprised to find her there. She swallowed, for the first time wondering if there wasn't something to this so-called psychic connection of theirs and that just maybe that connection filtered over to other things and people. Her in particular. This was the second time he'd found her hiding spot.

She dropped her hand from her neck with a tired sigh. That was just ridiculous. Wasn't it?

He crooked his finger, his attitude one of command and confidence. She could tell he expected her to comply, and part of her wanted to walk in the opposite direction just to piss him off.

She raised an eyebrow in challenge and did just that.

"Alana," he called out, but she ignored him.

Was it childish? Probably, but at the moment, it didn't matter. They were overwhelming her. The question was whether or not it was deliberate.

Noah came around the front of the truck, startling her. Her hand flew to her chest and she squealed in surprise. "Damn it, Noah," she snapped.

"You're not avoiding me, are you?" he asked with amusement as opposed to the annoyance she'd expected.

"Of course not," she replied. "That would be childish."

"Yes, it would," he countered, his luscious lips twitching.

She knew because she couldn't stop staring at them.

"I need to get back into the house. I left one of the audio recorders on the second floor."

"I'll go with you."

Knowing she wouldn't be able to convince him not to, she silently walked past him, not looking back to see if he followed. She didn't have to look. She could feel his stare—his hot, sultry, sexy stare as it bored into her back.

She could feel herself getting wet, imagining all the things he could do to her with his hands, his mouth, his body.

Rolling her eyes, she pushed through the front doors and headed for the stairs. He remained behind her, quiet until she reached the recorder on the second-floor landing and turned it off.

"Are we really going to keep playing this game?" he asked softly.

"What game?" she asked.

"The 'nothing happened, so let's ignore it' game, or the 'I'm still pissed at you' game, when we both know you're really not."

She turned to glare at him in disbelief. "You lied to me."

"You *think* I lied to you. I never said a word; you just assumed I was Aiden. My story isn't changing. What I told you earlier was true. Aiden and I are connected. Aiden and I like to share. We want to share you. It's that simple. Which one is it you have a problem with? The sharing or the connection?"

She slapped the side of her thigh in exasperation. "It doesn't matter. I don't have time for this, Noah."

He stepped forward, his eyes narrowed to tiny slits of deep blue. It wasn't anger that gave him that hard, dangerous look—it was hunger. Hunger for her that made her knees shake in weakness, made her heart flutter like a scared bird.

"I think you're making excuses," he murmured as he backed her against the railing that overlooked the main entry hall.

She glanced over her shoulder nervously at the black-and-white tile floor. Just how sturdy was this railing? She licked her lips and turned back to Noah. His body heat surrounded her, warming her, comforting her. It felt right to be this close to him, and that scared her. Something else that scared her was that at that moment, she was convinced she could feel his desire, his racing heart, his need as well as she could feel her own. How was that possible?

"Noah..." she began.

"I'm not giving in," he warned. "So don't even go there."

Her mouth dropped open, and some of her bravado returned. "Look, bossy. That kind of attitude might work with your men, but don't you dare—"

A door opened behind Noah as though the wind had blown it, slamming it hard against the wall with a loud bang. Alana squealed, and Noah quickly spun around, keeping her behind him as he turned to stare at the opening.

"What the hell?" he snapped.

Down the hall, they could hear other doors opening and slamming, one after another, over and over, the bangs actually rattling the windows. He rushed forward and into the hall. Alana followed, but he held up his palm indicating she should stay on the landing as the doors continued to open and close on their own.

Chapter Twelve

Aiden leaned against the back of the truck, rolling his eyes toward the sky. He'd wanted to go into the house with them, but he'd given them a few minutes alone. One at a time was probably a better approach anyway at this point.

"Where's Alana?" Tray asked as he stuck his head around the corner of the truck. "You okay? You look a little green."

"More like blue," he mumbled. *As in blue balls.* That's how bad they hurt at the moment. "Alana's with Noah. They're...talking."

"Like you and her were talking the other night on the terrace?" Tray asked with amusement.

Aiden narrowed his eyes, but Tray didn't back down. He continued to watch him with unbridled delight. "Wow, when you look at me like that, you look exactly like your brother. Even more than you usually do."

Aiden sighed and looked away.

Tray chuckled, but quickly stopped. "Do I need to be concerned about Alana?"

"No."

"Do you think you love her?"

"I've already gone through all this with Lisa, you know."

"I know, but now you're going through it with me," Tray countered, obviously not backing down.

Aiden pursed his lips then relented. "I'm not sure. I believe I could. I believe she's special, that she's probably perfect for Noah and me."

"What if she decides she can't handle it?"

"Then we let her go…albeit reluctantly."

"What if she decides she can handle it?" Tray asked.

Aiden smiled. "From your mouth to God's ears. I don't know what the future holds, Tray. None of us do. I just want to take this one day at a time and see where it goes."

"Whoa," Lisa mumbled from the back of the truck. Aiden and Tray turned to look at her as she stared wide-eyed at the screen. "You two have to see this!"

Tray jumped into the truck, Aiden close behind him.

"Look at what the doors are doing," Lisa said as she pointed to the screen.

"Holy shit!" Tray exclaimed as he took off out of the truck and headed toward the house.

"Hold up," Aiden yelled, close on his heels.

* * *

Alana stood back, staring in astonishment at the doors as they closed and opened on their own.

"This is... This can't be real," she whispered. "Noah, what the hell's going on?"

"I don't know."

Tray and Aiden came barreling up the stairs just as a young girl's voice cried out, "Stop him!"

Tray came to an abrupt halt, his eyes wide. As soon as the voice stopped, the doors went still, and they all stared at one another in shock.

Aiden glanced around warily as he pushed past Tray to get to Alana. "Are you okay?" he asked.

His touch was gentle as he pushed her curls away from her face. Alana nodded, but deep inside she still trembled. Through all the years she'd been investigating, she'd never experienced anything like that.

But despite what had happened, she felt safe standing between the twins. It was as if she knew instinctively they would never let anything hurt her. It was comforting and weird as hell.

"That was a heck of a disembodied voice," Tray said in awe.

Noah turned to look at Tray, a look of pure exasperation on his face. "A disembodied what?"

Aiden tried to explain. "It's a voice—"

"I know what the hell it is, Aiden!" Noah snapped. "This wasn't paranormal. A person did this. Human. Period."

"What the hell are you yelling at me for?" Aiden barked.

Alana quickly raised her hands, putting one on Aiden's chest, the other on Noah's shoulder, suddenly feeling the need to play referee. "Guys," she said with caution. "Let's settle down. Tray has a camera on this hall, so we'll be able to see if there was anyone here."

Noah looked at Tray. "Do they run all day?"

Tray shook his head. "No. We don't have the battery power for that, nor do we have the manpower. If they're on, someone needs to be here with them."

Noah nodded and turned back toward the far end of the hall. "Someone could have set this up while the cameras were off."

"For what purpose?" Tray demanded. "And what about the voice? It sounded as though it came from all around us."

Noah looked disgusted. "Speakers."

"Noah, you're being pigheaded," Aiden tried to reason.

"I'm not..." Noah scowled and put his hands on his hips, sighing in resignation. "Fine. I'm being pigheaded, but you can't seriously believe this was paranormal."

"I'll make a deal with you," Tray offered as he stepped forward. "We both work on this. You can even have Alana, since she's great at debunking things—"

"Hey," Alana snapped.

Tray held up his hand, silencing her. "I'll work on the paranormal end. Surely between the two of us, we'll figure it out."

"Where do I go?" Aiden asked with amusement.

Noah glared at him. "Do you really want me to answer that right now?"

"Look, Noah," Aiden snarled, stepping toward his brother.

Alana quickly stepped between them again, putting a palm on each chest. "I don't know what your problem is tonight—well, maybe I do, but I'm not playing referee here. I have better things to do with my time, so knock it off. If dating the two of you means I'm constantly stopping fights, I don't want any part of it."

Both men stared at her in surprise.

"Guess she told you," Tray murmured, trying his best not to laugh as he strolled past them.

"Where the hell are you going?" Noah asked.

"I'm going to get the camera," Tray replied as he kept going, his back to them.

"I promise you, we do not always fight like this," Aiden said softly.

"Then why now?" she asked, watching Noah as he followed Tray down the hall.

Aiden examined one of the doors, opening and closing it slowly, then running his hand over the edges, feeling anything around the hinges or the frame that would explain what happened.

"I think Noah's really stressed out," he replied.

"About what?"

"I think seeing that girl affected him more than he wants to admit. He doesn't like things he can't explain, and I think that also includes our reaction to you."

She stared at him, confused. "What reaction?"

"Just the whole strength of the connection between us. It's stronger with you. Stronger than it's ever been."

"My being with him wouldn't bother you?" she asked.

Aiden shrugged. "No."

Alana's lips twisted. "I'm not sure if that's a good thing or not."

"Why would it be a bad thing?" he asked, intrigued.

"Well, usually when someone you care about is with someone else, you feel jealous...competitive... something."

"We're different."

"Yeah, I see that," she said, letting out a tired breath as she watched Noah. She turned back to Aiden. "I'm trying to figure out how to tell the two of you apart. At first, I thought it was a good and bad thing. You were the nicer one, he was the naughty one."

Aiden grinned. "And now?"

"Now, like right now, I see a naughty side in you just like earlier, I saw a nicer side to Noah."

"We learned at a young age to make our personalities different. Noah's more the loner, the skeptic, the bullheaded one."

"And you're more the people person," she added.

"The patient one, more open-minded one. We both have tempers, we can both be unreasonable, but neither of us would ever hurt you, physically or otherwise."

Alana's lips thinned as she drifted off into deep thought. Could she really do something like this?

"What's your opinion of all this?" Aiden asked.

Alana stared at him in confusion, unsure how she should answer. "Opinion of what?" she asked, stalling for time.

He nodded toward the hall. "This."

She drew in a slow breath of relief he was talking about what happened and not about the three of them. "I don't know. I've never encountered anything like this. I never expected this." She shook her head. "I think I'm a little out of my league here."

"No you're not," he said with a smile. "Just look at it as you would any other investigation. Where would you start in debunking it?"

"I'd start where Noah's starting. Looking for anything that didn't belong."

"See. Maybe you're not in over your head as much as you think."

"Maybe."

She glanced at her watch. One in the morning. Wow. It was late, but early in their line of work.

"Alana!" Tray yelled from the other end of the hall.

"Yeah?" she asked, dropping her arm and looking toward the end of the dark hall and Tray.

"What do you suppose she meant by 'stop him'?"

"Good question. What do you say we try to figure that out?"

"I'm game," he replied, grinning from ear to ear.

* * *

"What the hell was going on up there?" Lisa asked, practically jumping up and down with impatience as Alana made her way toward the truck.

She'd left the three men upstairs, arguing with one another—about what, Alana had no idea and really didn't care at the moment. She just needed some time alone, some time to think things through, without the two most gorgeous men she'd ever seen watching her.

Alana looked at Lisa's expectant expression and stopped dead in her tracks. "What on earth..." She bit back a giggle. "You look like a kid at their favorite candy store."

Lisa rolled her eyes and waved her hand, dismissing Alana's comment. "I saw the whole thing on the camera. Did those doors really start opening and closing on their own? And what was with that voice? Alana! How can you stand there so calm? I would be jumping clear out of my skin."

Alana's smile faded. "I did plenty of jumping up there, believe me. I'm withholding judgment for now. Admit it. Have you ever seen a ghost do that?"

She walked around Lisa and climbed into the back of the truck.

Lisa jumped in behind her. "Does it really matter if we've seen it before or not? There is a saying. I've heard it. 'There's a first time for everything.'"

"True enough," Alana replied, grinning. "Did you notice anything on the computer screen before it started?"

"No. I actually didn't notice it until after they'd begun to move." She was quiet for a second, then asked. "What were you and Noah discussing so intently?"

"Oh God. Don't ask." Alana dropped her head into her hand and began to massage her forehead with her fingers. "Lisa. I'm such a weakling. I can't believe I..."

She dropped her hand and raised her head, scowling at the screen.

"I thought you didn't want me to ask. You can't say things like that and not expect me to ask."

"I know."

"Well?" Lisa pushed.

"I've lost my mind." Alana cringed. "I want to have sex with Noah...and Aiden."

Lisa remained silent for a few seconds as though taking it all in. "Well... They're both gorgeous. Can't say as I blame you, but is that what you told him? You looked a little pissed."

"That's not what I told him. Noah's bossy attitude is what pissed me off."Alana turned to look at her friend in surprise. "No lectures? No warnings or concern?"

"I'm not going to tell you what to do, Alana. I love you, but you have to do what you think is right for you."

"I don't know what's right for me."

"You will. In the meantime, I'm here if you need me."

"I know," Alana whispered, giving her friend a small smile.

Lisa nodded toward the computer and changed the subject. "Have you heard that voice before?"

"Tray has a recording of that same voice giving that same warning. I just wish I knew what it meant."

"Do you know who the girl is?"

"Not yet." Alana studied her friend. "Since you don't want to go in the house, do you want to do a little investigating?"

Lisa's lips lifted into a half smile and for the first time in a couple of days, Alana saw a spark of excitement enter her eyes. Lisa always loved doing investigative work.

"You want me to find out who the girl is?" Lisa asked.

"Yeah, and if possible find out if the guy she's warning us about is from her time or ours. If it's hers, it's residual. If it's from ours, it's an intelligent haunting, and I shudder to think what she might be trying to warn us of."

"You and me both. But how will we be able to tell?"

"I'm not sure yet. We might be able to tell by how she died, if we can even find her."

"It shouldn't be too hard."

"Famous last words." Alana smiled, but it quickly faded. "Can I get you to do me a favor?"

"Sure. What?"

"Make sure I leave with you and Tray tonight, not them."

Lisa tried her best to hide the grin that tugged at her lips, but failed miserably. "I'm assuming *them* means Aiden and Noah."

"Yep," Alana said with a sigh. "I think I've already proved I have no self-control where they're concerned."

"No kidding," Lisa replied, giggling softly.

Alana dropped her head in her hand, mortified. She just hoped to God the television crew kept this sexual tension stuff out of the show.

Chapter Thirteen

Alana tossed and turned amid the sheets. She could never get used to strange beds, and it was so hot. Sweat covered her limbs, and she kicked off the sheets, seeking relief from the humid air in the room.

Why was it so hot?

Soft lips touched her cheek, and she smiled. Oh, yeah. That's why it was so hot.

Turning her head, she smiled at Aiden as he gently brushed her curls from her sweaty brow. His eyes stared into hers, caressing her with a look and making her whole body tingle with awareness and growing need. How could he do that? How could he make her react so wildly?

On her other side, the bed sank, and she turned to see Noah place his weight on one knee. Her gaze took in his muscular chest and washboard abs. Strong, thick thighs flexed as he moved, and she reached out, running her fingers through the coarse hair covering his legs.

She feathered her fingers upward to his long, thick cock. Moisture glistened at the tip, and she licked her lips, anxious for the taste of him on her tongue.

He watched her, silent and tense as she softly trailed her finger along his length, smoothing the flat of her fingertip over the velvety flesh.

Beside her, Aiden cupped her breast, lifting it upward as he dipped his head. His mouth engulfed the aching tip, and she moaned, closing her eyes as the warmth from his mouth settled over her tingling breast. He swirled his tongue around her nipple and gently swiped it over the hard nub. She gasped, arching her back and thrusting her breast farther into his hot mouth.

She opened her eyes, catching Noah's gaze as he smiled down at her. A smile of pure animal lust that made her heart skip a beat in excitement. He had her exactly where he wanted her, and they both knew it. Sweat coated her flesh, cooling her and making her shiver despite the heat emanating from his eyes.

Was she dreaming? Had Lisa let her down and she'd left with the twins after all?

No. She was dreaming. She had to be dreaming. Right?

Aiden bit at her nipple, and she squealed, giggling as he opened his lips, playfully engulfing almost her entire breast in his mouth. At the moment, she didn't care if she was dreaming or not. It felt too good to make him stop.

Noah bent forward slightly, and inch by incredibly sensual inch, slid his palm up the inside of her thigh, spreading her legs as he went. Alana let them fall open, welcoming his touch against her throbbing sex. His fingers were gentle yet insistent as he slid them through the juices coating her labia, spreading them over her pussy as he teased and massaged.

The pad of his thumb brushed over her clit, and she gasped, bucking her hips toward his hands. Aiden continued to tease and lick at her breast, driving her insane with his wicked tongue. And Noah's fingers—his incredibly talented fingers—teased her entrance, making her moan for more.

Two men showering her with affection, touching her body, nibbling at her flesh. It was one of the most erotic, wildest things she'd ever experienced. Bombarded from all sides, she could feel herself falling, shattering into thousands of tiny pieces.

The sensations were overwhelming, intense, and smothering as she struggled to breathe, to hold on to consciousness as Noah thrust three fingers into her pussy. She cried out as her channel pulsed around the digits, pulling them deeper. Aiden's naughty, whispered words of encouragement echoed in her ears as he playfully bit at her neck and rubbed the flat of his palm over her nipples.

Alana tried to scream as her body careened into an orgasm that took her breath, but nothing came out. She struggled, digging her fingers into the sheets as she rode out wave after wave in tortured silence. Why couldn't she scream? Why couldn't she beg for more? Beg him to stop—to *not* stop.

With a loud squeal, Alana woke with a start and glanced around the room in startled surprise. She was alone, naked in her own bed, sweat glistening over her flesh. She shivered and wrapped her arms around herself as she tried to gather her thoughts.

God, it had been so real. She'd swear she could still smell their scents lingering on her skin. She'd swear she could still feel their touch.

Tray peeked around the corner of the doorjamb, and she grabbed the sheet, pulling it over her breasts. Tray had seen her naked before, so it wasn't that. Truthfully, she was embarrassed and could feel the heat of the flush as it moved over her entire body.

"Look at you," Tray drawled with amusement. "Moaning and squealing, all sprawled out like a Saturday night whore."

Alana sighed and dropped her head in her hands. "How loud did I get?"

"You weren't loud," Tray said as he came farther into the room and sat on the foot of the bed. He studied her with just a hint of concern as he watched her. "Nightmare or wet dream?"

Alana winced and glanced toward the sliding glass door that overlooked the small town.

Tray raised an eyebrow. "Why are you so embarrassed? I've given you blowjob lessons, using my penis. I've used your toys on you when you were so sexually frustrated, you couldn't stand it anymore."

"I know." Alana sighed, staring down at the sheets.

"You can't talk to me about this?"

"It was really weird, Tray," she whispered. "I'm not sure how to describe it. It's almost like they were in my mind, both of them." She glanced up at him frowning. "It's almost scary."

Tray reached out and touched her knee in comfort but said nothing.

* * *

Noah jerked awake, his balls throbbing. He stared toward the ceiling, trying his best to catch his breath. That had to be one of the most realistic, intense dreams he'd ever had. What the hell had just happened?

Again he could hear in his mind Karen's voice as she'd spoken softly. *"When you find your third, your power will intensify. The three of you will be one."*

Noah growled and dragged his hand down his face. His fingers lingered at his nose, and he inhaled, convinced he could smell Alana there. Why had Karen told him that? What had happened that weekend when he and Aiden had been separated? It had been Karen's idea, but why?

He frowned, trying to remember. He'd seen something—heard something—something in that house. It had frightened him—terribly.

Shaking his head, he pushed the growing fear aside and sat up, letting his feet touch the cold hardwood floor. He wouldn't be able to get back to sleep, so he might as well get up. He was hungry anyway.

With a sigh, he reached down and wrapped his fingers around his rigid shaft, squeezing hard. He hadn't gotten to finish the dream. He could still remember the look on her face as she'd exploded, the scream that had awoken him from the dream. He scowled. Or had she been the one to wake and sever the connection? Was that what this had been? Some sort of...

That was ridiculous.

Standing, he grabbed a pair of pajama pants that lay across the foot of the bed. He shook them out, then quickly stepped into them. With a tired sigh, he walked into the kitchen, unsure what it was he had even come in here for. He absently opened the fridge and studied the contents before deciding on bacon and eggs. Early morning sunlight streaked through the window over the sink, warming the floor beneath his feet.

Behind him, he heard Aiden enter the room.

"If you're cooking, I want some," he said tiredly.

Noah glanced at him over his shoulder as he placed two slices of bacon in the skillet. "Couldn't sleep?"

"I thought I was sleeping fine." He leaned against the counter and crossed his arms over his chest, watching Noah cook. "I had the weirdest dream."

"Yeah?"

"Well. Not really weird, I guess. I was having sex with Alana."

Noah froze but kept his head down, waiting for Aiden to continue.

"You were there. You made her come, and when she did, she screamed, and it brought me out of the dream. Thanks for that by the way. I have a woody hard enough to hammer a freakin' nail."

Noah snorted. "Like I truly had anything to do with what happened in your dream."

"I'm not so sure you didn't. I've never had a dream that fucking real. I've never been able to feel your reactions in my dreams. It was as though we were awake, and Alana was actually between us, and not just a dream."

Noah shrugged. "Weird."

Aiden remained silent for a few seconds. Noah kept his gaze on the skillet. He wasn't sure what to say. He didn't have the answers, so he chose to say nothing.

"Noah—" Aiden began.

"I'm changing to the night shift," Noah said. "I can't keep staying up until three or four, then getting back up at six."

"Yeah," Aiden sighed. "I know the feeling."

"You should probably do something along the same lines. Maybe take a leave of absence before you fall on your face from exhaustion."

"I don't know why you're doing this," Aiden snapped.

Noah looked up frowning. He knew what his brother was referring to, but he hoped he could get him to drop it.

"I can feel what you feel, Noah. I felt you tense a few seconds ago when I mentioned the dream. I felt your anxiety when you got out of bed and headed down the hall. I can feel you're keeping something from me, and for the first time in our lives, I don't know what that is."

"I don't even know what it is," he finally admitted. "I don't remember what happened." He scowled down at the skillet and moved the bacon around. "I get bits and pieces, and something about that woman feels familiar, but I can't place it. I can't fucking place anything!"

"That's what this is about?" Aiden asked.

"I don't know. I've been thinking about that weekend ever since I saw that woman. I remember Karen telling me I was the center. That when we found our third, the power would intensify."

Aiden shook his head. "Wait a minute. What power?"

"Our connection."

"And you think Alana is this third you referred to?"

"I don't know."

"Well," Aiden said as he once again leaned against the counter. "It would make sense, I guess. Our connection has been much stronger since Alana came into the picture. Did Karen tell you that weekend you stayed with her at the house?"

Noah shook his head as he turned the bacon. "I think so. I saw something... I think. Maybe. I believe she told me that after Gram called because you were upset. Something had freaked you out."

"Yeah, you."

Noah snorted.

"It's kinda like now," Aiden drawled as he reached around his brother to grab a plate to place the bacon on. "Something's got you freaked. We're sharing dreams, which is something we've never done, and somehow we've dragged Alana into it as well. Do I have it right, so far?"

One side of Noah's lips lifted. "Pretty close."

"Do you suppose she'll understand what happened?" Aiden asked as he held the plate level for Noah.

"I don't even understand what happened, nor do we know for sure she experienced the same dream. It might've just been between us."

"Right," Aiden drawled as he slapped Noah on the back of the shoulder.

Chapter Fourteen

"You want me to what?" Noah asked Lisa as she stood across from his desk.

He'd gotten a grand total of two hours' sleep the night before. The last thing he needed today was Lisa pestering him about ghosts.

"I want you to give a description of the woman you saw to one of your sketch artists."

Noah raised an eyebrow. "You're serious?"

She frowned. "No. I'm pulling your chain. Is it working? Are you wound up yet? Pissed, perhaps?"

"Almost," he growled.

"Come on," she said, before batting her eyes. "Please."

"Can't Tray or Alana do that?" Noah asked, agitated.

"They didn't get as clear an image as you did."

"What makes you think I got a clear image?"

"Are you telling me you didn't?"

Noah stared at her before sighing loudly.

"You've seen her more often and clearly than anyone else, and if I can find out what she looks like, it might make it easier to find her."

Noah snorted and shook his head. "I don't know how much I can help you, Lisa."

"You'd be surprised. Besides, Aiden told me how good your memory is. You notice things a lot of people miss, especially small details. My guess is it's what makes you a good cop."

"Oh, so now we're going to go with flattery?" he teased.

She shrugged. "Hey, whatever works. You know?"

Noah rolled his eyes as he closed his laptop. "How's Alana this morning?" he asked.

"Ah, so we've shifted to bribery?" she asked, grinning. "I tell you how she is, maybe even where she is, and you do what I want?"

"Hey, whatever works. You know?"

Lisa laughed. "Okay. Alana's tired and totally freaked. You two should lay off her for a while, give her some breathing room. Maybe take her out to dinner, get to know her. If she wants sex, she'll let you know."

Noah's lips twitched with amusement at Lisa's no-nonsense way of telling things.

"Hey, Alana's not shy. She's not above making the first move if it's what she wants," Lisa added.

"I don't doubt that for a second," he said. "I'll give what you're saying some thought. Fair enough?"

Lisa's eyes narrowed. "So...what? You two can't be with her without having sex?"

"Aiden's the only one that's slept with her. I've been with her three times now and not shoved her against the wall yet, although I'll admit the thought has crossed my mind."

"I'll bet," Lisa drawled, her lips twitching.

With a sigh, he leaned his chair back. "I have every intention of taking things slow, taking her out to dinner, letting her get to know us. So does Aiden. We would prefer to do it together, so we get to know her together."

"Are you just after her because your brother's attracted to her, Noah?" Lisa asked, her expression one of seriousness and concern.

"I'm after her because *I'm* attracted to her."

"Fair enough," she repeated, throwing his own words back at him and eyeing him skeptically. "So... Are you going to do the sketches for me?"

He chuckled. "Are you always like a dog with a bone?"

"Pretty much. Just ask Alana."

Noah nodded, still chuckling softly. "All right. I'll do it."

"You still don't think she's a ghost, do you?"

He shook his head. "No."

"So you give me the sketch, and while I'm researching the house, I'll see if she pops up as a recent missing person."

"I've already started looking into that."

"And you haven't found anything, have you?" Lisa asked, her lips spreading into an *I told you so* smile.

"Not yet."

"Keep hanging around us, and you may just become a believer yet."

Noah smiled as he stood. "How about I escape
with Alana and send you and that flamer you call a
tech guy packing?" he asked, teasing her.

Lisa snorted and turned to follow him from his
office. "Number one, Tray would probably kiss you for
recognizing him for what he truly is. If you think he's
flaming at work, you should see him on Friday nights
at the bar."

Noah stared at her over his shoulder, amusement
tugging at his lips. "I think I'll take your word for it. Is
there a number two?"

"Yeah." Lisa smiled. "Alana wouldn't allow it."

"Now *that* I just might believe." He opened the
door that led to the second-floor offices, which was
usually where their sketch artist could be found, and
waved his hand for Lisa to go through first. "Let's get
this shit over with," he sighed, making Lisa giggle.

* * *

Alana sipped the hot coffee Tray had brewed just
minutes before. Normally she loved this coffee, but at
the moment, she barely noticed the taste of the
Jamaican Blue Mountain. She couldn't stop watching
the footage from the night before.

She studied every second closely, slowing it down
to examine it frame by frame, looking for something,
anything out of the ordinary. Those doors didn't open
and close on their own. They couldn't have. Not like
that.

They swung open as though someone shoved
them, then banged closed so hard, the sound rattled
the windows. Alana stopped the recording and rubbed

at her tired eyes. Sleep had eluded her after that wild dream. Her body still tingled whenever she thought about it.

Why was she even stressing over this? She should just enjoy the ride, sleep with both of them. The thought of a threesome was a bit daunting, though. She'd often wondered about it, fantasized about it, but going through with it was another matter entirely.

Warm, strong hands gripped her shoulders, making her jump.

"It's just me," Tray said as he softly kissed the top of her head. He began to massage her tense muscles, and she slowly relaxed. "You're wound up too tight, Alana," Tray murmured.

"I know," she whispered.

"You're overthinking all this, I believe."

"What do you suggest then?" she asked. "Don't think about it at all?"

"If they were standing in front of you right now, what would you do? Don't think about it. Just imagine them there, both of them. What's your first instinct?"

"To go to them," she admitted.

"There you go," he said as though that was the answer to all her problems.

"It's not that simple. What if I fall for them?"

"What if they fall for you? What if they've already fallen for you?"

"Tray..."

"It's not that far-fetched an idea," he argued. "I saw the way they looked at you last night, and there was more than just physical lust there."

"Are you trying to push me toward them?" she asked.

"I don't know." Tray's hands worked slowly down her back, loosening the kinks. "I just remember all the times you and Aiden talked on the phone, all the e-mails back and forth, and all the times your eyes would light up. You liked him even before you'd met him. And obviously he liked you. There's something there, I think, and if a relationship includes that gorgeous brother of his, all the better in my book."

Alana snorted. "Let's change the subject. What do you think of this footage?"

"You know what I think of that footage. It's paranormal. Hands down."

"Whenever I think of that girl and that desperate voice, I get a terrible feeling. Like something really horrible is going to happen."

"Yeah," Tray agreed as he exhaled softly. He stopped rubbing her shoulders and pulled a chair over, sitting down next to her. "I get the same feeling. Have you noticed she seems to have a thing for Noah?"

Alana frowned as she turned to look at him. "What do you mean?"

"Well, Noah saw her first. Then we saw her that night, but Aiden was with us, so because they're twins, maybe she mistook Aiden for Noah. Then last night, he was the only one to see her in the window, then the doors started slamming when you two were upstairs alone."

"That's just coincidental," she said with a wave of her hand.

"I don't think so," Tray said. "I think later tonight we should do an experiment. Send a team in without Noah, then one with. See what happens."

Alana snickered. "That's crazy."

"That's genius," Tray said, grinning.

"Noah will think you're nuts."

Tray's grin widened. "He already thinks I'm nuts."

With a laugh, Alana lifted her coffee cup in silent salute. She blew to cool it off, then took another sip. "How do you know he's even going to be there?" she asked, telling herself she was only half interested in his answer.

"Oh, he'll be there."

Alana's phone beeped, indicating she had a text message. She flipped it open and stared at the screen in surprise.

Lunch?

"Aiden just invited me to lunch," she said, staring at the one-word question.

"Well, are you going to text him back, or just sit there and stare at it all day?" Tray asked.

Another text came in. *I promise my brother and I will behave.*

Alana snickered as Tray leaned in to read it over her shoulder. He nudged her gently, and she sighed, frowning back at him. "Okay, okay."

She sent a message back.

When? Where?

Instantly he came back with a reply.

Golden Dragon at 1.

Alana glanced at her watch, realizing she had less than two hours to get ready.

K, she replied back, letting him know she would be there before flipping her phone closed. "If I end up in bed with them," she growled, eyeing Tray through narrowed eyes, "I'm coming after you with a tire iron."

Tray laughed and leaned in to kiss her cheek. "Wear that cute purple turtleneck you have with the black slacks and those sexy-ass three-inch heels. You'll look killer."

Alana shook her head and closed her eyes. "You are so not helping."

* * *

He stood back, peeking around the corner of the bookshelf as the woman from the house sat in front of the library computer. Someone passed him and moved quickly by as though they found him to be distasteful or scary. He avoided public places as much as possible, especially in the daytime, but he couldn't seem to stay away from her. Her screams from the other night still filled his ears and tightened his loins.

He turned his attention from the wary people giving him a wide berth back to the young woman who seemed to hold his attention captive. The sunlight shone through the wooden blinds, streaking her black hair with silvery highlights. Her brown eyes twinkled with barely contained excitement as she set her papers beside her on the table and clicked the mouse to bring the computer to life.

He'd followed her all morning, watching where she went and who she spoke to. He couldn't seem to stop looking at her. With her dark hair, olive skin, and dark eyes that tilted up at the edges, she had a slight Asian appearance.

She ran her delicate hands down her thigh, rubbing them against the denim of her jeans as she waited for the computer to fully boot. The fan kicked on, blowing some of her papers off the table. He rushed forward and grabbed them just as she leaned over as well, causing them to almost bump heads.

"Oops," she said with a laugh as she quickly sat back up.

Her gaze landed on his face, and she gasped briefly, before quickly composing herself. It was a reaction he was familiar with, which is why he avoided the public.

He handed the paper to her, and she accepted it with a sweet smile that made his gut clench painfully. She didn't back away from him as most people did. That surprised him. The old familiar hunger roared to life as her fingers softly brushed against his. Her scent filled his senses as he imagined all the things he would do to her when he got the chance.

"Thank you," she said, but he didn't miss how she moved back, putting a little more distance between them.

"You have to watch those fans," he replied. He glanced down at the paper and the sketch of a young girl as she set it back on the table. "Are you researching something or someone?"

"Well, both actually," she replied. "You wouldn't happen to know anything about the Hayworthe House would you?"

"That big monstrosity out on Morris?"

"That would be the one."

He shook his head. "I'm afraid not. All I know is it's been empty for a long time. Sorry I couldn't help you more."

She shrugged, smiling slightly. "That's okay. I'm Lisa," she said, holding out her hand.

He stared at it for a second before grasping it within his. No one had offered to take his hand in a long time. Her skin was warm and soft. He brushed his thumb over the purple color of her nails as he continued to hold her hand within his grasp. It was the first friendly touch he'd experienced in years, and he didn't want to let it go.

"I'm Joshua," he replied, shocked that he'd actually told her his real name.

Revealing himself in any way was something he never did, and he'd done it twice today with her. Once when he picked up the paper, and the second when he'd revealed his name. She was dangerous to him. All the more reason to be rid of her in his own special way.

"Well, it was nice to meet you, Joshua," she said as she pulled her hand free.

He'd held on to her hand for too long. A slight wariness appeared in her gaze as she watched him, and he immediately tensed. She could feel something was off with him, so he needed to be careful. He would need to get close to her again if his plan of abducting her was going to work.

"It was nice meeting you as well," he replied. "I should probably let you get back to work."

She nodded but still smiled sweetly as he walked away, leaving her to the computer and her research. This wasn't the time or place for his plan, but if he stayed close to her, watched her, eventually it would be.

Chapter Fifteen

Alana opened the door to the Chinese restaurant and perused the dining area for the twins. She spotted them almost instantly sitting at the far side of the room, their heads bent close in quiet conversation. She wondered what they were discussing so intently. Aiden spotted her first, and he raised his hand, waving her over.

She drew in a quick, nervous breath. Already, her body hummed with the memory of how they'd made her come in her dream. Would it be that way in real life? Would they set her on fire as they had in her mind?

Noah turned to watch her over his shoulder as she made her way slowly across the room. The way his dark, sultry eyes raked over her body sent shivers of awareness to every inch of her flesh. Aiden, at least, kept his desire more under control. Noah left no doubt he wanted her and apparently didn't care who saw.

She approached the table, and both men stood. Aiden softly kissed her cheek while Noah pulled out her chair, allowing her to finally get off her shaky legs.

"We're glad you could make it," Aiden said as he returned to his seat.

Noah brushed his lips along her neck just below her ear, causing goose bumps to rise along her arms.

"I'm just glad you didn't tell us to take a flying leap," he whispered.

"The thought crossed my mind," she replied, her lips twitching slightly. "The two of you alone can be very persuasive. Together you're quite overpowering."

"We don't intend to be," Aiden said as he signaled the waitress to come take their order. "The buffet here is great. I hope you like Chinese."

"I love it," she said, swallowing down her jitters.

They were in a public restaurant. What could happen? She noticed the restroom sign at the far side of the dining area and almost giggled out loud as she imagined a stolen moment or two in a locked bathroom.

God, I'm so screwed.

An older Chinese man approached the table, waving off the young woman who was about to wait on them. "Sheriff, Councilman, it's good to see you today."

"Hi, Sam," Aiden replied before nodding to Alana. "This is Alana James, the young woman who's investigating the house."

His face lit up with a wide smile as he clasped his hands in front of him with excitement. "The ghost hunter?"

Alana smiled, always happy to meet a fan. "Yes."

"I just love to watch your show. It's so much fun."

"Thank you," Alana said with a chuckle.

"Lunch today is on the house," he said.

"Oh, no," Alana began to argue, wanting to pay for her food, but he waved her words away with a quick swish of his hand.

"I insist. Can I get you something to drink? Tea, soda..."

She glanced at Aiden and Noah. "Could I get a beer?" she asked.

He smiled and nodded. "Of course. Best in the house. Councilman, a beer for you?"

Aiden nodded. "Sounds great, Sam. Thanks."

"Sheriff?" Sam asked.

"I'm on duty, Sam. I'll just have sweet tea."

Sam nodded. "Coming right up."

Alana watched him go and shook her head with amusement. "He seems like a nice guy."

"Sam's great," Noah replied as he watched Sam as well. "He's been here a long time."

"He works with Noah a lot with the youth program Noah started," Aiden said.

"Youth program?" Alana asked, curious as to what made these two tick.

Noah shrugged, obviously trying to dismiss the whole thing as nothing. "It's just something I and a few of the business owners started to help keep the kids out of trouble."

"Does it help?" she asked.

"I like to think so," Noah replied, his lips lifting into a grin.

When he smiled, it softened his whole face, making him appear younger. She peeked over at Aiden.

He caught her watching him and winked. The heat of a blush moved quickly over her cheeks as Sam returned, placing drinks on the table.

She grabbed hers and downed two quick sips, hoping it would help to calm her nerves. The twins made her jittery, but not necessarily in a bad way.

What had her most frazzled was the fact that she wanted them. Right here, right now. How was it that they could do this to her without even laying a hand on her? She'd lost her mind, that's all there was to it. A temporary case of lustful insanity.

She welcomed Aiden's suggestion they check out the buffet. Choosing her food gave her something to think about other than being sandwiched between them. Once back at the table, she felt calmer and determined to learn a little more about them.

"So?" she began as she stabbed her fork into a bite of sweet and sour chicken. "What's the deal with you two?"

"What do you mean?" Noah asked.

"Well. Any other siblings, parents?"

"No," Aiden replied. "It's just the two of us. Parents died a long time ago. We were mostly raised by our grandmother. You?"

Alana grinned. She should have known they would want to ask her questions as well. "Mother lives in Florida. I'm an only child."

"How did you get involved in ghost hunting?" Noah asked.

She pointed her fork at him playfully. "That answer is easily found on my bio page on the Web. This is supposed to be an investigation into you two, not the other way around."

"I would think that would work both ways," he replied, his eyes twinkling with humor.

"Fair enough. I got into ghost hunting after investigating my first paranormal romance."

"That's right," Noah said with a nod. "I almost forgot you also write books."

"My newest one comes out in November. This is actually my last ghost-hunting adventure until next year. My publisher has me going on a book signing tour November, part of December, and January."

"Can that be postponed?" Noah asked.

"Why would I?" she asked, curious as to where he was going with that question.

Noah shrugged. "I was just curious. You never know what might happen between now and then."

His intense gaze held hers captive for a couple of seconds before she looked over to Aiden, who shrugged before taking a bite of shrimp.

"That sounds a little ominous," Alana said, turning back to Noah.

Noah snorted with amusement. "I didn't mean I was going to lock you away or bury you somewhere in the house."

"Well, that's good to know."

"I can't speak for Aiden, but this isn't just a one-night-stand deal for me, Alana, and I don't think it is for you, either."

"I agree," Aiden said.

"I don't know what this is," Alana replied. "I don't know what to think of any of it. I slept with Aiden not really seeing it as anything other than fun, then you approach me and offer a ménage relationship, which is something I've never even remotely considered in my life...at least until now. I don't understand this connection the two of you have."

"Neither do we," Aiden answered with a chuckle.

"How does it work exactly? You each feel everything the other feels? If one of you gets a paper cut, the other feels the pain?"

"More or less," Aiden replied. "We've learned over the years to block a lot of it out."

"What if Noah were to get shot?" she asked.

"He has been shot, and I felt it," Aiden said. "It hurt like hell at first, but after a few seconds I was able to block it, knock it down to a dull ache."

"But for whatever reason," Noah added, "I wasn't able to block Aiden having sex with you that night. Nor was he able to block it the other day when I found you at—"

"I get it," she interrupted. "Why is it stronger now?"

Aiden lifted his beer bottle and swirled it. "We don't know."

"We would like to find out, though." Noah reached out and rubbed his finger enticingly up her forearm, making her skin tingle.

"The two of you are insane," she whispered, only half meaning it. At the moment, she had to be just as insane to even consider such a relationship.

Noah grinned wickedly. "Yeah, but we're fun."

Alana giggled and shook her head in amazement.

"I promised your friend that Aiden and I would behave, take you out, get to know you. Ease you into this, if that's what you want."

"Ease me into it?" she asked. "How do you ease someone into this?"

Aiden's blue gaze twinkled with a devilment she would expect more from Noah. "There're lots of ways."

"Are you talking physical or emotional?" she asked.

"Both."

"The two of you never get jealous?"

"I don't know," Noah replied. "We've never had a threesome with a woman we had feelings for." Noah waved his fork. "Beyond the physical anyway."

"What happens if there is jealousy?"

"We would work through it," Aiden said. "We're not talking marriage, Alana. At least not now. None of us knows where this will go. You could hate it or it could fizzle. Noah and I can be demanding, overbearing, arrogant, and stubborn. It could all quite possibly be too much for you."

"No kidding," she murmured. "One man can sometimes be more than I can handle. Two? It's almost kind of scary."

Noah chuckled. "Just remember, Alana. We would never force you into anything you didn't want to do. We follow your lead. If you say no, it's no. Now." He gave her a sexy grin that made her stomach flip. "That doesn't mean we won't try to convince you from time to time."

"We're very good at convincing," Aiden said and she turned to stare into his deep blue, sexy gaze.

Oh, yeah. She'd been privy to their convincing firsthand and knew exactly how good they were at it. She doubted she could ever tell them no. At least not with any conviction.

She turned her attention back to her food and took a bite, barely tasting it. She swallowed and spoke. "I'm going to change the subject for a second."

"Okay," Aiden replied.

"How's the passage search going?"

"It's stalled," Noah replied. "I know there's an entrance into that second level passage, but I can't find the damn thing."

"Aiden said you spent time in that house as kids. Were you ever in the second level passage?"

"Once," Noah replied as he stared at his glass, thoughtful. "Karen or Gram, neither one liked it in there. They said it felt oppressive, like evil hung in the air."

"Considering what may have gone on there, can you blame them?" Aiden replied drily.

"Wait. What went on there?" Alana asked with curiosity. Whatever it was might explain the young girl.

"Karen's father kept sex slaves," Noah replied. "Not all the time, but at parties."

Alana's eyes widened. "Seriously? That would explain the girl. If she died there as a slave, her haunting is residual."

"Residual?" Noah asked.

"Her spirit could be reliving her death, warning of her own death, not someone else's."

Noah nodded in acknowledgment. "I suppose it makes sense if you believe in that sort of stuff. Besides, I thought you were the skeptic of the bunch."

"I am, but this sort of thing fascinates me. I've seen her. Aiden's seen her. We know she's there. Now all we have to do is find out why, and I think you may have just hit on it."

"If that is why she's there, can you help her?" Aiden asked.

"Help her? You mean put her spirit to rest?"

Aiden nodded as he took a bite of fried rice.

"Not if it's residual. Residual is like a recording, replaying itself over and over. Sort of like a memory of the house itself. Nothing more. Those you can't really get rid of."

"If you can't get rid of it, then what's the point of doing anything?" Noah asked.

"There's no point. It's just a fascinating mystery that I would love to be able to find the answer to."

Noah's lips twitched into a sideways smile. "I would prefer to find the answer to who attacked your friend. Has she remembered anything?"

"Not yet, but truthfully, I'm not so sure that's a bad thing. Whatever it was that happened up there scared the hell out of her. I don't want her to relive that. Even if it means we don't find who did it."

"Alana..." Noah began.

"I know we need to find who's responsible, but I really don't want her to remember if she doesn't have to."

Noah sighed and glanced over at Aiden, who nodded as though silently communicating with his brother. Aiden turned his gaze to her and smiled softly as his hand moved to rest over hers. A warmth traveled quickly up her arm, making her feel safe, protected—feelings that eluded her at night. They had ever since she'd been here; ever since she'd heard her friend's screams from the second floor of the house.

She licked her lips and pulled her hand free. All she could think about all morning was them touching her, kissing her. Her willpower was all but nonexistent where they were concerned.

"I, um..." She reached up and rubbed at the back of her neck, trying to relieve some of the tension.

"Do we make you nervous?" Noah asked.

She glanced over at him and frowned at the grin he tried hard to hide. "Actually, yes. You do."

"Why?" Aiden asked.

She gaped. "Seriously? I've had sex with you. I've been kissed by him." She pointed her thumb toward Noah. "I think it's safe to say I have zero control around both of you."

"It's the same for us," Noah replied. "If I had any control where you were concerned, I would've never kissed you back in Aiden's office and started this whole mess."

Shaking her head, Alana couldn't help but chuckle helplessly. "The two of you are killing me. You promised to behave."

Noah laughed. "We are behaving. I think you've seen us not behaving. Remember the house and Aiden's trip to your hotel room?"

Aiden joined him in the laughter while Alana dropped her forehead in her hand. She tried not to laugh, she really did, but eventually she gave in. The three of them chuckled until Sam returned, carrying their fortune cookies.

She smiled at him. "Lunch was wonderful, Sam. Thank you."

"I'm thrilled you liked it," he said with a bow. "Some of the girls were wondering if you would take a picture with them."

"Of course. I would love that," Alana replied, more than happy to take a picture with fans. Not to mention the distraction would help to take her mind off the twins and the things they made her feel.

AIDEN STOOD BACK and watched Alana with the girls at the restaurant. It was obvious she loved her fans, both of her books and her show. She took pictures, signed a couple of books that the girls had with them, and even a napkin for a woman who didn't have any books with her.

He liked watching her, and so did his brother if the interest shining in his eyes was any indication. But

Aiden had more of an indication than that. He could feel Noah's interest, his desire.

He could also sense Alana's hesitance, which was something that had him stumped. Why would he feel anything from her at all? Vaguely he wondered if there was a reason for that. Was that why he and his brother had never experienced such a sharp connection before? They'd been going after the wrong type of woman all this time?

Or was it all in his head, his imagination fueled by what he could see in her eyes? If she was hesitant, he could certainly understand. It was a lot to dump in someone's lap, especially someone who didn't know them well.

"Sheriff," a voice came through Noah's walkie attached to his hip.

Noah rolled his eyes and pulled it from the clip. Putting it to his mouth, he hit the Talk button. "Yeah."

"Are you about done with lunch?" the voice asked, and Noah frowned.

Alana turned to look as well, her expression one of concern as she heard the man's spooked tone through the walkie.

"Yeah, why? What's up?"

"I think you need to come by the station. You're gonna need to see this for yourself."

Noah's frown deepened. "I'll be right there."

He set the walkie into the clip. "I'll meet you guys at the house later." With a firm look, he pointed at Alana. "I better not catch you out there alone again."

"Noah," she countered, her brow creased with irritation at his dominant warning. "I'm not four."

Noah stepped closer and brought his nose close to hers, his lips twitching with a hint of amusement. "Trust me, darlin', I know. Just be careful, okay? I have a bad feeling about all this, and I'm afraid we haven't seen the last of the violence."

Worry darkened the green of her eyes. "Do you know something we don't?"

"No. Just gut instinct." He turned to Aiden and nodded before leaving the restaurant.

"What do you suppose that was all about? At the station, I mean," Alana said with a thoughtful expression as she watched him leave.

"Not sure, but if it's anything important, he'll let us know later. Are you ready?"

She nodded and turned to wave good-bye to Sam and his girls. Aiden put his hand at the base of her spine, leading her from the restaurant. It felt right there, like she belonged within his reach, his arms, his life.

"Tray wants to perform a little experiment later," she said as they came to a stop at her car.

He blinked at her change in topic. "An experiment?" Aiden asked intrigued.

"He believes the ghost has a fascination with Noah."

Aiden snorted. "Why Noah?"

"I'm not sure. I'm not even sure Tray knows why. I think he's just..." Alana waved her hand. "He's just looking for some sort of explanation as to why Noah sees her more than anyone else."

"Have you ever run across anything like this before?" he asked.

Alana shook her head as she pulled her keys from her purse. "Nothing to this extreme. I'm still skeptical. I still think this isn't all paranormal."

Aiden leaned against the truck and crossed his arms over his chest. "Now *that* I definitely agree with you on. Noah's worried. I can feel it even though he doesn't say it. He doesn't like loose ends and unanswered questions. It bothers him that we have zero leads on whoever that was in the house."

"Trust me, it bothers me too."

"I have to admit, though. I never imagined opening that house up to ghost hunters would be this much fun. I think your job is interesting as hell."

Alana laughed. "*Interesting* is one way to describe it. Another would be *tedious*. Most of the time we find very little, or we could spend hours watching videos and see nothing. The producer is already talking about turning this one into a three-hour-long special. He and Tray are practically salivating at the mouth. From what I understand, he already has the trailer ready to run."

"I also have the vendors, and everything else in place and ready to go for the Halloweenfest. All you have to do is say yes."

He could see the indecision on her face, the hesitancy in her eyes. "Businesswise, I would be an idiot to turn it down. Personally..."

Noah put his finger under her chin, forcing her gaze to meet his. "If it works between the three of us, it works. If it doesn't, it wasn't meant to be. I'm just asking for the time we need to figure out which one it is."

"We hardly know one another," she whispered.

Aiden nodded in agreement. "You and I know each other better than you and Noah. We've been talking longer, but honestly, we probably know each other just as well as anyone else who's just starting the dating process."

"True, but most women don't start the process with two men at the same time."

Aiden dropped his hand. "Well, I know some women who've dated two men at once."

"Not in the way you're suggesting, I'm guessing."

Aiden chuckled. "Probably not. Just think about it," he said as he rubbed the pad of his thumb along her jaw. Leaning down, he placed a chaste kiss on her cheek. "I'll see you at the house later."

She nodded, her cheeks blushing an adorable shade of pink. Aiden smiled, then walked to his own car, leaving her to think about what he'd requested.

Chapter Sixteen

Noah walked into the station and frowned at the three officers staring at his office as though the ghost of John Wayne was staring back at them through the glass.

Shaking his head, Noah stood next to them and crossed his arms over his chest, studying the closed door. "What am I supposed to be seeing?" he asked, only slightly amused.

The young officer next to him jumped. "Damn, Sheriff. I didn't even hear you come in."

"Obviously," Noah drawled good-naturedly. "What is it I need to see for myself, Danny?"

Danny nodded toward the office door. "But before you go in there, I think you should take a look at the video."

Noah frowned in confusion. "What video?"

Danny pointed toward the small camera in the corner. Noah's lips twisted as he stared up at it. "I forget that thing is even there."

"Yeah," Danny agreed as his face paled slightly. "Wish I could after today."

With a snort, Noah patted Danny on the shoulder. "Let's skip the dramatics, Danny. Just show me what happened. You've got me curious now."

"I can assure you, I'm not being dramatic. You'll see," he added with a nod that Noah found almost funny.

Noah followed Danny over to his computer. Several other officers joined them as Danny pulled up the footage. Noah glanced around in exasperation. "Don't you guys have cases to work?"

"Oh, no," John, one of the senior officers on the force, replied with a shake of his head. "We saw this firsthand. Now we just want to see your face when you see it."

Noah frowned, wondering just what the hell they were about to show him.

"Here it is," Danny said as he pointed to the screen.

Noah turned his attention to the picture of his office. At first, he didn't see anything, but as he looked closer, he noticed the papers flying just beyond the glass window. It was as though someone had turned on a fan, spreading papers everywhere.

"What the hell?" he murmured as he leaned in closer to get a better look.

As he watched, he realized it wasn't just papers. Books flew against the blinds, hitting the window that overlooked the parking lot. Two coffee cups slammed against the interior window, startling two officers as they walked past his office. They stopped and peered into the window, their eyes wide as they watched the papers fly all over the room.

"No one was in there," Danny said. "I checked the tape."

"Did anyone go in after things settled down?" Noah asked as he continued to watch the screen.

Eventually the paper storm died down and everything fell to the floor.

"No. We, uh...thought it would be best to wait for you."

Noah scowled at the young officer. Danny shrugged, his face turning red as he glanced toward the floor, too ashamed to look Noah in the eye. "It is your office, boss," Danny mumbled.

With a deep sigh, Noah stood straight. "What the hell do you think is in there, Danny?"

"Noah," John scolded softly from behind him. "You can't blame the kid. I didn't want to go in there either after seeing that."

Shaking his head, Noah strolled to his office door. "The whole lot of y'all are worthless," he grumbled.

Turning the doorknob, Noah had a split second of uncertainty. Was it possible this really was paranormal? He'd seen the footage with his own eyes: the papers flying everywhere, the cups hitting the window. No one had entered or left.

Or was it possible his team was playing some sort of elaborate Halloween prank?

Grumbling to himself, he opened the door and stepped into his office, now in a state of utter disarray. It would take him days to clean this up and put the files back together. He ran a hand down his face, becoming fatigued just thinking about the job ahead of him.

John made his way slowly into the room and came to stand next to him. His eyes were wide with shock, his expression one of caution, as though he expected something or someone to jump out at any moment.

"Is this your idea of letting me know I need to organize my office?" Noah asked.

John snickered. "Wish I had thought of that, but no. Besides, why do you need to organize it? You always know exactly where everything is. Or at least you did," John added as he carefully stepped over the strewn papers.

"Yeah, I did," Noah responded with a tired sigh. Now he wasn't sure where anything was. "Do you see anything?" Noah asked as he began to make his way slowly around the room, studying every corner, every inch of the wall looking for anything that would explain what happened.

John shook his head as he ran a hand through his short, dark brown hair. "I'm amazed we would see anything beyond this mess."

Noah pinned his old friend and partner with a stare he hoped came across as meaning business. "Are you sure this wasn't a joke, John?"

John scowled. "I can assure you if we were going to play a practical joke, it wouldn't be with police files."

Noah sighed and nodded. The officers loved to play pranks, but John was right. They wouldn't mess with official papers or files. They knew better.

"Were you working on something on your computer? Something with missing girls?" John asked as he leaned in closer to examine the screen.

"No."

Frowning, Noah walked over to see what John was staring at. On his screen, several Internet pages were open, one after another—pages of missing girls. Web sites put up by families more than likely, an attempt to find their missing child or wife. All of them were in their twenties, all dark-haired, all from different parts of the country.

"What the hell is this?" he wondered out loud as he hit the Minimize button, putting each page at the bottom of the screen so he could see the one beneath it.

Twenty-five in all. The last page was one he didn't expect to see and froze as he stared at the familiar face of Alana's friend, Lisa. It was her Web site page, her bio specifically. Why would that one be there?

"Do me a favor, John," Noah said as he handed John a pad he'd found at the corner of the desk. "Run these girls' names through the missing persons database."

John took the pad and nodded. "Okay. What about her?" He pointed to the screen and the picture of Lisa. "Isn't she one of the investigators at the house?"

"Yeah. She's also the one who was attacked that first night."

"Do you think there might be a connection?"

"A connection to what?" Noah asked in exasperation.

"Those other girls."

"The hell if I know," Noah replied. "None of this makes any sense. See what you can find out about the girls; make sure they're still missing. Sometimes they don't get taken off the list when they've been found."

"All right. Anything else?"

"I'm not sure yet."

* * *

"So...how was lunch?" Tray asked as he dropped onto the foot of the bed, shaking the mattress and forcing the headboard against the wall with a bang.

Alana glanced up from the laptop resting on her thighs and frowned. "What?"

"Lunch?"

"Oh. It went okay. Food was great."

She returned her attention to the screen and the sex scene she'd been in the middle of writing. Despite what she did or how she rewrote it, Aiden and Noah's personalities and skills kept creeping in.

"Working on the new book?" he asked.

"Yeah...I guess."

"Alana," Tray called, trying to get her attention.

She pushed the laptop closed with a sigh. "It seems like no matter what I do, it's me having sex with Aiden or Noah. I can't get it out of my mind. It's driving me nuts."

"Maybe that's not a bad thing. If the sex was good for you, it will be good in the book."

She shook her head, sighing. "That's not the point."

"I know it's not, but I'm trying to help."

Chuckling, she set the laptop aside. "I probably shouldn't have worked on this today. Now tonight when I see them, I'll already be horny."

This time Tray laughed. "I can take care of that for you," he teased. Smiling broadly, he wiggled his fingers. "I have great hands."

Alana threw a pillow at him playfully. "I'm not the right gender, remember."

Tray stood and spread his arms. "Hey. Like I said, just trying to help." He stared at her through his lashes and lowered his voice. "As I have in the past, numerous times."

"You're insufferable. You promised never to throw those times in my face."

His grin widened. "I'm not throwing them in your face. They're gentle reminders."

Alana returned his smile, knowing Tray was only teasing her. He was her best friend. Had been for years. They'd been through a lot—lost jobs, lost loves. He probably knew more about her than Lisa did.

"Have you heard anything from Lisa? I'm beginning to think that maybe we shouldn't have let her go alone." Alana steered the subject from anything sexual.

"Its broad daylight; she'll be fine. And yes, I talked to her about twenty minutes ago. She's on her way back and all excited about something she's found."

"What was it?" Alana asked with growing excitement of her own.

"Don't know. She wouldn't say. But if she's this excited, it's bound to be something really good."

"Hopefully it's something that will explain our little ghost."

"And her fascination with Noah," Tray added. "Although, truthfully, who could blame her. The man's a hunk and a half."

"He's straight, Tray," Alana said, grinning as she watched her friend study the books lying on top of the dresser.

"Hey, a man can dream, can't he?" Tray asked as he glanced at her over his shoulder, wiggling his eyebrows.

Alana shook her head in amusement as she reached for her cup of tea on the nightstand beside her.

"I have to admit, I'm jealous," Tray continued. "I would give my eyeteeth to be the person sandwiched between those two gorgeous brothers. I bet they have dicks the size of my forearm."

She choked on her tea, caught between laughing and coughing. "Oh my God, you're insane!"

Tray laughed along with her. "Maybe. But I bet I'm right."

"Well," Alana said as she set her cup aside and reached for a napkin to wipe the tea from her chin. "All I'll say is I had trouble taking all of Aiden at first."

"Oooh, yum," Tray teased, making her laugh again.

"This is so not an appropriate topic of conversation. I would die if they knew we talked about this, even jokingly."

Tray swatted her leg as he walked by. "Nothing's inappropriate between friends. Now get up off that lazy ass; I think I heard Lisa come in."

About that time, Lisa's voice carried through the room. "Guys? Are you here?"

"We're coming," Alana replied as she followed Tray to the living area.

Lisa stood at the dining table, dropping her papers onto the surface. "You guys won't believe what I found out," she said, barely able to contain her excitement.

"What?" Alana asked, curious as to what had her friend so thrilled.

"You wouldn't believe the history of this house. There have been at least seven deaths, four of which were young girls Karen's father brought in as sex slaves for private parties that he held. Some were even attended by politicians."

Alana snorted. "That doesn't surprise me. They probably still do that today."

Lisa held up a finger as she reached for a piece of paper lying on the table. "The woman the sheriff sees?" She handed Alana a sketch of a young girl. "That's her. I asked him to describe her to one of his sketch artists, and that's what they came up with"

Alana studied the woman's face and long straight hair. There was something about her eyes that looked familiar. "She looks familiar. Did you find out who she was?"

"Yep." Lisa grinned and rocked back on her heels. "You aren't going to believe this one."

Alana looked up, impatiently waiting for Lisa to continue. She raised her hand, shaking the paper Lisa had given her. "You're killing me, Lisa."

"It's Noah and Aiden's mother."

"What?" Alana and Tray both yelled at the same time.

Lisa handed them a picture along with an article she'd printed off the Internet. It was of a young woman, two small babies, and an older man.

"That's their grandfather," Lisa explained as she pointed to the picture. "He was mayor at the time. Apparently, there was some falling out with her family."

"What was the fallout over?" Alana asked.

Lisa shrugged. "Not sure, but one article claims she dabbled in witchcraft."

"And the family didn't approve, is my guess," Tray added.

"Probably so. But there's more," Lisa said as she handed them another article.

"More?" Alana asked with some dread.

She glanced down at the paper in her hand and groaned.

"How could Noah not know he's seeing his mother?" Tray mumbled.

"She disappeared when they were a little over one year old. It's possible he doesn't remember what she looked like," Lisa offered.

"Yeah, but didn't they at least have a picture of her?" Alana asked in confusion.

Lisa shrugged. "Who knows. But I think you should talk to Noah about it. See what he says."

"Well, that would certainly explain his seeing her. But why doesn't Aiden?"

"He saw her that night at the house when he was with us."

Tray nodded, conceding. "This can't be residual then. She's trying to warn him of something."

Alana shook her head, unsure she believed that line of thinking.

"She's warning Noah, Alana. That much is obvious. Why are you being so stubborn on this one?" Tray tried to reason.

"I don't know," she replied, shrugging. "But something isn't right with this. Am I the only one who feels it?"

"You probably feel it because you're closer to the twins, but I have to admit, it seems odd he would be seeing his mother and not even know it."

"I'll go by his office and talk to him later," Alana said, sighing. She definitely didn't like the bad feeling plaguing the pit of her stomach. Something wasn't right here.

"Okay," Lisa said as she waved her hands as though brushing their current topic away. "I know I'm jumping subjects here, but you guys should be used to how my mind jumps around. I met this really weird guy at the library."

Alana's head jerked up as concern tightened her chest. "What do you mean by weird?"

"I don't know. I just got a..." She rolled her hands, trying to find the right words to say. "A creepy feeling. Like I've seen him before, or I should be wary of him somehow. Nothing specific, just a feeling. I kind of felt bad for him. He was burned pretty bad. His face, his hands, even his neck. I couldn't see any more of him than that, but I'm wondering if the burns cover more of his body. He didn't look all that old, but his hair was white as snow."

"Was he bothering you?" Alana asked.

"No. He was actually very nice, it was just a gut instinct, I guess. He left, but afterward, I kept getting this feeling that I was being watched."

"Well, my mother always told me to trust my gut, and as for being watched, from now on, you don't go anywhere without one of us," Tray ordered.

Lisa snorted. "Give me a break. He didn't do anything; he just gave me the creeps."

"Lisa—" Alana began, but Tray interrupted her.

"Let me handle miss stubborn. You let Noah know what happened."

"Oh, speaking of which," Lisa said as she plopped onto the couch next to Alana, dismissing for the moment their pervious conversation. "How did lunch go?"

Alana rolled her eyes and opened her mouth to answer.

"It went well. Food was great," Tray repeated her earlier words in a dry tone that made Alana giggle.

"Actually lunch went very well. Both men were perfect gentlemen."

"Well, damn," Lisa teased.

"I know," Tray drawled. "My sentiments exactly."

"Ha ha. Both of you are just a barrel of laughs."

Tray and Lisa chuckled as Lisa put her hand on Alana's leg, giving it a gentle squeeze. "If you're happy with lunch, we are. We're just giving you a hard time."

"I know," Alana replied, smiling. "I don't know what I'd do without you guys. Especially now."

"We're here for ya, babe," Tray said as he leaned down to kiss her cheek.

"You betcha." Lisa kissed her opposite one, making Alana giggle.

* * *

Alana knocked softly on Noah's office door before pushing it open and sticking her head around the corner. "Got a minute?" she asked as he lifted his head to see who was coming in.

"Always," he said with a smile.

She pushed the door the rest of the way open and stared at the disarray in shock. Papers and files were everywhere, and she had to step carefully as she made her way into the room.

"Wow, I know men who are good at their job can sometimes be slobs, but..."

Noah snorted.

"What happened?"

"Well, if my staff is to be believed, your ghost paid a little visit to my office today."

Alana froze. "Excuse me?"

"I had someone make a copy of what happened and send it to Tray. He's probably got it by now."

"A copy?" she asked, a little confused.

He pointed behind her. "The camera mounted on the corner caught most everything."

Alana glanced at the camera then back to Noah. "She just ransacked your office?"

"No," he replied as he dropped two files onto his desk and reached for another. "She apparently sent me a message."

Alana's interest was piqued, and for the moment, she completely forgot what she'd come to talk with him about. She walked closer and took the file he handed her.

"When I came into my office, the Internet was up. Twenty-five pages in all, twenty-four of them pages on missing girls. I had one of my officers check the missing persons database. So far, all girls are still missing."

"You said there were twenty-five," she said as she flipped through the pages.

"Yep. Keep looking. You'll see it."

Alana came to the last page and took a shuddering breath as she stared at the face of her best friend. "I don't understand," she whispered. "Why is Lisa's Web page and picture here?"

"I'm not sure, but truthfully, I don't like what my gut tells me."

Alana moved to one of the chairs and sat down, her heart heavy and beating like a frightened rabbit. "Lisa said she met a man today that gave her the creeps. He didn't do anything, but she felt that she should be wary."

"Is she okay?"

"For now."

"Tell her she's not to go anywhere alone from here on out. I'll also post someone to keep an eye on her."

She shook her head. "Lisa's not going to like that at all. Tray and I have already had this argument with her. Last check, she was still fighting it."

He gave her a pointed look. "At this point, Alana, I don't care."

"Yeah, I'm not sure I do either. Do you think these girls are connected somehow?"

"They span over twenty years and come from several different parts of the country. If they are connected, that's a long time for someone to be getting away with whatever they're doing."

She sat silent for a moment, watching out the window and thinking. Was her friend in trouble? Was that why her picture showed up? They'd never dealt with anything like this. She felt out of her league and overwhelmed. Where did they go from here? How did Noah fit into all this? And what about Aiden? Why wasn't Aiden seeing it?

Noah moved around his desk and rested his hip against the corner. The toe of his shoe touched hers, and she felt a weird desire to reach out and touch his leg in comfort. For some strange reason, she felt as though she could sense his turmoil, his tension.

"Did you want to talk to me about something?" he asked softly.

"I'm sorry," she said with a shake of her head. "Actually, yes. If it's not too intrusive, I wanted to ask you about your mother."

She instantly felt a wave of tension tighten her chest, and she frowned, raising her hand to touch just under her throat in surprise. Where had that come from?

"What about my mother?" he asked.

"Do you remember her?"

"No," he replied, as he stood and walked around his desk, putting his back to her and a wall between them.

"What happened to her?"

Noah shrugged as he began to close down his computer. His discomfort was obvious to her, but was it because she could see it in the lines on his face or because she could feel it?

"She disappeared."

"That's it? Just disappeared?"

"Yeah, at one point there was a rumor she'd run off with someone, but we never found out for sure."

"You never looked for her? Were never curious as to what happened to her?"

"Why would we be?" he asked, his face empty of any emotion.

"I don't know. She's your mother. Do you have pictures of her?"

He frowned in slight confusion and shook his head. "We used to, but Gram said every time we would look at them, we would get upset, so she got rid of them."

Alana's mouth dropped open. "Did she not think you might want them one day?"

"Alana, what is all this about?"

She glanced down at the file in her hand. Should she tell him? "If you could find out the truth, would you want to?" she asked.

She slowly raised her head and stared into his eyes, still devoid of anything.

"No."

"Why?" she whispered.

"That was a long time ago. I've moved on, and so has Aiden."

"But you could have moved on from a lie."

He raised an eyebrow in disbelief. "A lie?"

Alana shook her head, now second-guessing her decision. "Maybe this isn't the right time."

"Right time for what?" he demanded.

Alana could sense his agitation and flinched. One of his officers stepped into the room, interrupting whatever she might've said, and at the moment, she didn't have a clue what that would've been.

"Sherriff, we've got a problem out on I-40 westbound. Tanker overturned."

"Oh my God," Alana gasped.

"How bad?"

"At least six cars, several injuries, possibly one death."

"Get all available on the scene and see if we can get Life Flight out there."

"It's already on its way."

Noah tipped his head in acknowledgment before glancing down at Alana. "I want to continue this conversation later." He glanced at his watch. "My and Noah's house around six thirty?"

"Sure," Alana replied as she stood to leave, still not knowing for sure what she was even going to say.

"I'll text you the address." He leaned over as he walked by and gently kissed her cheek, making her stomach flutter. "Take the back roads when driving back to the hotel. The interstate will be a mess for a while."

Alana watched him go, wondering if maybe she was about to open a can of worms best left closed.

Chapter Seventeen

Noah didn't have to hear Alana's truck door slam to know she had arrived. He could feel her, which was something that had him stumped. He'd also felt her nervousness earlier in his office and had wondered, more than once today, what it had all been about. Was it something to do with the questions she'd been asking about his mother? And why had she been asking those questions?

He glanced at his watch, wondering what was taking Aiden so long as he walked to the door, opening it just as she was about to knock.

Her eyes widened in surprise, and she took a step back, startled. He grinned. "You're early."

"It didn't take me as long to get here as I thought it would."

He stepped aside, allowing her to walk past him into the small entrance hall.

"Nice house," she said, glancing around his and Aiden's home. "A sheriff in a small town makes that much?"

He chuckled. "Aiden and I bought this place together. We modified it a little. There're two master suites, the whole basement is a den and workout room, and then of course there's the outside." He waved for her to head to the sliding glass door off the breakfast nook.

She gave him a strange look, then walked toward the door, setting the file she had in her hands on the kitchen island as she went. He should've been curious as to what was in it, but all he could focus on was the soft sway of her ass, and his balls tightened instantly. Walking became difficult, so he tried to ignore the throbbing and focus on her reaction. Most people were surprised with what they'd done outside, and he was sure she would be as well.

"Good Lord," she sighed and opened the door, stepping out into the back patio area.

Light steam lifted from the pool and hot tub, filling the backyard. Their pool, spa, outdoor kitchen, and rocky waterfall probably cost more than the house itself, but it was money well spent in Aiden and Noah's minds. It had gotten a lot of use.

"This is amazing," she said before giggling.

"Aiden and I grew up with a pool; we just improved on the idea. I also have pool parties here for some of the troubled teens and kids in the area. They enjoy it."

"I would imagine so." She turned to smile at him. "Your work with kids actually surprises me a little."

"Why?"

"I don't know. You just don't seem the type. You're hard, sometimes cold—"

He raised an eyebrow in amusement. "Rough around the edges?"

She smiled and pointed at him. "That's it."

"Aiden and I both like kids and enjoy working with them."

He let his gaze wander down her curves, her breasts hard and firm beneath her tight sweater, her long legs encased in the stonewashed jeans. God, he wanted her. He could even feel her desire, her nipples hardening, her pussy moistening.

His stare met hers, and the desire darkening the green of her eyes made his cock jerk within his pants. She'd come here to talk to him about something. Something important—he could feel it—but at the moment all he could think about was ripping her clothes off.

He walked toward her slowly, not wanting to scare her off, not wanting to startle her into fleeing. He gripped her waist, tugging her toward him with gentle pressure. She came willingly. In her eyes he could see what he felt coming from her: her confusion, her lust and need, her uncertainty.

He dipped his head, stopping just short of her mouth. He could feel her heat, her pulse as it pounded through her veins. Could she feel his?

"This is too weird," she whispered.

"This is nothing," he countered before covering her lips with his.

She whimpered and raised her hands to the back of his arms, holding tight as he deepened the kiss, sliding his tongue between her lips to taste her sweet mouth. He slid his hands around her back, flattening them to push her against him so that every inch of their bodies touched.

Her body felt so good in his arms. Her scent reminded him of coming home, of belonging.

She broke the kiss with a reluctant moan. "I came here to talk to you and Aiden about something."

"We'll talk later," he growled before capturing her mouth again in a deep kiss that made even his heart race.

Her tongue twirled around his, returning his demands with some of her own. He gripped her ass, lifting her slightly and pressing his hard cock into the vee of her firm thighs. He groaned and dropped her back to her feet, moving his hands quickly to the bottom of her sweater. He lifted it, shoving it over her head quickly and dropping it to the floor.

The cleavage of her full breasts fought to spill over her bra, and he tugged the lace down, capturing one pert nipple in his mouth. She gasped and dug her fingers into his hair, tugging him closer and trying to force more of her breast into his mouth. He obliged, licking and sucking till she dropped her head back with a loud cry of delight.

She shivered from the cool air, and for a second he wondered if he should take her inside, but the other part of him was afraid if he stopped, she'd come to her senses and put an end to the blessed torture of her in his arms.

He returned his mouth to hers and reached to undo the clasp at her back. The bra fell to the floor as he moved his hands back around to cup her firm mounds. She filled his hands and then some as he massaged and gently pinched at her nipples. Her mewling sounds were lost in his kiss as he deepened it further, never giving her a chance to protest or remember why she'd come here.

Shaking fingers moved to the buttons of his shirt, and he let go of her breasts to help her. He wanted to feel her flesh against his, wanted to feel her body with nothing between them. It was like he couldn't breathe, couldn't get enough. It was like she was a part of him that he needed to be whole.

Her palms smoothed over his chest, sending hot currents of sensations to his balls that almost had him losing control. He gripped one of her hands and placed it over his throbbing cock.

"Feel this?" he growled against her mouth.

She nodded and tightened her fingers around the bulge through his jeans.

"I want to fuck you with this."

ALANA FELT A tinge of excitement at his words. She liked the rough edge to his voice, the desire shining in his eyes when he looked at her. She could feel how much he wanted her—or was that just her imagination? And where was Aiden?

Part of her thrilled with the idea he might walk in on them and join in the play. It made her more excited, wetter, hotter—although at the moment, she wasn't sure she could get much hotter. Her skin felt more on fire than it ever had in her life.

She rubbed her palm along his thick length, pressing gently, and he growled in pleasure before slanting his lips back over hers, making her forget everything but the feel of his hands on her as he swiped his tongue between her lips.

She pushed his shirt off his wide shoulders, exploring his hard muscles as she went. God, he was hard and hot. She barely felt the cool breeze as the heat off his body seemed to encase her, warming her.

His hands were everywhere, stroking down her back and over her ass before moving to the zipper and snap of her jeans. Oh God. What was she doing? But heaven help her, she couldn't stop. She didn't want to stop. Her pussy throbbed from wanting him so badly; she felt like screaming. She wanted to wrap her legs around his hips and grind herself against him until she came.

This was so crazy, so intense. She shuddered from head to toe as Noah shoved her jeans and panties down over her hips. His hands lingered at her ass, squeezing and kneading the muscles with his strong fingers.

"Noah," she sighed as he lifted her and set her on the wooden outdoor dining table.

Noah moved back slightly so he could grasp her pants and remove them along with her ankle boots, tossing them somewhere to the ground. Where, she had no idea and didn't care.

"Lie back," he ordered.

His voice was gravelly, deep, and sensual, making goose bumps rise along her flesh as she slowly lay back. The cold of the table penetrated the skin of her back, making her shiver, but the heat of Noah's mouth as he gently slid it up along the inside of her thigh sent heat coursing through her veins, warming her from the inside out.

He used the tips of his fingers to separate her labia, and her whole body tightened in anticipation.

Even her hips lifted in excitement as hot breath from his mouth brushed over her pussy.

She put her hands over her eyes briefly, groaning as his tongue swiped over her swollen nub, then lower to dip into her passage.

"Oh God," she gasped, dropping her hands back down to her sides.

Her fingers flexed and unflexed; her nails dug into her palms as he used his tongue to tease her aching pussy, lapping at the cream that coated her swollen lips.

The sensation of being watched washed over her, and she opened her eyes and stared directly into Aiden's hot gaze. She drew in a sharp breath, expecting anger and jealousy, but instead seeing and sensing desire, lust, hunger.

"Aiden," she whispered, wondering what he would do but hoping he would join them.

The idea felt strangely right.

As he watched them, he removed his shirt and tossed it over the back of the closest chair. Her gaze wandered down his chest, then lower as he unzipped his slacks, freeing his thick, engorged shaft.

God, he was big.

Noah continued to lick her pussy as though no one had come in, making her writhe and moan. Aiden stepped out of his slacks and shoes and came to stand over her, watching. He took her hands in his and placed them over her breasts. With his hands over hers, he squeezed.

She arched her back, enjoying the feel of their hands together, touching her body. He lowered one of her hands and pressed against the underside, lifting it as he bent down to wrap his lips around her nipple.

She cried out as his teeth bit into the sensitive bud, the sharp sting sending currents of liquid heat to her womb.

"I like watching," he whispered as he rubbed his palm over her stinging nipple, soothing it and driving her crazy. "I like watching your face as Noah eats your pussy."

His words sent shards of hungry lust tingling up her spine. Could she really get more turned on than she already was? It almost felt overwhelming as not only her desire coursed through her body, but it felt as though theirs did as well, making everything more intense and surreal.

Noah pulled away from her pussy, and she murmured a protest. Aiden soothed her, placing his palm over her sex and applying gentle pressure, but not enough to satisfy her. Her hips bucked upward, trying to force him to press harder, to make her come and put her out of this sweet misery.

"All in due time," he whispered as though he knew exactly what she wanted.

She heard a chair scrape along the concrete, and she looked, watching as Noah removed his pants and sat down. What was he doing?

He gripped his cock, staring at her through eyes so dark, they were almost black.

"Bring her here," he commanded.

Aiden grabbed her hand and helped to pull her upright. Her legs were so wobbly, she had to hold tight to Aiden as they walked over to where Noah sat in the chair, stroking his cock.

As she approached, he twirled his finger. "Turn around."

She frowned in confusion as she put her back to him. Aiden lifted her, catching her by surprise as he placed her on Noah's lap, her back against his chest, her thighs resting over the arm rest. Her pussy rested against Noah's balls, and she sighed, thrusting her hips backward slightly, trying to get a firmer touch.

Noah moaned and let his cock rest between the cheeks of her ass. The tantalizing move surprised her, sending white-hot shards of pleasure along her nerves. His hands rested at her waist, holding her still as he slowly and gently stroked the tight opening that seemed to come alive with his touch.

She watched as Aiden bent over and licked at her clit, making her cry out in surprise. With her legs spread this wide, he could easily tease the swollen bud. She wanted to beg, but she wasn't sure she could string two words together at the moment.

He rose back up and slanted his mouth over hers. She could taste herself on his tongue, and she moaned, licking her own juices from his lips.

She felt Aiden's hand move Noah's cock from between her globes and placed the head of it at her dripping entrance.

"Take him," he whispered as he slowly helped guide Noah's cock into her aching channel.

Noah was so thick and hard. His girth stretched her amazingly tight, especially from this angle. She dropped her head back, groaning as he pressed deeper. Her walls wrapped around his hot length, encasing every inch of his shaft.

Aiden's fingers brushed over her clit, and her hips bucked, making Noah curse and grasp her waist tighter.

"She's tight, Noah," Aiden whispered as he swiped his tongue over her nipple.

"No shit," Noah ground out as he slowly pressed even deeper, forcing all of himself inside her. "But, God, it feels good."

Aiden stood to his full height in front of her and positioned himself so that his cock was directly at her mouth. Alana leaned forward slightly, swiping her tongue over the tip and licking away the drops of precum that glistened against the tight skin.

He groaned, and his mouth spread into a sexy grin as he used his thumb to press his cock toward her lips. She opened her mouth and wrapped her lips around the head. She swiped across it with the flat of her tongue and felt a wave of excitement at the sound of his moan.

"I like that," he murmured.

Noah gently rocked her hips, pressing upward with his cock as he shifted her pussy backward. Alana moaned around the thick cock in her mouth and scraped her teeth across his sensitive tip. Grasping the base of his cock, she tilted it upward and ran her tongue along the underside all the way to the tip.

Aiden dropped his head back and hissed. "This is going to fucking drive me insane."

Noah grasped her hips, lifting her slightly before dragging her back down along his length. Alana squealed, sighing as he pressed upward, filling her even deeper with his huge cock.

"Oh my God," Alana gasped as Noah did it again. "The two of you are insane."

Aiden grasped a handful of her hair and tugged her head back, forcing her to meet his sultry eyes. "Do you want us to stop?"

"Oh God, no!"

Aiden smiled and slanted his mouth hungrily over hers. His tongue invaded, mimicking sex as he dominated her mouth and what felt like her soul.

Noah began the rocking motion, this time a little faster, working her hips over his in a tantalizing motion that made her womb tighten. Aiden broke the kiss and stood straight, returning his cock to her mouth.

Alana grabbed the base, opened her lips hungrily and sucked his thick girth as far into her mouth as she could. She was so close; she could feel the tension beginning to build, feel the need rising.

"Make me come with you, Alana," Aiden murmured as she twirled her tongue around his shaft, sucking gently at the tip. "That's it, baby. Like that."

Her jaws ached as she widened them as far as she could, forcing the tip of his cock to the back of her throat. Aiden's fingers tightened in her hair, his nails digging into her scalp as she swallowed, sucking hard against the engorged head.

The sensations licking at her spine were suddenly becoming too much. She squeezed her eyes shut and tightened her jaw around Aiden's cock as her own womb exploded, rushing currents of screaming pleasure over every inch of her flesh. She moaned, sucking and licking at Aiden's cock until she tasted his stream of cum as it spurted down the back of her throat.

Turning her head away, she screamed as Noah brushed his fingers over her clit, gently massaging as another wave of pleasure coursed through her, almost blinding her with its intensity. Noah tensed below her, his groan of pleasure vibrating across her back as he came as well.

She took a shuttering breath of surprise, convinced she could feel each of their hearts beating within her own chest. This was insane. It had to be her imagination. There was no way she could feel them like that, was there?

Aiden cupped the back of her neck and leaned down to kiss her forehead. Alana smiled at the tender touch she'd come to recognize in the gentler twin.

Noah had his moments as well, just like Aiden had his intense moments. Maybe they weren't as different from each other as she'd initially thought. Maybe they were more alike than either of them wanted to reveal.

Alana tried to move her foot and gasped at the numbness from her knees down. "My legs are asleep," she whispered.

"Wrap your arms around my neck," Aiden said as he bent forward, putting an arm around her back between her and his brother.

Noah helped her slide her legs off the arms of the chair and over Aiden's awaiting arm. He settled it behind her knees and lifted, carrying her toward the house. The cool evening air hit her bare skin, and she shivered, snuggling closer into Aiden's arms.

"Cold?" he asked.

"A little."

"We'll get you warmed up."

His lips touched the top of her head, and she smiled, thinking just how right all of this felt.

Chapter Eighteen

Noah strolled into the kitchen, his legs shaking as he walked. His reaction to Alana had shocked the hell out of him as well as left him weak as a newborn fawn. His legs struggled to hold him upright as he wobbled into the kitchen.

The file lying on the counter caught his attention, and he placed his palm on it. Whatever was inside was what Alana wanted to talk to them about, and he had a sinking suspicion it was about his mother.

Why would Alana be dredging his mother up, and what did she have to do with all this? Were the answers inside? He wasn't sure he wanted to know.

She'd left them when they were babies. What kind of mother left their children?

Gram never talked about her. Neither did Karen. He frowned, thinking back to that night so many years ago. The night Karen had told him he was special, that he was the center. Noah sighed. Whatever the hell that meant.

Had she mentioned his mother then? He couldn't remember.

What did it all matter anyway? She was gone. They'd accepted that years ago.

Alana's squeal carried down the hallway, and Noah winced at the needle pricks in the muscles of his legs. He glanced down in surprise. Alana had said her legs were asleep. The blood was rushing back, sending sharp, slightly painful needle pricks throughout the muscles of her legs.

What the hell? This only happened with Aiden. Why was he feeling Alana's pain?

Shaking his head, he closed his eyes and tried to block out the sensations. It took a second, but they eventually subsided. He quickly grabbed the file and headed down the hall toward Aiden's bedroom at the back of the house.

Alana was on the bed, lying on her back. Aiden was on his knees, rubbing at her calves to ease the ache.

"You okay?" Noah asked, chuckling softly as he leaned against the doorjamb watching them.

"I'm okay now," she replied, turning her head to the side so she could look at him.

Her hair was a riot of red curls against the cream color of the pillowcase, her skin lightly tanned, her eyes a vibrant green. She was so damn pretty Noah couldn't keep from staring at her like an idiot.

"I shouldn't have kept you on the arms of the chair for so long."

She shrugged, her lips twitching just a little as a light blush moved over her cheeks. "I'm not complaining."

Noah smiled. "Good thing. If you complained, I would've had to spank you." Her eyes widened, and a spark of interest darkened the green. "Unless of course you like the idea, and then we may just spank you for the hell of it."

Alana snorted, making Aiden chuckle as he dropped his hands from her calves.

"And just what was that snort for, missy?" Aiden teased.

"Nothing," she replied, a small, coy smile tugging at her lips.

Aiden put his hand at the back of her thigh and pushed it back, exposing one hip. He slapped it hard enough to make a loud *pop*, and she squealed before falling into a peal of laughter and forcing her leg back down.

"All right, you two. Stop messing around. Alana came here to talk with us about something. Maybe we should let her."

He dropped onto the bed and leaned back against the leather headboard. He held the file up and stared down at Alana. "What's in this?"

Her smile faded, and she sat up, grabbing the sheet to cover herself. "It's what Lisa found when she was researching the girl you see."

"Really?" Aiden said as he grabbed the file and opened it.

The second he did, he froze, staring in silence at the first page, which had the picture of their mother and grandfather, each holding one of the twins.

"This is um..." Alana took a deep breath before continuing and watched Aiden wipe nervously at his mouth. "This is you and your mother." She pointed to the description under the picture. "It has your names here."

He looked at Alana with a confused frown before glancing back down at the picture. "I don't know that I've ever seen a picture of her."

"You have, you just don't remember," Noah replied.

"We were one when she left. We never really knew why." He stared back at Alana. "Why did Lisa dig this up?"

"Because the woman in the picture is who Noah sees." She reached forward and pulled a piece of paper from the bottom of the file, putting it on top. "This is the police sketch that Noah did of the ghost he's seen."

Aiden pulled it to the side, studying both pictures. "My God. They're identical."

"Yeah," Alana whispered.

Aiden frowned as Noah sat silent. "But that would mean she's dead."

Noah tensed, not sure he really wanted to reopen this wound. "It doesn't matter, Aiden."

"What the hell do you mean it doesn't matter?" Aiden snapped. "Aren't you curious as to what happened to her?" Noah remained silent. "You're not, are you?"

"No."

"I am," Aiden snapped.

"Why?" Noah snapped back, making Alana jump. "Where the hell was she all those years, Aiden? Not with us, that's for damn sure."

"It's because she was dead."

Her voice was so soft, so uncertain, Noah wasn't even sure he'd heard her correctly. "Excuse me?"

She leaned forward and grabbed another page from the file. With uncertainty making her forehead crinkle, she handed it to him. "She was found dead."

Noah stared at the article in shock, numb of any emotions except confusion.

"What does it say?" Aiden asked.

Noah took a deep breath. "It's an article about the murder of a Jane Doe five counties over. She was beaten and mutilated, everywhere except her face. A sketch artist did a composite. The sketches match."

Aiden snatched it from Noah's hand and quickly read it. "My God. Do you know what this means?" Aiden asked as he looked at Noah. "Maybe she didn't leave willingly at all."

Noah shook his head stubbornly. They didn't know that. They didn't know why she left. For all they knew, she hadn't been kidnapped and had left willingly with the man who'd killed her, leaving her sons behind to grow up motherless.

Alana placed a palm on his thigh. "Noah."

"No," he said with more calm than he felt. "I've gone my whole life living with the idea that our mother left us deliberately. Nothing here changes that notion. Gram never said anything bad about her, but she never denied our mother ran out on us either."

"Maybe she didn't know," Alana offered. "Maybe your mother was kidnapped, and everyone just thought she ran away."

"I'm not going to second-guess what happened or hold hope that will never be verified. Our mother left us, Alana. That's that."

"Why are you seeing her?" she asked. "Maybe she's been here all along and you just didn't realize it."

"That's ridiculous."

ALANA WATCHED NOAH as he climbed from the bed and headed toward the door. She felt a lump of sadness in her throat at his determination to continue to believe the worst.

"Where are you going?" she asked.

"To shower. We have a house to investigate."

"We're taking the night off," Alana called.

Noah paused before continuing toward his own room.

"Is he always so stubborn?"

Aiden still sat at the foot of the bed, studying the file. "Yeah, but honestly, I understand how he feels. We've gone our whole lives believing what we did of her. It would be hard to change that now, especially when we still don't know the whole truth."

Alana sighed with regret. "Maybe I shouldn't have even brought it up."

Aiden glanced up at her and placed a reassuring hand on her calf, gently rubbing it. "No. It'll be fine, Alana. He just needs to brood a bit. I'm glad you brought this. I'm not sure I believe it yet, but I'm glad to see it." His lips spread into a slight mischievous grin that made her heart flutter. "So we really have the night off?"

Alana leaned back against the headboard and crossed her arms over her chest, holding the sheet in place. "Yeah. I insisted so I could have time to talk to you guys about this. Besides, it gives Tray and our producer time to get some editing done. They changed the idea for the show. We've gotten so much usable footage, instead of a three-hour show, they plan on splitting it up into three two-hour shows and running the first of the three-part series in one week."

"No kidding?" Aiden said, smiling. "That soon?"

She snorted softly. "Are you kidding? The network is salivating over this one. It's some of the best footage we've ever gotten. And it's right before Halloween. Timing couldn't be any better, ratings-wise. They also want to incorporate more of the history of the house. The sex slaves and deaths will make the house even more intriguing."

Aiden chuckled. "It's all about the mighty dollar, isn't it?"

"It always is."

She sighed and glanced toward the door. Despite what Aiden had said, she remained worried about Noah. He'd appeared upset when he'd left. Truthfully, it was more than appeared. She could feel he'd been upset, more so than he'd wanted to admit.

For the hundredth time since this afternoon, she regretted bringing up the subject of his mother.

"Hey," Aiden said softly as he laid his hand against her leg. "If you're that worried, go check on him."

Her eyes widened in surprise. "What makes you think I'm worried?"

"I can tell," he said before removing his hand and glancing down at the file still in his hand. He looked back up at her, his eyes a shade of blue that reminded her of sapphires, dark and intense. "Noah may not want to right now, but I would like to delve a little deeper into this. Why don't you go check on him? Distract him if you want."

He wiggled his eyebrows, and the heat of a blush moved over her cheeks. She liked the idea of distracting him. Even though they'd just had sex, the thought of Noah touching her again sent her libido into overdrive.

She licked her lips and frowned. "It doesn't bother you?"

He shrugged, his lips twitching in amusement. "Why would it bother me?"

"I don't know," she whispered. "I'm afraid I've never done this sort of thing before. Two guys at once. Together."

Aiden set the file aside and leaned forward, placing his hands on the mattress by her hips. His face was close to hers, so close she could see the tiny flecks of black in the blue of his eyes, feel his hot breath as it brushed her mouth when he quietly spoke.

"I think you're handling it quite well," he whispered. He brushed his lips over hers, and she inhaled a sharp breath of air. "The thought of you in the shower with Noah is truthfully very arousing. I may decide to join you."

Alana swallowed as he nipped at her bottom lip playfully.

"Or I may give you time alone. After all, I've had you for a night to myself. It's only fair I return the favor for Noah."

He grinned and placed a quick kiss against her lips. She huffed in surprise as he pulled away, once again grabbing the file he'd set aside. He stood and grinned down at her.

"So that's that? You're just handing me over?" she asked, unsure what it was about the whole situation that settled funny on her stomach.

"I'm by no means handing you over. We share, and only if you want. You don't have to go in there." He used the pad of his finger to tip up her chin. "You do what you want to do. Noah and I will follow…if that's what you want."

"I have no idea what I want."

She felt breathless, staring into Aiden's pretty eyes—those beautiful deep blue, understanding eyes. She could drown in them, lose herself for a night, a week, an eternity. Was it really that simple? Just do what felt right to her and they would follow.

"In some ways, the two of you scare me."

Aiden gently brushed his thumb over her cheek, and she tilted her head toward his touch.

"You have no reason to fear either of us, Alana. Apart or together."

She knew that. Somehow, deep down, she knew that.

Aiden chucked her under the chin and left the room. As he entered the hall and headed toward the

front of the house, he called back over his shoulder.
"Holler if you need me."

Alana snickered at the thought. Need him? Sure.
Want him? Absolutely. These two could seriously
become addictive. Biting at her lower lip, she glanced
through the door toward Noah's bedroom. Should she
go in there? Was he mad at her?

She scowled. It didn't feel as though he were
angry. At least she didn't think so. She could feel
something, deep in her gut like a sixth sense. Instead
of anger, she felt resignation, confusion, even desire
simmering beneath the surface. Was that desire for
her? Or her own desire for him?

She didn't understand any of this.

Sighing, she brushed her hair back and threw the
sheets off her body. She spotted a shirt thrown over a
chair by the window and grabbed it. She quickly slid
her arms through the soft cotton and wrapped it
around her. Glancing down, she studied how well—or
not so well—it fit. The blue material barely covered her
ass, but it covered it at least.

Drawing in a deep breath for courage she wasn't
quite sure she needed, she headed into Noah's
bedroom.

* * *

Noah didn't have to open his eyes to know she
stood inside the bathroom door, watching him. He
glanced around the corner of his oversize tile shower
anyway, curious. She stood just a few feet away,
wearing one of Aiden's shirts. It barely covered her,

leaving her long, well-defined legs fully exposed. His lips twitched along with his cock.

"Aren't you an adorable sight," he murmured. Gripping his cock, he glanced down at his thickening girth, then back at her. "See what you started."

One of her eyebrows rose, giving her a cocky, playful look that did nothing to lessen the pain now tightening his balls.

"Are you sure it wasn't already in that state before I came in the room?"

"Maybe...but I doubt it." He crooked his finger. "Come here."

"Come here?" she teased. "I came in here to check on you."

"Then check on me." She licked her lips, and he groaned. "Keep it up."

Her lips spread into a saucy grin. "You're such a rogue."

Noah laughed. "I'm a horny rogue." He held his hand out and spoke softly, coaxing her to join him. "Come here, Alana."

She slowly opened the shirt, exposing her creamy breasts and shoulders. "You're not upset with me?" she asked, watching him closely.

"Do I look like I'm upset with you?"

Her brow crinkled in annoyance, and he couldn't help but notice how cute it made her look. "Don't answer a question with a question."

"I'm not upset with you," he replied softly, impatiently waiting for her to finish removing the shirt and join him in the steamy shower.

She dropped the shirt, and he watched it fall to the floor, allowing his gaze to linger on the lips of her shaved pussy before continuing their travel upward. She stepped forward, and he took her hand in his, leading her into the steam.

"I didn't mean—"

Noah put his finger over her lips, silencing her. He knew his reaction had worried her. He could sense it, and he wanted to ease her distress. Not because he wanted her, but because he didn't like seeing her upset.

"Don't worry about this. These are my demons, and I'll deal with them. You did nothing wrong."

She opened her lips and gently bit at the tip of his finger. Blood rushed to his cock, making it harden with a need that almost strangled him. What was it about her that had him so desperate?

He lowered his finger to her chin, tipping it up. "I think I know of a way you can make it up to me, though," he whispered as he brushed his lips over hers.

Her sharp intake of breath made his heart race. She was so damn adorable—so perfect.

"But I did nothing wrong," she reasoned, mischief sparkling within the depths of her gaze.

"Pretend," he countered, grinning.

He moved his lips to her neck, softly nibbling the flesh just below her ear. He could feel the pounding of her blood through her veins along with his own. It was an unusual but not unpleasant sensation. He actually liked it. He liked how it heightened his own sexual desire, his own need to feel himself buried deep inside her again.

Her hands rested at his waist before moving lower along his hips. He held his breath as the fingers of one hand wrapped around his cock.

"Does making it up to you have anything to do with this?" she asked, her voice barely above a strained whisper.

"Most definitely," he moaned.

He took her earlobe between his lips and gently sucked. Her soft gasp sent a tingling shiver down his spine to settle in his balls. He reached down and grasped her ass, lifting her as he shoved her against the tile wall.

Her long legs wrapped around his waist, allowing his cock to settle against her wet pussy. Her giggle made him smile as he slowly stroked her labia with the length of his engorged shaft.

"You're wet," he murmured.

"We're in a shower," she countered, her lips lifting into a sexy grin.

The lids of her eyes lowered sensually as he continued to slowly rock against her, teasing them both. He wasn't sure how much longer he could keep this slow seduction up. He wanted her badly. So badly he could easily slam into her, forcing her to take all of him in one quick, deep thrust.

"Smart-ass," he whispered as he pushed the head of his cock into her opening.

Chapter Nineteen

Noah stopped, and her hips bucked forward, forcing more of him inside her. He groaned but kept his gaze on her face. Her mouth fell open in a soft gasp of surprise and pleasure. A flush moved over her cheeks as water from the showerhead covered her face in a soft drizzle. The curls in her hair sprang to life, making tight ringlets around her cheeks.

"Don't stop there," she sighed, trying to push her hips out farther.

He pulled back slightly, leaving just the tip of his cock in her channel. She moaned and arched her back. She was so passionate, so damn responsive. With a growl deep in his chest, he pressed his hips forward, burying himself deep inside her tight, hot passage.

She gasped at the sudden invasion. Noah had to close his eyes for a second as her tight walls squeezed at his length, sucking him as they pulsed around his shaft. Her cream eased his way as he pushed farther inside her, going as deep as he could. He wanted to be so deep, he became a part of her. He already felt as though he was. He could feel her desire, her pleasure, her need coursing through his veins, mingling with his own. It was the wildest, most erotic thing he'd ever felt, and he wanted more.

"Hold on to me," he growled.

He wrapped his arms around her back, holding her wet body against his own as he turned her away from the wall.

"Wait, the water," she panted.

He stopped, allowing her to reach out with one hand and turn off the water. She put her arm back around his shoulders and leaned her face into his neck. Her hot breath washed over his flesh, and he silently moaned, unsure he would make it to the bed. Maybe he should just drop her to the floor here.

He took a step, and she moaned as their hips moved against each other in tantalizing bumps and grinds. Her hard nipples rubbed his chest, teasing his skin. The bed was just a few feet away. He could make it.

The walls of her pussy quivered along his length, and he gulped. This wouldn't be gentle. Not by a long shot. She felt so good, so hot and slick against his cock, he wanted to shout, to slam himself into her over and over until he couldn't fucking move.

Finally at the foot of the bed, he set his knee on the mattress and bent forward, laying her on the comforter. He had to pull out of her so she could position herself, and he hissed as the cool air of the room washed over his shaft.

He glanced down at her, licking his lips at the sight of her glistening pussy so ready for him, so eager. She rose up on her elbows, starting to push back, but he gripped her hips, dragging her to the edge of the bed.

She squealed in surprise but became quiet, watching in anxious regard as he lifted her legs over his shoulders. Standing straight, he watched her face as he positioned the head of his cock at her entrance. Her eyes widened slightly as she realized his intent. Her fingers fisted in the comforter, holding tight as he slowly slid his length into her tight passage.

Inch by inch, he pressed forward as her walls clamped down on him, sucking him deeper. His hands shook slightly, and he gripped her thighs, holding his own lust in check to give her pleasure. Once she came, then he'd let loose, fucking her like he really wanted to.

He looked into her face. Her cheeks were flushed pink; her lips were swollen and parted. Breath huffed past her lips in short bursts, the sound a mixture of pleasure and surprise.

Her breasts bounced slightly as he thrust his hips forward. He reached out and pinched one of her rose-colored nipples, and she moaned, arching her back and forcing her breast toward his hand. He gave her what she wanted, cupping the entire mound and squeezing. He liked the feel of her breasts in his hands. They fitted perfectly, even spilling over a little as he squeezed.

He pulled back, coming almost all the way out of her before sliding back in. His eyes closed as his length moved along her walls. He went deep, pressing his balls against her ass as he pivoted his hips, rubbing his groin over her swollen clit.

She moaned and let her head lull to the side.

"God, you feel good," he growled.

Using his palms, he pushed her legs backward toward her shoulders and out, spreading them wide. The position put him even deeper, and he moved his hips in small, tight circles, massaging her swollen nub.

Alana gasped and tried to lift her hips, but he held her down, held her still as he teased and tormented her. Her walls tightened and trembled. She was close; he could feel it.

"Like that?" he whispered.

She swallowed and nodded, making Noah smile.

"I like this too," he murmured. "I also like this."

Pulling out, he thrust back in hard, taking her breath. She squealed, lifting her hips as best she could to meet him, to take him deeper inside her.

"Do it again," she panted. "Oh God."

He did it again, this time grinding into her as he thrust back in. Juices slid from her opening to coat his balls, easing his way as he thrust once more and then again. He lost himself in the feel of her body cradling his, the way her pussy sucked at his cock, the feel of her walls as he came closer to that edge.

Her hands reached up to grasp her breasts, and Noah groaned, enjoying the sight of her squeezing her own breasts.

"Don't stop," she cried.

"Damn that's hot," he growled as he thrust faster. "Come for me, baby."

He didn't have to encourage her. Her body was already in the beginning throes. He could feel it. Her walls quivered around him, and her body tensed. He could even see it in her face, her wrinkled brow, her narrowed eyes, her flushed skin.

He gritted his teeth, holding his own release back until he heard her scream, until he felt her body erupting beneath his. Her scream of pleasure washed over him, and he pounded harder, allowing his own orgasm to wash over him, joining hers. The two mingled into one as he spewed what felt like his soul within her walls.

The grip he had on her thighs released, and her legs fell, hanging limply off the edge of the bed. Noah dropped forward to his elbows and buried his face in the side of her neck. He couldn't speak through his erratic breathing and the sated feeling that left him weak.

"Wow," Alana sighed. "Is sex like this what I can expect for the rest of the night?"

Noah chuckled. "If you want more right now, I'll have to call Aiden in here."

Alana shook her head. "I think I need a few."

Lifting up, he brushed her hair from her brow and smiled. "So...does that question mean you're staying the night?"

She studied him as though she could read his mind. "Are you asking me to?"

He grinned. "Don't answer a question with a question. Isn't that what you told me?"

She snickered softly. "Yeah, it is." She remained silent for a few seconds, as though thinking. "I'm hungry."

"Hungry?" Noah asked with amusement.

"Yes. Hungry. Sue me."

Noah laughed and kissed the tip of her nose. "By all means. Let's eat. I'll go see what Aiden's up to. You can use the shower if you want. I'll bring your clothes in from outside. Or if you like, I have several in the closet I think you would look great in."

Alana returned his smile. The spark of devilment in her eyes made his balls tighten. She would be the death of him; he could feel it in his gut. No matter what they did, or how often they did it, he had a feeling he would never get enough. She would be an addiction he would always be fighting against and submitting to.

"I'll surprise you," she whispered.

Noah dropped his head to kiss her brow. His lips lingered as he inhaled the sweet scent of her hair. He really needed to get up, or he'd be hard as a rock again in no time. Poor girl would be raw by the time morning came between him and Aiden. Would they scare her off? God, he hoped not. The more time he spent with her, the more he liked her, and the more he found himself falling for her.

"I'll leave you to it, then."

With a grin, he pulled himself free of her body and stepped into the bathroom to clean himself up and grab a pair of sweats from the walk-in closet. As he stepped back into the bedroom, he caught Alana's stare as she watched him walk toward the bed.

She lay on her side, her knees drawn up, one hand under her cheek. She appeared deep in thought, and he wondered what was going through her mind. If he concentrated hard enough, would he be able to tell, or could he only gauge her emotions, her stresses?

He winked and turned to leave the room, giving her some privacy. He found Aiden at the table, his eyes glued to the laptop.

"What are you looking at?" Noah asked, but he had a feeling whatever it was, he wouldn't like.

Aiden sighed and slowly closed the laptop. "Why didn't we look into this sooner?"

"What are you talking about?" Noah asked as he opened the fridge and reached for the steaks he had inside.

"You don't need to cook. I ordered pizza."

Noah sighed and put the steaks back in the fridge. He noticed Alana's clothes folded on the counter and realized Aiden must have retrieved them already. He walked over and grabbed them.

"Noah—"

"I really don't want to talk about this, Aiden. They both left us. Mom, then Dad. Let it go."

Noah headed down the hall, but Aiden's words stopped him cold.

"What if I don't want to let it go?"

Turning to stare at his brother, Noah wasn't sure how to deal with this. He wanted to let it go. He wanted to forget either of them had ever existed. Finally, he sighed and said, "Do what you want, Aiden. Just leave me the hell out of it."

"What are the two of you fighting about?" Alana asked worriedly from behind Noah.

He turned and smiled slightly, trying to brush it off and lessen the troubled look in her eyes. "We're not fighting," he replied as his gaze wandered down her long legs, visible beneath the hem of one of his flannel shirts. A pair of his socks covered her feet, and he tried to fight a chuckle.

She crossed her arms over her chest and glared at him in disbelief. "You're upset with him."

Noah stepped closer and put his palm against the wall, leaning in. "Are you trying to take up for him?" he asked in amusement.

Her chin rose in defiance. "Maybe." Her chin dropped a little as a cloud moved over her face. "It's the weirdest thing. I sensed you were upset. I can't explain it."

Noah could, but he chose not to say anything. Instead, he took her hand and led her back to the living area, laying her clothes on the recliner as he passed by.

"Aiden ordered pizza for dinner. It should be here shortly."

"Good, I love pizza. I think I could eat it every day."

Noah grinned. "Me too."

ALANA WATCHED AS Noah and Aiden tried to appear relaxed in front of her, but she could tell things were tense. Had she made a mistake bringing up their mother? She wished she could take it back. She wished she hadn't mentioned it and done a little more research on her own.

"Aiden, is everything okay?"

Aiden strolled toward her and used the pad of his finger to lift her chin. "Don't second-guess yourself," he whispered. "You did what you thought was right."

She opened her mouth to ask how he could read her so well, but Noah walked in carrying the pizza. The smell filled the air, making her stomach growl, and she followed him to the table while Aiden went to retrieve plates.

"I didn't even hear someone knock at the door," she said in surprise as she stared at the bags in Noah's hand.

"I saw his headlights when he pulled into the driveway," Noah replied.

"How does Tray feel about this night off?" Aiden asked with a smile.

Alana chuckled. "Oh, he's fine. He's going through the footage and editing. He has just as much fun doing that as he does investigating."

"How did you get started in this?" Noah asked as he opened the pizza box.

Alana took the piece he handed her and set it on her plate. "It started out as a special that went along with one of my books. It got such good ratings, the network approached us about doing a series." She shrugged. "The rest is history."

She glanced around at them before taking a deep breath. "What about your dad?" she asked. "Is he still around? Maybe he knows something about your mother."

Noah and Aiden looked at each other briefly before Aiden turned to her and spoke. "Our dad disappeared on us several years ago. After our mother left, he withdrew and was hardly ever around until eventually he just disappeared altogether."

"So you had both parents disappear on you?"

Aiden nodded. Alana glanced at Noah, and her stomach tightened at the haunted look in his eyes. He dropped his gaze, staring at his plate as he slowly picked at the pepperoni. She reached out and touched his arm. The muscles twitched, and his flesh warmed beneath her fingers. Something was wrong—wrong with all of this. Something just didn't feel right, and she could tell that Noah struggled with it as well.

"At least we know now what happened to your mother," she offered.

"No we don't," Noah replied with a shake of his head. "We know she was murdered a few days after she disappeared, but that's all. I'm not going to speculate that she was kidnapped. She could have left with him willingly."

She pointed at him. "You're stubborn, do you know that?"

He looked at her with a lopsided grin on his face that seemed to erase some of the worry lines and tension. "I appreciate your trying to help, but we've lived with this for a long time. No point trying to change how we feel when we can't get true answers. We would only be guessing at this point."

"So we just don't look into it at all, is that it?" Aiden asked, slightly miffed.

"I told you," Noah replied. "If you want to look into it, be my guest. But keep me out of it."

Alana sighed and set her napkin next to her plate. "I say we change the subject. The two of you can work this out when I'm not around. I have two gorgeous, hunky men at my beck and call, and I would prefer to find other things for the two of you to do rather than fighting."

"Really?" Aiden asked as his brow raised and desire sparked in his dark eyes.

A shiver of delight ran down Alana's spine.

"I think I could think of a few things too," Aiden purred.

She could feel the wetness between her thighs grow as she imagined the two of them on either side of her, bringing her body to life once again. She took a bite of her pizza and slowly chewed. As she did, she kept her gaze on Aiden's, and he smiled devilishly, which made her nipples harden in anticipation.

"Just watching the two of you is making me get hard," Noah drawled.

Alana choked back a chuckle as she swallowed her bite of pizza. Once down, she covered her mouth and couldn't stop the laughter that bubbled up.

"We're not that bad," she said with a giggle.

Noah scoffed. "Please. You're looking at him like you could rip his clothes off, and he's looking at you like he wants to throw you on this table and fuck your brains out."

"I do," Aiden said, grinning.

"At least you're honest," Alana said with a snicker.

"No point mincing words at this point," Aiden drawled, making Alana giggle.

He was right. After what they'd done, why beat around the bush about things? She would have sex with them again tonight, maybe even more than once. They were incredible and made her feel things she hadn't felt in...well, a long time, if ever.

The only thing that gave her pause was all the times she believed she could sense their feelings. Was that even possible? It was what they claimed happened between the two of them, but why would she be feeling it too? It had to be all in her head.

She frowned.

Right?

"Is something wrong?" Aiden asked.

Alana eased her facial muscles, making the frown disappear. "No," she replied with a shake of her head. "I was just thinking."

Noah reached out and gripped her chin, forcing her to face his penetrating gaze. "What were you thinking about that made you frown like that?"

She swallowed, knowing without a doubt that she couldn't lie to him. He watched her as though he expected her to tell the truth. She would bet he never even considered the possibility that she would lie to him.

"I was just thinking about how sometimes I think I sense what you feel. There're times I know I can feel that you're mad or upset or worried. It's weird, I know."

"Trust me," Noah said with a snort. "My brother and I are very familiar with weird."

"How long have you been sensing that?" Aiden asked.

She turned back to him as she reached for another napkin. Pizza could be incredibly greasy, and she hated the feel of grease on her fingers for too long. "Just a few days. Truthfully, I think it's just all in my head."

"We used to think that too," Aiden said as he reached for another piece. "It didn't take us long to dismiss that idea."

"Why? What happened?"

"Lots of things. Things we couldn't explain. Things we couldn't ignore. The sex thing was the most annoying. That's when we started sharing. Made things easier and definitely more interesting."

Alana grinned. "I bet. So...just how many women have you shared?"

Aiden's lips twitched in amusement. "Jealous?"

The heat of a blush moved over her cheeks. "No," she said, glancing down at her plate. "Just curious."

"You really want to know?" Noah asked.

She sighed in silence, thinking. Did she really want to know? "On second thought..." she murmured.

Noah chuckled and leaned over, letting his lips tease the side of her neck, sending a shiver of excitement down her spine. "All you need to know," he whispered, "is that we know what we're doing."

"I think you've already proven that," she drawled softly.

Noah's smile widened, and her heart skipped a quick beat in her chest. God, she was such a goner where they were concerned. Two men at once. She'd considered it, daydreamed about it. Earlier she'd gotten a little taste of what it would be like, and she loved every second of it. But both of them inside her at the same time? Just thinking about it made her pussy clench in need.

Could they tell?

Chapter Twenty

Alana stared into Noah's dark gaze and had a gut feeling that they could. She quickly dropped her eyes and pulled a piece of pepperoni off her pizza. Hunger was the last thing on her mind at the moment. Sex was foremost. She opened her lips, placed the pepperoni on her tongue, and slowly chewed. As she did, her mind kept skipping back to the patio, replaying every touch, every kiss, and the way his cock had stretched her walls, filled her deep. She could still taste Aiden on her tongue as she swallowed the food.

She glanced at him through her lashes. His hair was slightly mussed, a day's growth of whiskers covered his cheeks, and she imagined what they would feel like as they scratched against her skin. He wore a button-down shirt, but it was open, exposing his hard chest. She licked her lips as her gaze moved lower, taking in his washboard abs and strong hands—hands that had made her body shudder in delight, fingers that had teased her and made her want to scream for more.

Her heart pounded as she let her fork rest against the edge of the plate. She pushed her chair back, letting it scrape along the floor. Both men looked up at her in surprise as she walked over to Aiden. He sat back, and she draped one leg over his thighs, straddling him.

Aiden's hands slid beneath the edges of the shirt and gently stroked the outside of her thighs, igniting a fire so bright, she thought it might eat her alive.

"I like this," he whispered.

Placing his hands at her ass, he tugged her forward, settling her pussy directly over his hard cock. She wiggled against the ridge beneath his jeans, sighing as the rough material rubbed against her sensitive lips.

He reached up with one hand and opened her shirt, spreading it wide so that her breasts were exposed. With a wicked grin, he leaned forward and licked across her nipple, making her shudder in delight.

Behind her, Noah gripped her hair at the base of her neck and tugged her head backward. His mouth landed over hers in a kiss that nearly sent her head spinning out of control. It was dark, sensual, deep, and hungry. His tongue delved into her mouth, taking complete control and demanding a response.

She gave him one, greedily returning his kiss. She couldn't remember ever being this turned on. The intoxicating sensations left her feeling light-headed and brazen.

Aiden's mouth latched onto the tip of her breasts, sucking it into her mouth. He bit down and the slight bite of pain mingled with pleasure made her gasp in surprise, but the sound was swallowed by Noah's kiss—Noah's incredible kiss.

He broke away and growled close to her lips. "We haven't prepared her at all."

"Then do it now," Aiden murmured around the tip of her breast. "Before I undo my pants and take her here."

"Don't move," Noah whispered.

"Fat chance of that," she sighed as Aiden continued with the licking and biting of her nipple.

His words of preparing her barely penetrated her subconscious as Aiden lifted a hand, cupping her breast and pushing it upward toward his mouth. Her whole body tingled with pleasure and hunger that grew to a deafening roar within her ears.

They made her crazy. That's all there was to it. Crazy and wild and horny and brazen. Had she really just walked over and sat on Aiden's lap? She smiled, letting her head loll to the side as Aiden's lips moved up along her neck. His teeth gently nipped at the sensitive flesh beneath her ear, and she shivered.

"Cold?" Aiden whispered.

"No. Far from it."

Aiden's hands settled around her waist, holding her close as his thumbs gently brushed over her ribs.

"Are we making you hot?" Aiden teased.

She scoffed. "You can't tell?"

"Maybe I should check."

Aiden's hand slid between her legs from behind. Her mouth opened on a silent cry as his fingers gently stroked through the juices leaking from her labia. Her hips shifted backward, trying to force his fingers inside her, but he pulled them back, smearing her cream between the globes of her ass.

He brushed over the tight opening to her anus, and her muscles clenched in anticipation. The thought of him taking her there was surprisingly exciting.

"Nice," he murmured against her lips.

Alana's mouth opened in anticipation of his kiss, but instead, he teased her by swiping his tongue over her bottom lip.

Noah's hand rested against her shoulder, then slid slowly down her spine. Her skin tingled in response to the gentle touch.

"I don't want to hurt you," he whispered softly. "So I'm going to stretch you first. Do you trust me?"

Alana nodded, unable to string two words together. She was out of her mind with lust. She knew it. They knew it. It was likely she would come the second he slid whatever it was he planned to slide inside her.

Her fingers gripped Aiden's shoulders as Noah lifted a clear plastic anal wand up for her to see. It was long but not as thick as Noah and was covered in cream so that it would enter her body easily.

Her breathing became even more erratic as Aiden used his hands to spread the globes of her ass. Noah placed the toy at her entrance and gently pushed. The tight ring of resistance gave way, allowing the toy to slip inside. Moaning, she leaned forward just a little so Noah could slide the toy deeper.

The cold, hard plastic stretched her walls, rubbing against her channel from the other side, and nearly sent her over the edge. She panted, trying to hold off her release. She wanted to be filled with both of them before she came. She wanted the three of them to be as one as they came together.

She believed she could sense that's what they wanted as well.

Noah buried his face in her neck. His breath blew against her skin as his lips parted and his teeth scraped across the column of her throat.

"So hot," he whispered. "Now take Aiden."

Noah grasped her breasts from behind, holding her back as Aiden freed his thick, engorged shaft. Alana had a brief second of trepidation at his size and the equal thickness of his brother. Would this work? Could she take both of them?

Her heart raced almost out of control as Aiden placed the head of his shaft at her opening. All thought of worry or fear fled her mind as he began pushing his way inside her. Noah pinched her nipples, making her cry out in pleasure as Aiden went deeper, stretching her tight around his girth.

"Fuck, she's tight," Aiden groaned as his fingers dug into her hips, trying to hold her up and keep her from sliding down his length and taking every last inch of him inside her.

She could barely breathe and she gasped for air as she struggled to keep herself from screaming. Not from pain. Yes, there was a little, but the pleasure outweighed it by a long shot. Aiden spread his legs, which in turn spread hers, and she screamed as her weight dropped down on him, forcing him inside her balls-deep.

"Ah, yeah," Aiden moaned. "That's all of it, baby."

She was full, consumed and so ready to burst, she could barely contain her need for more. Experimentally, she shifted her hips, and Aiden sighed his pleasure. Noah lifted a breast, offering it to Aiden, and he leaned forward, engulfing the tip in his mouth. Alana let her head fall back against Noah's chest, completely trusting he'd be there to support her, to catch her if she fell.

"You're so damn sexy, I could just stand here and watch," Noah whispered. "But I want to feel that body too. I want to be buried in your ass when you explode between us."

She swallowed and ground her hips against Aiden, forcing his cock deeper. Noah's finger slid between the cheeks of her ass and tugged at the toy before pushing it back in, filling her deeper, forcing her to take even more.

"Like that?" he purred, knowing good and well that she did.

"Oh, yes," she hissed.

He did it again, and she giggled around a cry of rapture. Wow, this was insane. She felt everything. Aiden's heartbeat in his cock, the gentle slide of the toy, even the rapid rise and fall of Noah's chest as he breathed shallow behind her.

"I can't stand this," Noah growled as he pulled the toy free of her ass suddenly.

The loss of fullness took her by surprise, and she gasped, wanting it back. Startled she would find she craved such a thing, Alana swallowed at her own growing dark desire.

"Stand up," he commanded of Aiden.

Aiden wrapped his arms around her waist and stood slowly. "Hold tight to me," he whispered just before his mouth covered hers in a sweet kiss that, if she had been standing, would have made her knees buckle.

She could hear Noah behind her but wasn't sure what he was doing until he moved in close and placed the head of his cock at her anal opening. She tensed, knowing he would be much bigger than the toy, but at the same time wanting to feel both of them inside her more than anything.

"Are you ready for him?" Aiden asked against her lips.

"Yes," she said, nodding rapidly.

Noah pressed forward past the tight opening. A sting of pain made her gasp at first.

"Relax," Noah whispered.

"I don't think I can," she cried, her nails digging into Aiden's shoulders.

He stopped, and she held her breath. She couldn't move, couldn't feel anything beyond the moment and the need to have him take her completely.

"Noah," she gasped, gulping in air.

"Am I hurting you?"

"Damn it, no! Just do it. Take me. Noah, please."

He grasped her waist and pressed forward, burying himself deep with one, hard thrust. She screamed, and her head fell back against his shoulder as pleasure unlike anything she'd ever felt spread through her body.

"Son of a..."Aiden groaned, and his eyes rolled back.

Sweet Lord, what had she been missing? Two men, consuming her every thought, her every breath. It was incredible, and she didn't want it to end. But it would. She could feel it.

Her release built from her womb, tightening her stomach and working its way outward through her limbs. Blood rushed through her veins, warming her flesh and making her ears roar.

"Oh God," she whimpered.

Aiden reached up and pinched one of her nipples. The pleasure intensified, and she squeezed her eyes closed, forcing the water that had gathered there down her cheeks. The heat from their bodies warmed hers, making sweat bead across her skin.

Slowly they began to move. One in, the other out, then they would push deep together, practically taking the very breath from her lungs and leaving her feeling weak and ridden hard.

Her whole body tensed as the pleasure built, stronger and more intense than anything before. What started as a moan from low in her throat crested at a scream as every muscle in her body trembled with pleasure. Wave after wave raced through her as her pussy and anus pulsed around the invading rods. Her clit quivered as it brushed against Aiden's groin, and she shuddered against the massive sensitivity that settled there.

She could feel the tension in both of them as they each shouted out their own orgasm. Hot jets of cum coated the walls of both channels as their hips jerked against her, burying their cocks. It was strange she could feel what they did, strange that she knew the exact second they came and how it felt for her walls to suck at their rods.

Why was she feeling this? Was it the intensity of the situation, the tightness of the fit—or was it their connection? Was she somehow connected to them like they were connected to each other?

That wasn't possible, was it? It couldn't be. It just couldn't.

"Alana," Aiden whispered as he cupped her cheek and tilted her head so he could place a soft kiss against her cheek.

"Oh..." she breathed. "Just shut up and get me to bed."

Aiden's eyes widened while Noah chuckled.

"I may be too sore to do this again tonight, but I am definitely not through with the two of you."

Aiden's mouth opened, but he didn't say anything. Noah moved closer, pressing his hips into her and pushing his still hard cock farther inside her. She sighed and leaned against him.

"That's three times for me. Twice for Aiden. What do you think we are? Teenagers?" Alana could tell by the teasing tone of his voice he was only kidding.

She smiled and glanced at him over her shoulder. "What are you saying, Noah? Can't handle me?"

His lips lifted into an amused one-sided grin. "Hardly," he drawled. "I can assure you, if fucking all night long is what you want, that's what you'll get."

* * *

He stood in the shadows of the lobby, watching his latest obsessions, Lisa, as she strolled across the lobby with two members of her crew. After finding out her name at the library, obtaining her had become even more important, but that was going to be harder than he'd anticipated. She never went anywhere alone, and his frustration was about to get the better of him.

His gaze wandered down her curvy figure, and he clenched his fists, stepping farther behind the potted plant he hid behind. He couldn't afford for her to see him. At least not yet. But soon. Soon they would slip up and she'd be alone, or he'd take her anyway, killing whoever stood in his way.

It wasn't the way he normally did things, but she was different. She was beautiful and vibrant. He wanted to watch that life fade from her eyes. He wanted to be the reason she screamed in fear as he sank his blades into her warm, supple body.

His cock hardened at the image, and he glanced away, trying to force the beast back down. If he didn't he would lose control. The beast would consume him, and he'd make mistakes—mistakes he couldn't afford to make.

He couldn't remember anything before the beast had taken over. Had he been normal? Had he had a life that consisted of things other than blood and pain? He couldn't remember—couldn't remember who he was or how he'd come to be. All he knew was he had to feed the beast. Feed it flesh. Beautiful, vibrant, bloody flesh.

His gaze moved back to Lisa as she stepped into the bar at the far side of the lobby.

The beast wanted her, and he'd get her.

Chapter Twenty-one

Alana awoke struggling to breathe. Pressure wrapped around her throat, and she lifted her hand to pull it away but felt nothing. She sat up, frowning as her fingers groped for whatever gripped her windpipe. Fear sped up her spine, and her eyes widened, searching for the assailant she would swear stood directly over her.

Warm hands touched her shoulders, and she struggled to free herself of the restraining grip. Aiden jumped in front of her and grabbed her shoulders, giving her a firm shake.

"Alana!" he yelled. "It's us."

She stared up at him, stuck somewhere between her fear and relief.

"It's okay," he said a little softer. "It was just a dream."

"My God," she sighed, dragging a hand down her face.

The hands on her shoulders began to massage gently, and she sat back, letting her shoulders slump in defeat.

"I've never had a dream like that before."

"What was it?" Noah asked.

She heard tension in his voice, and she turned to look at him. His haunted eyes met hers, and she almost flinched at the pain reflected in his gaze.

"Why are you asking me? You already know... Don't you?" she demanded.

She wasn't sure how, but she knew. He'd had the same dream she had. She could feel it in her gut. She shivered and wrapped her arms around herself.

"There was a man," Noah began in a soft voice. "I couldn't see his face—"

"His eyes were...evil," Aiden added. "There was nothing inside him. Nothing but anger, torment."

Alana swallowed as her gaze moved from Aiden to Noah. "He tried to choke me, but it wasn't me." She glanced at Noah. "It was you. This is your memory. How the hell am I experiencing your memory?" she yelled. "And how the hell did I know that?"

"I don't know," Noah replied.

He was telling her the truth. To her it was obvious. She reached out and touched his arm in comfort.

"I don't understand what's going on," she said with a sigh.

"This is what happened to you when we were separated that weekend," Aiden suggested. "That thing you can't remember."

Alana gasped. "Oh my God. This is what happened? You were attacked?"

"I don't know," Noah said, this time a little more firm. "I don't remember."

"Have the two of you always shared dreams like this?" Alana asked, changing the subject for a moment to keep Noah from losing his temper—something she felt that was close at hand.

"No. Well...at least not until you," Aiden replied, and Alana frowned at him as though he'd grown three heads. "When you came along is when it started. This isn't the first dream you've shared with us either."

She raised an eyebrow, and her heart skipped a beat. She had a feeling she knew which dream he would say it was. "The sex dream," she whispered.

Aiden nodded. "Yeah."

Alana dropped her hand from Noah's arm like a dead weight. "Okay, this is just getting to be way too weird."

"No kidding," Noah grumbled.

She narrowed her eyes as she looked at Noah. "Back to the dream tonight. You knew your attacker. I felt it."

Noah shook his head. "I honestly don't remember. If I did know the person, I have no idea who it is now."

"Well then why—"

Noah slung the covers back and stood so quickly, Alana almost jumped out of her skin.

"I'm going to take a shower," he mumbled before heading to the bathroom.

"Haven't you already had a shower?" she called after him.

"I need another."

Alana watched him go, shocked at his sudden exit. "What the hell just happened?" she whispered as she stared wide-eyed at the closed bathroom door.

Aiden leaned his back against the headboard and readjusted the covers around his waist. "He just needs some space. For whatever reason, he's fighting the memory."

She glanced at Aiden over her shoulder. "Why?"

Aiden shrugged. "Whatever it is he's trying not to remember must be terrible. I remember bits of the dream. The anguish, the surprise. If he does remember, it will be bad, that much I can tell."

"Wouldn't it be better if he did?"

"Depends."

"On what?"

Aiden pursed his lips for a brief second before answering. "On who it is."

Alana huffed and turned on the bed to face Aiden. Despite all that had happened and seemed to keep happening, she couldn't seem to stop staring at his chest. His hard, smooth, tan...

Okay, she had to stop this.

Rolling her eyes, she moved to lean her back against the headboard next to him. Grabbing the sheets, she lifted them to cover her breasts and tried to make herself comfortable and, above all, indifferent to the hunk beside her.

"You seem a little distracted, sunshine. What's up?" Aiden asked.

She slanted a look through the corner of her eyes. "This all isn't strange to you? The dreams. The memories. The weird connection between the three of us."

"Noah and I have had this weird connection for years now. To be honest, the added third doesn't feel off at all, but right. It's sort of like we're complete now, whereas before we weren't."

"Do you realize how crazy that sounds? How crazy all this sounds?"

"Yeah, but I was kinda hoping you wouldn't notice."

Alana snickered. "Kind of hard not to, Aiden."

Aiden took her hand in his and lifted it to his mouth, kissing the back of it. His lips were warm against her skin, and she couldn't stop the tiny shiver of delight that ran up her spine.

"We take things a day at a time. That's all we can do. The connection may weaken with time, or it may strengthen. We have no idea. We just have to roll with it, get to know one another, and see where it all takes us."

Alana's lips twitched slightly. She wished she could be as assured as Aiden appeared to be. She worried about Noah, though. Something terrible was about to happen. She could feel it deep in her gut and didn't have a clue what to do about it.

* * *

"Oh my God! She's alive!"

Alana dropped her purse into the chair and slanted a look of annoyance toward Tray. He sat in one of the office chairs they'd brought into their suite, swinging it back and forth and grinning at her like the cat who'd just eaten the canary.

"Well, it looks as though you can still walk. How's sitting?" Tray asked.

Lisa snorted and almost choked on her coffee. She lifted her hand and covered her mouth quickly before swallowing and bursting into a peal of laughter.

"Both of you are impossible," Alana replied.

"Not impossible," Tray countered. "Easy."

Alana rolled her eyes. She loved Tray, but sometimes he could be a real pain in the backside. After a night of little sleep and exhausting sex, she really wasn't in the mood.

"How's the editing?" she asked, changing the subject.

"Slow. Interesting. Enlightening."

Unzipping her jacket, she raised an eyebrow. "Enlightening? How so?"

"There's a lot of activity in that house, some of which I'm not so sure isn't human."

She walked over to the table, intrigued. "Like what?"

"Check this out," Tray said as he twirled the chair back around and turned on the laptop with the infrared footage. His fingers flew quickly over the keys, opening the program he needed.

Alana watched the screen as a picture came up. "Where is this?" she asked, trying to make out the images she was seeing. The only bad thing about infrared was unless you knew what you were looking at, sometimes it was hard to make it out.

"This is the second-floor hallway."

As she watched, a heat signature in the shape of a man walked across the hall, then a few seconds later, he stepped from one of the bedrooms and into what appeared to be the wall.

Alana drew in a sharp breath. "That's not paranormal. Are you sure no one was up there?"

"Look at the time stamp. We were all in the front yard, present and accounted for."

"Someone was in that house," she murmured. "But who? Do you think it was the person who attacked Lisa?"

"I don't know, but at least we know where the entrance is to the secret passage on the second floor. All we have to do now is figure out how to open it." Tray smiled devilishly. "Want to head out there?"

"What? Now?"

Tray shrugged. "Sure. Lisa can stay here and help finish up the editing—"

"Thanks for consulting me, Tray," Lisa called.

Tray waved a hand, ignoring her. "Besides, the time alone will give us a chance to talk."

"Don't think I can talk to you in front of Lisa?" Alana teased.

Tray leaned in close. "You tell me more than you do her, and you know it. I just thought you might want to talk, especially after last night."

"I'm fine," she whispered, giving him a pointed look. Her gaze softened, and she leaned and kissed him on the cheek. "But I appreciate the concern. And honestly…sitting is a little rough today."

Tray chuckled. "Welcome to my world."

"Really?" she purred. "And here I always thought you were the pitcher."

This time Tray laughed. "I sometimes like to mix it up a bit." He chucked her affectionately under the chin.

"What are the two of you over here plotting?" Lisa asked as she walked over and dropped a flash drive onto the table.

"I'm trying to convince Alana to make her little threesome a foursome," Tray replied.

Alana snorted. "I don't think I could handle another penis wagging in my face, thank you very much. Two is quite enough."

Lisa giggled. "What I wouldn't give to have your dilemma."

"I have to admit," she said, thoughtfully. "It wasn't quite what I expected."

"Is that good or bad?" Lisa asked with concern.

"Good, I guess. There's just some things I'm still not sure about."

Like their connection. The strange feelings of contentment and belonging. The weird way she could tell what they were thinking. Last night, it had all felt completely overwhelming, but now that there was some space between them, some distance, the feelings had lessened, allowing her to think a little more clearly.

In the beginning she hadn't really believed them about their connection, but now...now that she'd experienced it herself...

She should be honest with herself. She still didn't know what to think. Who would've ever imagined such a thing?

Tray stepped behind her and wrapped his arms around her upper arms, holding her close in a comforting hug that always made her feel secure. "Hey," he whispered. "We're here for you if you want to talk, vent, or otherwise let off steam. 'Kay?"

Alana smiled and patted his arm. "'Kay."

He placed a quick kiss on her cheek before dropping his arms. "Are we headed to the house, or are you chickening out?"

"I don't want to leave Lisa alone."

"I'm not alone," Lisa replied as she poured herself a cup of coffee.

"Well, you're not alone right now," Alana reminded her good-naturedly.

"Well, duh," she mumbled, making Alana giggle. "I meant the other tech guys are here. I'll be fine." She smiled at Alana as she placed the coffeepot back onto the counter. "I promise. Go on, have fun, explore."

Alana could tell by the tone of her friend's voice the smile was mostly fake. She walked over and placed her hands on her shoulders.

"You're not fooling me or anyone else," Alana said.

"I know," Lisa said, then sighed. "I'm just tired of being babied. I still don't remember anything, so to me it all seems silly."

"It's not silly. Whoever attacked you is still out there. The last thing I want to happen is for him to get his hands on you again."

Lisa nodded reluctantly, and Alana gave her a hug.

"At least take a couple of cameras and get some footage. If I can't be there, I can live through the two of you vicariously."

Alana laughed. "Deal."

* * *

Lisa stared at the computer screen and let out a long, tired sigh. Alana and Tray had left over an hour ago. They had a couple of stops to make for supplies, then they were headed to the house. She would give anything to be with them. She had become so tired of sitting on the sidelines, watching one of their best investigations ever from a distance. She hated this.

One of their many producers, Steve, looked over at her and grinned.

"That sigh sounded awfully dramatic."

She rolled her eyes. "Sorry. I'm just bored out of my mind."

He raised an eyebrow. "You're kidding, right?"

With a slight smile, she shook her head. "Well, not really. I have to admit, this stuff is amazing. We've never gotten anything like this before. It's just..."

"You want to be in that house."

"Yeah, I do. Unfortunately, whenever I try, I can't seem to make my feet move," she replied, sadly. "I still don't remember much about what happened. I've gotten little bits and pieces, but nothing I can really grasp onto. It's gone as quickly as it comes."

"Have you told Alana? About the flashes?"

She shook her head firmly. "Absolutely not. She worries enough as it is."

"She's your friend; of course she worries. We all worry. You may not remember what happened, but I can assure you, everyone else does."

"I need some coffee," Lisa said as she quickly stood.

"We're out."

"Great. I'll run downstairs and get some from the coffee shop across the street."

She started toward the door, grabbing her purse as she passed by the table.

"Whoa," Steve growled. "Not alone, you're not."

"Oh, come on," she snapped. "It's just across the street and besides, Noah sent officers over to keep an eye on me."

"When?" Steven asked in disbelief.

Lisa opened the door showing the two officers standing outside. "That's who called just after you got here."

The two officers turned to look in the room and stared at them in a mixture of interest and confusion. "Where are you headed?" one of them asked.

"Out...before I lose my mind." She held out her hand. "I'm Lisa."

"Jake," the young one on the right replied.

He had blond hair and pretty blue eyes but was a good inch shorter than her, not to mention a few years younger.

"John," the other replied as he took her hand, giving it a firm shake.

John was older with hazel eyes and a hint of gray in his dark brown hair. She loved older guys, especially ones who kept in shape like he obviously had.

She gave him her best smile. "Nice to meet you. I assume the two of you are going to follow me."

"I will," John said. "Jake will stay here and watch the door."

"Fair enough," she said with a nod as she stepped out the door.

She headed down the hall toward the elevator without looking behind her to see if John followed. She knew he did, and she also had a feeling he stared at her ass. Peeking around her shoulder, she caught his stare right where she knew it would be.

His eyes lifted and met hers. He gave no apology, showed no sign he was embarrassed about being caught. Instead, one side of his mouth lifted in a devilish grin that made Lisa's stomach flutter.

She turned away as the heat of a blush moved over her own cheeks. What the hell was that about? She never blushed. With a huff, she pushed the button for the elevator, feeling somewhat off-kilter. She had no problem flirting, no problem making the first move, but for some reason this guy suddenly had her feeling as though she were on a Tilt-A-Whirl, spinning out of control.

Thank God, the coffee shop wasn't far. She really needed a shot of espresso. Maybe two. Alcohol would be better, but the bar wouldn't be open until later, and all the stuff they'd brought with them was gone. They all drank way too much.

The elevator opened, and the two of them stepped inside. He stood next to her, tall, buff, silent. She glanced over at him.

"How long have you been a cop?" she asked.

"Ever since I got out of the service. About four years now."

Ex-military? She let her gaze wander down his tall form. No wonder he was in shape.

"Let me guess. Marine?"

He nodded. "Good guess. I was an officer, planned to go career, but was injured overseas and took the medical discharge. I preferred that to a desk job. After about a year of rehab, physical therapy, and hard work, I was able to get a job as a police officer. It's a small town; not much goes on here. Until you arrived, that is. Apparently you big city people bring it with you."

Lisa chuckled. "I would've preferred this time we left it at home."

The doors opened, and they stepped out into the lobby. John put his hand at the small of her back and waved toward the front door. His touch felt comforting. She moved just a bit closer to his strong presence as they made their way across the lobby.

Once outside, the cool fall air hit her arms, and she realized she'd forgotten her jacket. Even though the sunshine felt warm against her skin, the breeze could cut like a knife. Wrapping her arms around herself, she shivered slightly and picked up her pace. John stayed close but didn't hover as his long stride kept up with her easily.

She quickly stepped into the front door of the coffee shop and sighed in relief. The temperature felt much better in here than outside, especially with her short sleeves.

"It gets a little cool here this time of year. I should've told you to get a jacket," John said as he rubbed his hands up and down her arms.

She jumped in surprise but found his touch to be right, so she didn't make him stop. Instead she took a step back, moving closer to his heat.

"Better?" he asked close to her ear.

The deep timbre of his voice sent tingles up her spine, and she swallowed.

"Yes," she croaked, then cleared her throat to try again. "Yes. Much, thank you."

She really needed a minute to compose herself. There was a long line at the counter, so she had time to run to the ladies' room for a second to find her spine. This guy made her feel...odd, and she wasn't so sure that was a good thing. She liked being in control but with him, she felt small and out of control.

She spotted the restroom tucked away around the far corner. She pointed with her thumb. "I'll be right back."

He stared at the corner then back to her with a frown.

"I'm just going to the restroom. It's right there. I'll be fine."

He appeared hesitant, but finally nodded. "What do you want? I'll get it ordered while you're in there."

"White chocolate mocha," she replied. "With whole milk and whipped cream."

Yeah, she knew it was fattening, but her mochas were the one thing she refused to skimp on. She quickly turned and headed to the bathroom, anxious for a second or two of breathing room.

She rounded the corner and for a second had reservations. He couldn't see her, nor could she see him. She placed her hand against the bathroom door and tried to shake off the feeling of impending doom.

It's nothing; just my vivid imagination working overtime.

John was right outside. He would hear her if she screamed. Taking a deep breath, she shoved the door open and stepped inside. Sunlight shone through the large frosted window, warming the tiles and the small room. She turned to the mirror and studied her makeup. The breeze had messed up her hair, so she ran her fingers through it, attempting to tame the thick tresses.

The door behind her opened, and she glanced over her shoulder to smile a welcome at the woman who entered, but it wasn't a woman. Her heart jumped at the sight of the man she'd met at the library—the man who'd given her the creeps and who now stood before her with a look of utter evil.

She opened her lips to scream, and he rushed forward, clamping his hand over her mouth. She struggled against his hold as a bite of pain pinched at her neck. A drugging warmth spread through her body, and she sagged against him.

Fear was gone. The only thing that remained was the pang of regret as his eyes faded from her view, and she slipped into the deep, dark sleep of the damned.

Chapter Twenty-two

Alana climbed out of the truck and shut the door. The weather had cooled as it got closer to sunset, and she squinted up at the bright blue sky before turning back to the house. It looked different in the light of day. Not nearly as scary, but thinking about what or who might be inside its walls made her shiver, despite the warmth of the late-afternoon sunshine.

"We took way too much time at the electronics store. We're going to lose the light soon."

Tray walked around the front of the truck and handed her a handheld camera. She fixed the strap around the back of her hand and opened the side. The camera came on with a loud *ding*, and she almost flinched as the noise seemed to disturb the quiet of the country mansion.

"I think we'll be fine. Besides, they've turned the power on if we need it, remember? So it's not like we're going to have to cut it short at sunset. Ready?" Tray asked.

She pursed her lips and took a deep breath through her nose, letting it out loudly. She was beginning to have second thoughts, but wasn't sure why. A gut instinct maybe. "Noah's told us never to come here alone."

"We're not alone. We can watch each other's backs."

She stared up at the third-floor windows. She had a strong sensation of being watched and frowned at the curtain blowing through the open window at the far end of the third floor, close to the tower. "Did someone leave a window open last time we were here?"

Tray shook his head and looked up to see what she looked at. "We don't normally touch the windows."

Her stomach tightened with discomfort at the thought of going through that house. Someone was up there, watching them. She could feel it. It was as though he stood behind them, his hot breath on their necks. She shook her head, trying to dislodge the sensation. "I have a bad feeling about this, Tray."

Tray jerked his head around and frowned down at her as though she'd grown another head. "Since when do you get the creeps?"

"Since today, apparently. It's weird. It's as though something...or someone...is telling me not to go in there."

Tray turned to fully face her, his expression thoughtful but also disbelieving. "Okay, you gotta explain that one."

She leaned her back against the truck door. "I can't. Sorry."

"Do you want to leave?"

She looked into Tray's eyes and knew the last thing he wanted to do was leave. He would, of course. If she said she did, he'd go with her. That was just the way he was. He would never make her do something she wasn't comfortable with. He'd take her back and get one of the cameramen to go with him instead.

Shoving the unease aside, she bolstered her courage. "Let's do this."

"Yes," Tray said with a grin and turned to head toward the front steps of the house.

"Did you bring the key?" she asked, following close behind.

He jiggled his keys. "Got it."

Tray slid the key into the front door lock, and Alana stood behind him, nervously shifting from one foot to another. He eyed her with amusement over his shoulder, and she immediately stopped. "What?" she snapped.

Tray snickered but said nothing as he pushed the front door open. It squeaked, and Alana once again shivered. The grand staircase came into view, and she immediately understood why Tray and Aiden wanted to turn this into a bed-and-breakfast. It was beautiful, and when all their planned renovations were done, it would be stunning. Add to that the label of haunted, which it most definitely was, and the place would be constantly booked.

Tray stepped inside, and Alana reluctantly followed. This was stupid. It really was. She'd never in her life been afraid like this. But truthfully, she'd never known anyone who'd been attacked the way Lisa had either. Maybe she should be afraid. Running in headfirst without looking both ways often got you into trouble. If she'd learned anything at all on this trip, she'd learned that.

She held up the camera and spun it around the entryway as they headed up the stairs. They were halfway up when the sound of a truck outside caught their attention.

"Who do you suppose that is?" Tray asked.

Alana tensed. She knew who it was, and he wasn't happy at all.

Noah stomped through the front door and stopped in the middle of the room, his hands on his hips and glared angrily up at them.

"Busted!" he snapped.

She dropped the camera down to her side and returned his glare. Her own anger rose to the surface as she faced down the more intimidating of the two brothers. "Excuse me?" she replied angrily.

Where the hell did he get off?

"Oh, boy," Tray mumbled from behind her, but she ignored him.

"Didn't I tell you not to come here alone?"

"How did you even know I was here? And I'm not alone."

"I saw your truck, and I'm sorry, but Tray isn't exactly my idea of protection."

"This is stupid, Noah. What are you going to do if this guy is never caught? Are you never going to allow anyone to be here alone? What about your guests or your staff?"

Noah dragged his hands down his face in agitation. "Once construction starts on this place, if someone is hiding out here, he won't be for long." He wagged his finger between the two of them. "One strong, resourceful man could easily take down the two of you, and you both fucking know it."

"Wow," Tray drawled. "Ye of little faith."

"Don't be a smart-ass, Tray," Noah snarled.

"Don't treat me like a child," Tray replied.

The menace in Tray's voice surprised Alana, and she glanced with surprise at her friend over her shoulder before turning back to Noah. "Okay, guys. Seriously. Don't you dare come to blows and make me have to choose who to pull off who."

Noah's eyebrow rose, and he snorted as though he found what she said to be amusing.

"Don't make me regret coming to your defense with Alana," Tray said.

Noah rolled his eyes. "Tray—forget it. I've been trying to get a hold of you for almost two hours now. Where the hell is your phone?"

"My phone?" Alana replied, then gasped. "Damn. I left it at the hotel to charge."

"Where's yours?" Noah asked Tray.

"It went dead earlier, and I haven't had a chance to recharge it. Why? What's going on?"

"You two need to come with me. I'll explain at the station."

A blood-curdling scream made everyone freeze. Alana's heart stopped at the sound of the alarming cry, and she began to glance around the entrance hall to determine its origin. The very sound gave her the chills. It wasn't loud but sounded more muffled, as though it came from deep within the walls.

"What the hell was that?" Alana asked, her voice breathy and shaking. It didn't sound like the other noises they'd heard before. It was human...real.

"Jeez," Tray whispered. "You have stuff like that happen when you have guests in this thing, you'll either be rich or bankrupt."

"That's not funny, Tray," Alana whispered as she walked over to the wall and placed her hand against the stained wallpaper. "That wasn't paranormal."

The scream had stopped, and she held her breath, waiting to see if it would start back up again.

"I agree with Alana," Noah said as he stood still, listening.

The scream sounded again, and Alana gasped at the tortured sound. She jumped from the wall then turned, wide-eyed, toward Noah. "It's coming from inside the walls."

Noah pulled his gun. "Both of you out, now."

"What?" Tray and Alana cried in unison.

Lifting the walkie to his mouth, Noah scowled at both of them as he spoke. "This is Noah, I need backup at the mansion."

"Backup's on the way. What's up?" someone asked on the other end.

"Not sure yet. Tell them to be prepared for anything."

Before Noah could place his walkie back in its holder, Aiden's voice came over the speaker. "What's going on, Noah? Did you find Alana?"

"Yeah, she's here. Get your ass out here," Noah replied.

"What the hell's going on?" Tray asked as Noah pointed toward the door, indicating he wanted them to leave.

"Come on, Noah! You can't make us leave; I know where the entrance is on the second floor. The one we've all been searching for."

Noah scowled. "Damn it, Tray. We don't have time for this. Lisa's missing."

Alana gasped. "What? Since when?"

"Since this afternoon."

"Are you kidding me?" she snapped before turning to head up the stairs toward the second floor. "That could be Lisa screaming."

"Oh, shit," Tray said as Noah sped past to catch up with Alana.

"Tray, I swear to God. You better get your ass out there and let them know where to go when they get here."

Alana didn't wait to hear Tray's response. Instead, she ignored her fear and headed toward the portion of the hallway where they'd seen their figure disappear earlier on the tape.

"Lisa!" she screamed.

Noah grasped her arm, slinging her against the wall as they both came to an abrupt halt. Tears escaped to slide down her cheeks as she stared pleadingly up at an angry Noah. But she could tell, could feel deep down, he wouldn't be swayed. He was pissed.

"You need me to find that entrance," she said, narrowing her eyes. "I know where it is." She was determined to argue her point. That scream they'd heard definitely wasn't paranormal and could be Lisa.

"You're bluffing. You wouldn't dare keep silent and leave your friend down there and you know it. If it's even her."

"You know as well as I do it's her. Please don't send me away. She'll need me, and you'll need to get whoever's doing this."

Noah closed his eyes for a brief second. "I can't do that if I'm having to watch out for you as well, Alana."

"Accept it, Noah," she snarled as she raised her chin in stubborn defiance. "I'm going with you."

He drew in a deep breath through his nose and pointed his finger at the tip of hers. His eyes were dark and angry. She would pay for this later, she had no doubt. But it would be worth it. She couldn't stand by and do nothing.

"I swear," he snarled menacingly. "If you get in my way, I'll have your head."

"Deal."

She turned and started running her palms down the wall, looking and feeling for anything that appeared out of place.

"It's here?" Noah asked.

Before she could even nod, he grabbed her arm and pulled her out of the way. He ran a finger down the edge of the door frame and something clicked free in the wall. It popped open and Alana stared in surprise.

"It's right in the seam of the wallpaper," she whispered. "Clever."

"Stay behind me," he ordered as he pulled the door open and stepped inside the darkened passage.

Alana glanced around quickly, looking for something she could use as a weapon. She snatched a heavy candlestick from one of the hall tables and wiped the cobwebs away as she followed Noah into the passage.

Chapter Twenty-three

Aiden sprinted up the front steps and almost ran into Tray as he stepped out the front door. He jumped back and searched the entry hall behind Tray for Alana. When he didn't see her, his heart almost stopped. He'd been worried sick since Lisa had disappeared, and they hadn't been able to get hold of Alana by phone.

"Where is she?"

"They went into the passage. I was told to wait here for you so I could show you where they went," Tray responded.

"What passage?"

"Long story." Tray turned and waved his hand for them to follow.

"What's going on, Tray?" John asked as he followed Aiden into the entry, three other cops behind him.

"We heard a female scream from somewhere in the house. Alana and Noah think it might be Lisa."

Aiden took a moment to study Tray. His pale face showed every emotion, every worry, every fear. He tried to hide it, tried to appear brave, but Aiden knew how hard that could be. He reached out and patted Tray's shoulder.

"If it's Lisa, we'll get her out," Aiden assured him.

Tray nodded but remained silent.

Aiden followed him up the stairs, John and the other officers close on their heels. They made it midway down the hall when Tray stopped and pointed toward the wall. "They went in here...I think."

With a frown, Aiden studied the solid wall. The only thing to indicate anything was a thin seam in the wallpaper. That was it—the seam.

He rushed forward and ran his fingers down the seam. The doors were set to close on their own, so if they went in here, the door shut behind them. He would have to find the mechanism to reopen it.

He felt with growing frustration. Where was it? Noah knew these tunnels much better than he did.

"How did they find this?" Aiden asked as he slid his fingers along the wainscoting.

"We saw someone enter it on the infrared camera we'd left running the other night."

Aiden turned and looked at him in surprise. "Are you serious? It wasn't paranormal?"

"No." Tray nodded toward the door. "Could you hurry, please?"

Aiden shook his head and once again began running his fingers along the wall toward the closest door frame. "So whoever this is was here the whole time we were in the house."

"So it would seem."

"How the hell was he getting around?" John asked.

"The passageways," Aiden replied as he slid his fingers up the outside of the door frame.

"I thought Noah went through all of them."

"He went through most of them. We couldn't find the entrance to the second floor, and it's cut off everywhere else. He told me he believed the passages have been changed but couldn't remember enough about them to know where."

"Changed?" Tray asked, worry in his voice. "Who would change them and why?"

"Good question." The mechanism clicked, forcing the door to pop open. "Bingo," Aiden said with a smile.

He started to step into it, but John grabbed his arm, holding him back. Aiden turned to look at him, and John held up his gun. "Cop. I go first. You go second."

"I don't care who goes where, just go."

John nodded and stepped into the very narrow and dark hallway. He held up his flashlight, pointing the light toward the end. He motioned with a tilt of his head for the others to follow as he stepped inside.

"It's a tight squeeze, guys, so go slow."

"Fuck slow," Aiden mumbled.

* * *

Alana followed behind Noah as they made their way down a set of stairs so narrow, she had to turn sideways to get down them. They creaked and groaned under their weight to the point she became nervous and grasped the thin railing down the side of the wall. The beam of light from Noah's flashlight illuminated the corridor below them. Dust floated through the beam like dancing fairies. There was so much dust, she had to resist the urge to sneeze.

Noah held up his hand, indicating she should stop. He stopped as well, and she held her breath, wondering what had made him come to a halt. He shut off his flashlight, and her stomach jerked at the darkness around them. As her eyes adjusted, she noticed a dim ray of light making its way down the hall, softly illuminating the rock walls and dirt floor at the bottom of the stairs.

"Where's that—"

"Shh," Noah hissed harshly as he placed a finger in front of his lips.

Alana bristled at his tone but quickly realized he'd been right to use it. She should be quiet. She should know better, but she was so worried about her friend all she could think about was finding her. The danger around them hadn't really even entered her mind...until now.

The cold hand of dread worked its way up her spine, and she shivered. Wrapping her arms around herself for a brief second, she tried to listen to the soft noises coming from somewhere in front of them.

This was the third set of stairs they'd gone down. Apparently, the passageways continued well underground beneath the house as well as the barn a few yards away in a nearby field. They were extensive and winding like a labyrinth. Noah moved through the maze as if he knew where he was headed, and she'd followed behind, keeping quiet and trying to pay attention. Despite that, if she had to find her way out, she doubted she'd be successful. She was beyond lost. And, at the moment, beyond terrified.

"What is that?" she whispered as soft music filtered down the hallway toward them.

He shook his head. "I don't know, but stay behind me." He glanced back at her with a menacing scowl she believed had more bark than bite. "I mean it."

"I get it," she mouthed and waved her hand, indicating he should continue on.

Her fingers tightened around the candlestick as she followed Noah to the bottom of the stairs. He left the flashlight off so as not to warn anyone of their approach. Alana just hoped they hadn't already tipped someone off.

She swallowed and glanced back up the stairs. She stiffened as she imagined someone up there, staring down at them through the darkness. She squinted, almost convinced she could actually see something or someone. Shaking it off, she turned back to Noah and walked down a step.

The wood creaked beneath her feet, and she froze, fearful it had been too loud. Noah waved her on. There was no point stopping now. They'd come too far. Her heart beat faster as fear-backed adrenaline flowed through her veins. She'd faced ghosts head-on, even overzealous male dates, but never anything like this.

They were potentially about to face a killer. A man who preyed on women. A man who did God knows what to his victims.

Was this the same man who'd been responsible for the disappearance of all those girls on Noah's computer? And what had happened to those girls?

As they went farther down, the damp air took on a putrid smell that made her stomach turn. She winced and put her hand over her mouth. The air smelled of rotting animals and urine.

What in God's name was that?

Noah glanced back at her with a worried expression as they hit the bottom, then went around the corner as the tunnel took a turn to the right. It seemed to never end, going into what felt like a complete circle, sloping downward as they went. The light became brighter and the music louder as the circle straightened out.

They stood in the hall, just outside the light from the numerous candles burning inside the room. At the far end, Alana could see a spiral staircase that she assumed led to the barn above them. Aiden had told her about the passages that led to the barn when he'd initially told her about the house and its history, but it had been so long since they'd been in them, they hadn't been able to rediscover the entrances.

"I should've done what I first thought about and ripped that damn barn down," Noah growled softly.

"Do you see anything?" she whispered.

Noah shook his head. Her nerves rattled her entire body, making her shiver. She must have been temporarily insane to come along. She wanted to help her friend, but she wasn't a cop. She wasn't trained for this. Her fingers tightened on the candlestick for what must have been the fifth time since coming down the stairs.

Noah leaned to one side, trying to see inside the large room. Candlelight flickered off the damp rock walls. A scene that might've been pretty was ruined by the stench filling the air. She shuffled slowly forward and leaned so that she could peer around Noah's shoulder. To the left of the room was a wooden table with tools, clothes, and jars half full of various items. Stains covered the clothes, the deep brown color either dirt or dried blood.

Alana cringed at the idea.

She moved to the other side, peeking around Noah's other shoulder. He moved in front of her, blocking her view, and she shoved at his back.

"Don't scream," he said, his voice tense.

Alana stiffened as he shifted, allowing her to see what his body blocked. Her eyes widened as a scream climbed her throat. She put her hands over her mouth to try to hold it in, to keep the cry from escaping.

Who could do something so morbid?

A female body hung on the wall to the right, her arms held over her head by a pair of rusty shackles. Her body ghostly white and lifeless, the only color was the blood that had dried on her skin. It was everywhere, covering every inch. That had to be the smell.

My God. How long had she been down there?

"Where's Lisa? Do you see her?" Alana whispered.

"Not yet."

Tears streamed down her face as she imagined what might've been done to her friend. Would whoever this was mutilate her like he'd done that poor woman hanging against the wall?

"We need to find Lisa," she pleaded, her voice cracking from fear.

Noah didn't acknowledge her, but the stiffening of his body indicated he'd heard her. His hand grasped hers as he nodded toward the far right of the room. Alana shifted trying to see, but became frustrated when she didn't see anything other than two feet and calves.

Whoever it was appeared to be lying on the dirt floor, motionless. A lump rose in Alana's throat as she imagined all sorts of morbid things. She swallowed it back down, determined to be brave for her friend. She had to be. Noah might need her help.

A noise sounded from above them, and Alana jumped, searching the darkened stairs behind her.

"Would Aiden have gotten here that fast?" she whispered.

"Possible," Noah replied and motioned for her to follow him. "Be careful and keep your eyes open. I don't see any indication he's in here, but just be cautious nonetheless."

Alana nodded and swallowed down another lump of fear that threatened to choke her.

They moved forward slowly, Noah with his gun raised, his body tense and ready. Alana moved behind him, her hands shaking and nausea threatening to consume her.

Alana moved slowly toward the body, her heart breaking as she got closer and realized it was Lisa. She'd hoped it wasn't her, that somehow her friend had gotten away. Her lips trembled, and she clamped her hand over her mouth before rushing forward to check on her lifeless friend. She knelt on the floor and brushed Lisa's hair aside to better see her swelling face. Lisa was unconscious, her clothes ripped, blood drying on her cheeks and neck from her busted lip and broken nose. Alana touched the side of her throat and felt frantically for a pulse.

"Is she alive?" Noah asked.

Alana nodded, breathing a sigh of relief. "Yes. But she's out cold. How are we going to get her out of here?"

She turned to look at Noah, who stood a few feet behind her studying all the tools lying on the far table. From the corner of her eye, she noticed a figure move from the shadows toward Noah. She screamed, alerting him, but he turned too late.

ALANA'S SCREAM SENT ripples of terror through Noah. He turned but didn't see the face of the man who slammed into him, shoving him against the rock wall.

The back of his head bounced off the rock with a sickening thud. Pain sped down his spine and lightning flashed behind his eyes. He struggled to keep conscious as darkness threatened to consume him. He blinked, then widened his eyes, trying to hold on to the moment and keep himself in the present. Alana couldn't fight this guy. He was strong and had shoved Noah against the rock with enough force to take his breath.

He looked forward, and what he saw made his heart stop. Alana had stood and was creeping toward them.

"No!" he yelled just as the man who'd attacked him turned and backhanded her across the face.

"Alana!"

She grunted and fell sideways, landing on the ground with a groan. Even with his blurring vision he could see the blood oozing from her lip and nose.

"I'll kill you, you dirty son of a bitch," Noah growled, blinking to try to clear his eyesight.

The man turned back to him, and Noah gasped. His face was contorted in rage, his eyes a weird shade of amber, his lips snarling and cracked. Burns had scarred his flesh, leaving him grossly deformed. No wonder Lisa had said he wasn't human that first night.

The man stared at Noah, and the color of his eyes changed, going back to a softer brown. He shook his head as though inwardly fighting against something. His breathing was harsh and shallow. As Noah watched him, he realized there was something about him that was familiar. It was the eyes.

Quick as a flash, the eyes turned back to amber, and he snarled. Whatever he'd been fighting had appeared to win as he stepped forward with a growl of rage and placed his hands around Noah's neck before Noah could even respond. This guy moved with superhuman speed and held his grip with a strength Noah struggled to fight against.

Noah lifted his hand, placing his palm just under his attacker's chin, and tried to force it up. As he did, there was something about the way his attacker looked at him that sparked a memory. He gasped as images began to pour back into his mind.

He was a teenager and had gone into the barn late at night, when he should've been in bed. Gram and Aiden were out of town. He'd decided to stay behind. While trying to get some sleep, he'd remembered he'd left something in the barn earlier and had gone to retrieve it.

He'd walked in on something very similar to this—a deranged man, a battered woman, and blood everywhere. Noah's eyes narrowed as he stared into the rage-filled eyes of his attacker. Despair unlike anything he'd ever felt raced through him, and his chest shook with a soft sob of disbelief.

This man had tried to kill him then, years ago, in the barn directly above them. He'd been in this same position, his hands around his neck, recognition tearing his heart from his chest.

It was his father!

"Noah!" Alana yelled.

"Get out," Noah shouted hoarsely. "Alana, get out!"

His attacker turned back to Alana briefly, and his fingers loosened around Noah's neck. "Look at me," he snarled at his father. "Look at me. You know me."

He turned back to Noah, a look of confusion in his eyes as the amber again began to fade. Noah didn't believe in the paranormal, but there was definitely something going on here. Karen had always talked about the veil of evil within the house. Had that evil somehow taken over his father? Was his father somewhere inside this beast who had him pinned to the wall?

Behind his father Noah could see the wavering image of the same woman he'd been seeing ever since Alana arrived. Were they right? Was she his mother? And was she here to help?

His eyes widened as more memories came rushing back. She'd been there that night. She'd helped him, protected him. She'd done something to him, made him different. What had she done?

Noah let go of his father's face and put the backs of his hands against the wall. He concentrated hard, keeping his gaze on his mother just over his father's shoulder. In his mind, he envisioned shoving his father. It's what his mother had told him to do that night, and it had worked. It had saved him, allowing him to get away.

Noah shouted as he concentrated harder. His father's hands fell away from his neck, and he flew backward with a gasp as though something pulled him from behind. Noah stared in shock as his father flew over twenty feet, landing against the far wall with an inhuman squeal of pain.

He glanced down at Alana's startled expression and felt a pain deep in his chest. There was fear in her eyes. Was it fear of him?

"Alana, get out of here, now!" he shouted.

He couldn't think about anything other than making sure she was safe. In such a short time, she'd come to mean everything to him. If she left him and Aiden—if she died—it would be as if a piece of his soul was ripped from him.

She climbed slowly to her feet and staggered to Lisa's side. Bending, she tried to lift her, but without Lisa's help, the body was too heavy for her. John appeared from what seemed like nowhere and lifted Lisa in his arms and headed quickly toward the spiral staircase in the far corner that led to the barn.

Help had finally arrived, so he could take his mind off Alana and focus on this man who he believed was his father. Noah stiffened as the man climbed slowly to his feet. What the hell was he supposed to do? If it were anyone else, he'd arrest them or look for a way to shoot the son of a bitch. Who did this to women? And how many had he done it to?

This monster couldn't be his father. He couldn't.

The man raised his face and glared at him in rage. His eyes seemed to glow with an inhuman light and hunger that made Noah cringe. Drool slid from the corner of his mouth, and Noah watched as he lifted the back of his hand and wiped it away.

"I should've killed you years ago," the man snarled. "But he was weak. He couldn't go through with it."

"Noah?" Aiden murmured as he slowly crept toward them.

Noah held up his hand, stopping him. "Who are you?"

The man's lips twisted. "You know who I am."

Noah shook his head. "No. You may have his body, but you're not him."

ALANA SLOWED AS she reached the top of the stairs. Lisa was safe with John, so she paused and held tight to the railing as she watched the dirt floor below. Noah stood against the wall; the murdering monster crouched a few feet away like some animal ready to strike. Aiden was close by, watching everything with a cautious and confused eye. Behind him was another cop she didn't recognize, his gun poised and ready, his aim on the man stalking Noah. Behind him stood a pale-faced Tray; his ever-present camera raised and recording the whole event.

She sank slowly to the step and watched everything through the iron railing. Her fingers gripped the cold metal so tightly, her knuckles began to ache. She couldn't leave the spot. She had to see what happened.

She swallowed as emotions of fear, disbelief, and staggering hurt shook her entire body. They were coming from Noah. They were so strong she could almost believe they were her own.

"Noah," she whispered.

As though he'd heard her, he glanced up briefly. He would be pissed she'd stayed behind, but she couldn't leave.

The suspect snarled like an animal, then shouted something in a language she didn't understand before screaming and hurling himself toward Noah. The officer fired, sending the attacker staggering sideways before falling to the ground, lifeless.

"No!" Noah yelled, startling everyone.

A vibration shook the ground, and Alana gasped as the stairs creaked beneath her. On the floor, a black smoky image began to lift from the bloody body lying on the floor. It swirled as it lifted upward, towering over everyone. A low growl sounded from all around them, and Alana sank lower, hoping to remain unnoticed.

Noah backed against the wall, Aiden next to him as the black mist moved closer to the brothers, and the sounds grew louder and more menacing.

From nowhere a young woman appeared. Her body of clear white mist moved between the brothers and the black smoke as though to protect them. The scent of jasmine filled the room as the mist separated and surrounded the shadowy black form.

Alana watched as they circled each other before mingling with a loud cry of pain that made her cringe before disappearing from sight. The room was as silent as death as they all stared toward the empty center.

Noah sank to the floor, sick regret showing clearly on his face. Alana wanted to run to him, to comfort him somehow, but she couldn't move. She was too afraid and confused to move. Something terrible had just happened, and it appeared Noah was the only one who understood it all. She didn't know how, but she knew that was it. She could feel it.

She glanced toward Tray, who slowly let the camera fall to his side. His eyes were wide, his face pale.

"Holy shit," he said.

"What the fuck just happened?" Aiden snapped, breaking the stunned silence.

* * *

Noah sat on the exam table, letting the doctor stitch the small cut on his shoulder. It had apparently happened when he'd hit the wall, but at the time he hadn't noticed it. All he could remember was the look on Alana's face as she'd stared down at him. The pain and anguish in his father's eyes.

He still struggled with the idea that this man was his father. What had happened to him? What would make a man attack his own child? And what the hell was that thing that had come out of him in the end?

The only thing he was sure of was the white mist was his mother, his and Aiden's.

She'd saved them just like she'd saved him all those years ago in the barn when he'd first run into this monster that was supposedly his father. She'd done something to him; something she said would help protect him.

He knew now what this connection between him and Aiden was. It was him. He was a sender as well as a receiver. He could send out his emotions and needs to those he was closest to, but he could also receive their needs as well. Which explained his connection to Alana.

He was in love with her, so it made sense he would connect with her. The fact that the connection happened so quickly only led him to believe she was the right one for him and his brother.

But how did she feel? He hadn't seen her since the house. She was with Lisa.

He glanced over his shoulder at the doctor. "Any word on Lisa?" he asked.

"Last I heard they took her for a CAT scan. She took a pretty hard blow to the head. Other than that, I haven't heard anything."

Noah nodded, satisfied with that for the moment.

A knock sounded at the door, and the doctor paused briefly to reply, "Come in."

Alana stuck her head inside, and Noah's heart gave a little jump but instantly sank the second he felt her distance. She stepped inside hesitantly and handed him a small journal.

"They found this in that room and thought you might want to see it before it's cataloged as evidence."

He took the small leather journal. "Thank you. Are you okay?"

She nodded but for some reason wouldn't look at him.

"Alana," he began, watching her closely. "Are you afraid of me?"

Her startled gaze met his. "No. Never of you. I'm just... I just need a little bit to digest all this. I still don't understand what happened down there or what's happened between..." She glanced at the doctor as her words trailed off.

"Can you give us a sec?" Noah asked, and the doctor nodded.

"I'll give you about a minute, then I need to finish this whether you're finished or not."

Noah nodded as the doctor left the room and shut the door softly behind him.

"Talk to me, Alana," he said.

She sighed and rolled her eyes. "I don't know what to say, Noah. This has all just been so...so strange and overwhelming. It scares me. Whenever I'm close to you physically, I feel as though I'm being bombarded with emotions that aren't mine. It's unnatural and freaky and just plain...scary."

"I get it," he said. "I do. But don't walk away from this."

"I need to, Noah. For a while, for my own sanity. Please understand."

He shook his head. "I don't understand."

"We're going to be here for a while longer. Our producer has put his foot down and is making us stay for the Halloween thing," she murmured. "Plus Lisa will be here for a couple more days for observation."

"How is she?" he asked.

Alana nodded and tilted her head. "She's struggling. They found a small bleed in her head, and they're watching it, but other than that, she's fine physically. Emotionally is another story. John and Tray are with her right now. I think John might be a little smitten."

Noah sighed. "Alana—"

"Don't." She put her palms up. "Just give me the space I need, Noah, then we'll go from there. Okay?"

Noah pursed his lips. "Fine."

With a nod, Alana turned and left the room, taking what felt like his soul with her.

Chapter Twenty-four

"Have you lost your mind?" Tray demanded.

Alana rolled over in her bed and stared at him as he glared down at her.

"Not only is it almost noon—and Lisa is worried sick about you, by the way," Tray said as he climbed onto the bed and settled on his side facing her. "But you've pushed Noah and Aiden away. Those two are the catch of a lifetime, and you're pushing them away."

"I talked to her on the phone this morning. John's with her. She really likes him."

"I know," Tray whispered as he brushed her hair from her brow. "What are you doing, honey? It's not like you to hide out like this."

"I feel like I need to hide. I feel like I need to cover myself so they can't see into my heart. It sounds crazy, I know, but..." A single tear slipped free to dangle from the edge of her nose. "I don't want them to know how confused I am and how much I miss them."

"Ah, honey," Tray cooed as he gathered her in his arms.

"They scare me," she murmured, her face buried against his chest.

"Why? What about them scares you?"

"That...that connection thing."

Tray snorted. "That? Seriously?"

Alana rose onto her elbow and looked down at him. She scowled at his amused expression. "This isn't the least bit funny."

"I'm not laughing," he replied. "Alana, you've driven the two of them to beg for my help. Aiden I could maybe see doing it, but Noah? Noah actually came to me for help getting through to you. They love you. It's all over them, it's so obvious."

"Yeah, but there's something really odd between them, between the three of us."

"Odd? Are you nuts? Do you have any idea how lucky you are? Do you have any idea how many women complain that their husbands or boyfriends don't have a clue? Not only do these guys have a clue, but they adore you. I swear, if you walk away from this, I'll wring your neck."

"It's not that simple."

"It is that simple. Do you care for them?"

She nodded.

"Do you think you might love them?"

After a brief moment, she whispered, "Yes."

"Then what the hell are you still doing in bed? Go tell them."

"I don't know," she sighed.

"Oh, for the love of God." He climbed from the bed and grasped her hand, pulling her to her feet. "Come on."

"Where are we going?" she asked.

"To shower."

Tray pulled her into the bathroom and began to unbutton her pajama top. She slapped at his hand, making him chuckle. "Oh, come on. It's not like I haven't seen you naked before."

She frowned and rebuttoned the top. "That's not the point."

Tray snorted. "That is the point." He once again reached for the shirt, slipping the button free. "You're going to get in the shower, then go see them. If you want, I can even get you all turned on so when they see you, they'll sense it and be all over you like white on rice."

"What the hell does that mean anyway?" she grumbled as she pushed Tray out of the room. "I can shower on my own, thank you, and I definitely don't need you to turn me on."

She shut the door and smiled as his laughter filtered into the room. Tray was right. What the hell was she doing? She had two men any woman would love to have. Why would she turn away from it? Maybe she should talk to them, see if they were open to taking things a little slower for a while.

With a sigh, she turned back to the shower and almost had second thoughts. She'd been doing this yo-yoing for the last two days. One minute she wanted to run to them, say she was sorry and stupid for being scared. She wasn't a person who normally got scared, but she'd also never been through anything like this before, either.

She had a right to a little trepidation, didn't she?

"Oh, good grief. Maybe Tray's right. Of course Tray's right," she tried to reason out loud. "Tray's always right."

* * *

Aiden sat and stared out the window of his office, his mind on everything but the work in front of him. Neither he nor Noah had gotten much sleep. They both missed Alana, and Noah had a few things to work through. Aiden wasn't sure of all of it, but he was sure his brother would talk sooner or later.

He struggled with the fact that...thing had been their father. Noah had it worse. That thing had tried to kill him. Not once, but twice.

A knock sounded at his door, and without turning around, he called, "Come in, Noah."

Noah stepped into the room and shut the door behind him. Aiden kept staring out the window, but he could hear his brother's footsteps as they crossed the room. Something landed on his desk with a loud *pop*, and he jumped before turning to look at his brother.

"What did you throw?" he asked.

He pointed to a book lying on the desk. "That."

"What is it?" Aiden asked as he picked up the worn leather and flipped through the yellowed pages.

"It's a journal. Our grandmother's journal. Her friend cast a spell that made me forget that night. That's why I could never remember it until now."

"Why would she do that?"

"Because she didn't want me to remember that my own father had tried to kill me."

"So they knew it was our father?" Aiden asked.

"Yes. They knew all along."

Aiden sighed and squeezed his temples between his thumb and forefinger. "This makes no sense."

"Oh, it gets better," Noah said with sarcasm. "When our mother disappeared, our father tried to use magic to find her. Did you know our parents dabbled in witchcraft? I didn't. I knew our grandmother did a little but never dreamed our parents dabbled in the stuff as heavily as they did. But apparently dear old Dad didn't have a clue. He didn't cast the spells properly, and something went wrong. He became mad...possessed. Possessed! The evil that had its hold on him was so strong and so evil, it deformed him physically. Not only are we dealing with witches and ghosts, we're dealing with demons too," Noah said angrily.

Aiden raised an eyebrow but remained silent as Noah continued his rant.

"They tried to save him, but whatever it was that had its hold was too strong. He disappeared after that night but apparently returned at some point and took over the tunnels under the house. It looks as though he rerouted some of them too. That's why we could never find some of the entrances. He'd blocked the damn things off and made new ones. We never knew about what he was doing because he never took women from here...until Lisa."

Aiden stared at his brother, shocked at the guilt he could feel eating away at him. "You can't blame yourself for this, Noah. We're not responsible for the things that they did. They shouldn't have tried to help him and turned him in instead, but that was years ago. We were kids then."

"How could he have been running around this town and we not see him?"

"Noah, I'm not sure if he was standing in front of us right now that I would recognize him. We were so young when he disappeared. Not to mention the fact he was covered in burns. He looked nothing like his pictures."

Noah sighed and shook his head. "Except the eyes."

"So does this mean we're witches?" Aiden asked. "Since it appears everyone else in our family is."

Noah snorted. "I can't cast magic. Can you?"

Aiden shrugged. "Never tried."

Noah narrowed his eyes into angry slits. "Don't."

"Can't argue with that," Aiden replied drily. "But what's with our connection?"

"It was something our mother did that night. It was a way of protecting us by always having us connected to each other." Noah waved his hand. "More magic."

Aiden scoffed. "But why is Alana drawn in?"

"Not sure, but I do remember Karen saying something about one day I would find a third, then I would know she was the right one. At the time I didn't understand it. I think now I do. Karen must've known what spell our mother had used."

"So what we have is a spell, not something natural?"

Noah sighed and dropped into the leather chair facing Aiden. "So it would seem."

"That's...interesting."

"That's one way of putting it. If things get any more interesting, I'll have to be committed."

Aiden chuckled. "Now you're just being ridiculous."

"I miss Alana."

Aiden blinked. "That was random. Talk about a one-eighty in topic of conversation."

"What one-eighty?" Noah asked with a frown. "It makes perfect sense I would go from talking about being committed to talking about Alana. She drives me crazy. This whole 'space' thing drives me crazy."

Aiden sighed heavily. "Yeah. Me too. We can't push her, though. She'll come around."

"You're awfully calm about all this," Noah said with disgust.

"I've always been the calmer one. Besides, if you weren't so distracted, you would sense it. I've noticed over the last couple of days, this connection has gotten stronger. She's nervous, hesitant because she can sense it getting stronger too."

Noah stared at him in surprise.

"What?" Aiden asked.

"She's here," Noah replied softly as he held up a finger. "Wait."

A knock sounded at the door, and they grinned at each other.

"Come in," Aiden called.

The door opened, and Aiden smiled at Alana as she stuck her head inside. He'd known it was her, but his heart still stopped at the sight of her pretty eyes and adorably curly hair.

"Can I come in?" she asked.

"Of course," Aiden said as he came to his feet.

Noah stood as well. Alana appeared nervous, so both he and Noah kept their distance—at least for now.

"I saw your truck outside and was hoping you were here too," she said as she came inside and shut the door.

"Really?" Noah replied. "I hope this is good news and not bad."

"Well," she said as she clasped her hands in front of her and twirled her fingers nervously. Her eyes shone with uncertainty that made Aiden want to run to her and reassure her. "I guess that depends on how you look at it."

Aiden walked around the desk and leaned his hip against the edge, close to where Noah stood. He wanted nothing more than to grab her, rip her clothes off, and kiss every inch of her flesh. It was at that moment he realized just what an advantage they had with their connection.

He could feel her desire as well, but he could also feel her tiny bit of uncertainty. She was still nervous, still scared. And truthfully, he didn't blame her. If he hadn't been dealing with this connection for as long as he had, it would probably make him a little uncomfortable as well.

Noah took a step forward and Aiden remained where he was, watching. If both of them made a move toward her at once, she would probably run. She did just what Aiden expected her to—react with trepidation, at least at first.

Her eyes widened, and she took a small step back before stopping. She kept her gaze on Noah's as he tilted up her chin with his finger.

"I see you wanting to give the three of us a try as good news," Noah said.

"And how did you know that's what I was here for?" she asked, then twisted her lips. "Wait. Stupid question."

Aiden chuckled.

"What brought about the change of heart?" Aiden asked.

She glanced over at him and shrugged sheepishly. "Tray chewed me out."

Noah laughed and wrapped her in his arms. Alana slid her arms around Noah's waist and returned his embrace. Aiden could feel her touch on his own back as well as his brother's arousal. Wow, this thing was definitely stronger.

Suddenly, as though remembering something, she pushed away from Noah and put some distance by moving a few feet to the other side of the room. "I want to take things a little slow, though, okay."

"Slow how?" Aiden asked. "If you mean sexually, you should know I already had plans to fuck you here."

"Well...I mean..." Alana stammered, making Aiden grin. "I meant more along the lines of you know, going on some dates—some real dates—and getting to know one another better."

"Oh, but the sex is still okay, right?" Noah asked, teasing her.

Her cheeks turned a dark shade of red. "Well...maybe we should take that a little slow—"

Noah grasped her hand and tugged her to him. He quickly covered her mouth with his, stopping whatever she was about to say. Her arms lifted to wrap around his neck, and Aiden smiled, shifting to adjust his hardening cock within his pants.

"Maybe the sex is okay," she sighed against Noah's lips.

Aiden's smile widened. Everything felt right for the first time in a long while. She was back where she belonged. If she wanted slow, they could do slow, but in the end, she would be theirs...forever.

THE END

Trista Ann Michaels

Trista lives in the land of dreams, where alpha men are tender and heroines are strong and sassy. When not there, she visits the mountains of Tennessee. Not a bad place to spend a little spare time when she needs a break from all those voices in her head. Unfortunately they never fail to find her.

Loose Id® Titles by Trista Ann Michaels

Available in digital format at www.loose-id.com and other retailers

Blood Rite
Darkness Falls
Dead Reckoning
Deadly Crimson
Leave Me Breathless
Shutter
Their One and Only

* * * *

The ENTWINED FATES Series
Captive
Destined for Two
Remember Me
Mercenary
Slaves

Available in print at your favorite bookseller
Blood Rite
Darkness Falls
Dead Reckoning
Leave Me Breathless
Their One and Only

CPSIA information can be obtained at www.ICGtesting.com
Printed in the USA
LVOW07s0442050416

482059LV00001B/2/P